# VELVET TOUCH

## ZARA DEVEREUX

piatkus

PIATKUS

First published in Great Britain in 1996 by X Libris
This paperback edition published in 2012 by Piatkus

A CIP catalogue record for this book
is available from the British Library.

ISBN 978-0-349-40043-3

Typeset in Sabon by M Rules
Printed and bound in Great Britain by
Clays Ltd, St Ives plc

Papers used by Piatkus are from well-managed forests
and other responsible sources.

MIX
Paper from
responsible sources
FSC® C104740

Piatkus
An imprint of
Little, Brown Book Group
100 Victoria Embankment
London EC4Y 0DY

An Hachette UK Company
www.hachette.co.uk

www.piatkus.co.uk

# Chapter One

'We're spending the summer on the Greek islands. D'you have to take that job? Why not come with us?' Jeremy pleaded, using that little-boy-lost expression he had learned at his nanny's knee.

Karen grinned, knowing this ploy worked wonders with female students and lecturers alike. Not with her, however. She recognised their relationship for what it was – mutual lust and nothing more. Not for her the agony of sighing after this handsome, feckless young man, the jealous pangs, the heart-breaking wait by the phone for calls that rarely came.

*Thank God he doesn't affect me that way*, she thought, resting back against the flat corduroy boat cushions as he poled the punt along the placid surface of the Cherwell. *I can admire his well-shaped head, bleached-blond hair, broad shoulders, slim waist and lean hips, and his tush, balls and cock are ten out of ten. He's fit, muscular and tanned, but I'm not in love with him, whatever that means.*

'By "us" I suppose you mean Pete and half a dozen hangers-on?' she asked, idly trailing her finger in the river. It was deliciously cool, and she relished the sensual caress of the swirling water on her bare skin, a striking contrast to the hot sun beating down on her head, turning her chestnut hair to flame.

Milton's verse ran through her mind: 'See here the olive grove of Academe – There Ilissus rolls his whispering stream.'

She had enjoyed her years at university, indulging to the full her passion for history, revelled in the rich social life, the plethora of red-blooded males, and had come out with brilliant grades – but it was time to go.

'My parents have a villa in Corfu. They'll be in Miami, and we can use the place as a base.' Jeremy jabbed the pole into the greenish water then lifted it out. Diamond drops sparkled from it at every stroke. He regarded her from under thick fair lashes hedging pale-blue eyes. He was sweating, though they had not been out long. Karen was sure his body heat had something to do with the fact that her thin cotton skirt had become wet when she climbed into the unstable craft. It was sticking to her, outlining the curves and angles of her bare legs.

With a smile tugging at the corners of her generous mouth, she deliberately let her eyes rest on the solid bulge straining the zipper of his tight denim jeans and then looked up into his face. So intent was he on trying to make out the dark triangle at the apex of her thighs, he very nearly overbalanced from his precarious perch at the back of the punt.

'Whoops! Steady!' she warned, laughter bubbling up in her throat. It amused her to see him showing off for her benefit and to guess at the discomfort of his swollen phallus confined by Levi's.

Jeremy Hurst-Pemberton, popular athlete and champion oarsman, the darling of the campus, pursued by a horde of doting women, had tried everything to win her over. Bouquets, champagne suppers, windswept rides in his Ferrari, even a long weekend at his aristocratic father's Scottish castle.

Win her over? She smiled to herself at the old-fashioned phrase. It sounded vaguely Victorian – all hearts, flowers, chaperones and blushing maidens. The reality had been very different.

Karen had seduced him after a select dinner party given by a university professor and his wife whose soirées were renowned in academic circles both for the cuisine and the engaging conversation. It was she who had taken him to her room, eased him out of his tuxedo, lured him into bed and shown him how to pleasure her.

He had been disappointing, she remembered. Though living off a reputation as a stud, his knowledge of female arousal had been abysmal. He wasn't much better now, needing constant reminding that slam-bam-thank-you-ma'am just wouldn't do.

He steered the punt into a secluded creek, screened almost entirely by overhanging willows. After shipping the pole and tying the painter securely, he slid over to where Karen was sitting. He rested a hand on her knee, started to move his fingers up under her skirt, heading towards the damp, cotton-covered mouth of her sex. He was eager to probe the entrance to the liquid centre of her being, but she closed her legs, not ready for him yet. He was always so precipitate, grabbing at her breasts, homing in on her clitoris. She made him wait.

Karen sat up and took the velvet scrunchie from her

hair, shaking out the tumbling mane of Medusa curls till they flowed across her shoulders and halfway down her back. Jeremy watched her, biting his lip in frustration. She was like a woman from a Rossetti painting – tall, full breasted, with an almost barbaric beauty, an exotic bloom who captured attention wherever she went, admired, envied, even disliked, but never ignored.

Although he had known her carnally, drawn into the vortex of her tumultuous orgasms, he still shuddered with a feeling akin to awe whenever she was close. He was mesmerised by the enticing perfume that emanated from her skin, frightened by the fierce light in her green eyes, chastened by her intellect and biting sarcasm. Karen was clever, quick-witted and confident. A free spirit who took no prisoners.

Jeremy had only to crook his little finger to summon a bevy of girls panting to have him shaft them. They flattered him, made him feel macho and virile, but none was as exciting as Karen. She was a potent drug, too powerful for all save the strongest personality. The need to convince himself that he could tame her forced him to attempt it again and again.

He took the tartan rug stowed under the seat, stepped on to the bank and held out a hand to her. The willow formed a perfect bower; the blanket spread on the short grass invited fornication. Karen sank down on it, linking her hands under her head and looked up at the bright dazzle filtering through the swaying branches.

How she loved summer; she became listless and droopy during the dull rainy days of winter. Now energy poured through her veins, revitalising her, running like quicksilver along every nerve, inflaming her senses.

From beneath curling dark lashes she considered Jeremy, who sprawled beside her, propped up on one elbow. He leaned over, and his mouth caressed the smooth, petal-soft skin of her cheek. She turned her head and their tongues met and tangled. He grunted and pulled her closer, the tips of her breasts bunching as they brushed against the material of her flimsy blouse. She was warming to his kisses, her juices already pooling at the opening of her vagina, the ripe, sweet scent of her rising into the warm air.

Jeremy might not be a ideal lover, but the afternoon was filled with a golden haze, heavy with langour. The sound of water, the rustle of leaves, the birdcalls and distant voices of other boaters combined to rouse in her a deep and enticing longing for fulfilment, and a heaviness gathered in her groin.

Had she been there alone she would have lifted her skirt, pushed aside her briefs and played with her clitoris, stroking, petting, rubbing it, bringing herself to climax in that entirely satisfying way that no man had yet surpassed. She suspected that another woman might, but had not yet tried, merely fantasising about it sometimes when she masturbated.

She relaxed in Jeremy's arms, and he lowered his mouth, fastening his lips around her nipple, sucking it through the cotton till it stood up in a needful little peak, hard as stone. She gritted her teeth and closed her eyes, drawing in a sharp breath at the delicious friction of his tongue. Her hand smoothed the outside of his jeans, tracing the large, elongated shape of his cock that throbbed urgently, demanding release from its imprisonment.

Gently but firmly she unfastened the metal button at his waistband, then seized the zipper tag between thumb and forefinger. Tantalisingly slowly, she pulled it down, the gap widening till it freed the pulsing member, which sprang out to nestle in her palm. Her hand closed round it and she applied pressure, her touch slippery smooth, enjoying the sensation of the damp, hot hardness jerking and moving as if it had a life of its own, a thing apart from Jeremy.

He opened her blouse. She was not wearing a brassière. Her breasts bared to his gaze, beautiful in form and colouring, firm and high and lightly tanned, with faint blue veins and luscious nipples ringed with darker brown.

He cupped her right breast in his hand, his thumb revolving on the tense tip. Then he bent his head and sucked it into his mouth, teasing and tonguing it before moving to the other, while Karen moaned her appreciation of this tribute. Such attention was irresistible, but it made her clitoris ache. She wriggled her hips, attempting to rub her inner lips together and put pressure on her rampant nub.

Jeremy responded to her need, one hand straying below her waist, across the flat bowl of her belly and under her panties, easing them down. Karen kicked them aside, and he brushed the abundant tangle of brown pubic hair, a finger finding its way into the deep avenue between. It parted to reveal her labia, swollen now, her clitoris standing out from its hood, glistening like a silver-pink pearl, quivering with want.

Karen closed her eyes, her hand working up and down his engorged phallus, but aware that she must not rouse him too soon or he would lose patience and plough into her, forgetting that she, too, needed orgasm. She slowed the movement, caressed him gently, though lost concentration as she waited breathlessly for him to bring her off.

Jeremy was panting, nibbling at her breasts, his finger dipping into the scented pool of her vulva, then, once moistened, moving upwards along her crevice to spread silkily over the sensitive head of her lovebud. She could feel herself spiralling as he settled into the slick, wet rhythm she so desperately needed to carry her over the edge.

Up she rode, up and up, waves crashing hard on one another. 'That's it,' she whispered hoarsely, clutching at his cock. 'Don't stop! Go on! Go on! Oh – oh! Yes! Yes!'

She was peaking. She was there. Sensation washed over her, tingling from the tips of her toes to the recesses of her brain, glorious release provided by that tiny organ existing solely for delight, her precious, delectable, wonderful clit.

Jeremy pushed between her relaxed thighs, his thick member plunging to the hilt in her warm, convulsing depths. A couple of strong thrusts, and she felt the twitch of his cock as he came, clasping her tightly to him. After a moment, she freed herself from his weight, shifting to lie with an arm across her eyes.

Karen was filled with a sense of well-being, the rolling spasms of pleasure receding, leaving her limp and momentarily satiated. Her thoughts wandered aimlessly. Fragments of music floated in her head – ideas, plans. She was aware of the lovely sounds of nature, the lapping of the river, the fussy cheep of the moorhen calling her fluffy black chicks. Summer in England, and where more summer-like than magical Oxford?

At the same time she was aware of her juices bedewing her thighs and puckered folds. She could smell Jeremy's sharp, male sweat cutting across her familiar female fragrance which carried the odour of seaweed and shells. Sex, raw and untamed. Sex and only sex. She felt a pang of loss, of regret. Was there nothing more?

Poems, music, great works of art all spoke of something deep and meaningful. Whenever she listened to symphonies or opera her throat constricted and tears pricked her eyes. She had not yet found this elusive, heart-stopping element during her congress with men, and her experience had been considerable.

Fastidious and choosy, she had applied her intellect to her experiments with a number of them. Each had been carefully selected, but even so, none had moved her beyond satisfying the yearnings of her loins. There seemed to be an emotional block. She was aware that some accused her of being cold but knew this to be untrue. If anything she was too sensitive, too vulnerable, and this made her afraid to lower her defences. Too often she had comforted women friends devastated by callous males, and she had vowed it would never happen to her.

Karen pulled herself up, leaning back against the bole of the willow, and Jeremy shifted over to lie with his head in her lap. She pushed her fingers through his rumpled curls. A pattern of leaves dappled his face and spilled across his eyes.

'You'll come to Greece?' he asked softly, seizing her hand and running his tongue over her fingers, sucking each digit with absorbed concentration.

Karen frowned, withdrawing her hand. His licking was too canine to be pleasant. 'I can't,' she said. 'I've told you before. There's a post waiting for me in Devon. If I turn it down, I'll never get another chance like that. It's just what I want.'

'Why so keen to work?' He rolled on his stomach, his head to one side, resting on his folded arms, regarding her with a sulky expression.

'It's not a question of keenness. I have to earn a living,'

she replied crisply. 'We don't all have rich parents, you know.'

'Yours can't be badly off.' Jeremy was in a perverse mood. She guessed he was annoyed by her refusal, probably more upset than he cared to admit. 'Your mother's just had another book on archaeology published, hasn't she? And your old man appears on BBC2 regularly in those philosophy programmes.'

Karen was decidedly bored by this. When he could not get his own way, Jeremy displayed the less attractive side of his character. She picked up her discarded knickers and stuffed them in her pocket, then scrambled to her feet, parted the peridot veil of leaves and dropped down into the punt. It wobbled dangerously.

'I don't have to explain anything to you,' she said, lowering herself on to the seat. 'Come on. It's time we went back. I've packing to finish.'

In silence they drifted up the river, sometimes hailed by fellow students on other boats. The shadows lengthened and the bells chimed from spires poking admonishing fingers into the plum-blue dusk. They left the punt moored under Magdalen Bridge alongside several others, then strolled through the Botanic Gardens towards the High Street. It was busy as always, but with an extra frenetic buzz about it – it was the end of the teaching year; for some, like Karen, the end of an era.

It seemed incredible that it was over four years since she had obtained sufficient A levels to be accepted at this, the *crème de la crème* of universities. She had spent three years as an undergraduate, finally achieving degrees in history, art and English with an additional familiarity with Latin. This had not been the end, however, for she had stayed on to take a postgrad course in archive administration. This might have led to the position of records manager's assistant in local government of a big company, had not Tony come up with the invitation to work as his aide at Blackwood Towers.

Just because her parents were famed intellectuals, it had not been easy for her. In fact it had been hard – a case of the cobbler's children. They had expected her to do well simply because she was their daughter and had never had the time or inclination to give her extra tuition themselves.

Standing by the archway leading to her lodgings, Karen said goodbye to Jeremy, aware of the cool air breathing on her bare thighs and naked pussy. He was aware of it, too, and she felt the heat of his hand on her backside, curving round the tight globes, pushing into the crease between in a proprietorial way that she found offensive.

'You'll write?' he persisted anxiously, a sullen expression spoiling his near-perfect looks.

'Yes,' she lied. 'Have a good summer, Jeremy. Be happy.' She rested the back of her hand against his cheek in a casually affectionate gesture.

He gripped her arm, tried to stop her going, but she broke free and disappeared into the passageway. Jem, the porter, stuck his head out of his cubbyhole of an office.

'Letter for you, Miss Heyward,' he said cheerfully, handing over a white envelope. She was going to miss Jem, perpetually optimistic despite the weather, the recession, the peculiarities of dons, the behaviour of students. Nothing ruffled him.

'Thanks,' she said with a smile.

'You off then, miss?' Jem lingered to talk. His ruddy face with the bushy walrus moustache would be etched on her memory.

'Tomorrow morning.'

She ran lightly up the dark, winding staircase leading to the rooms she shared with Alison Gray. Alison had finished, too, but she was taking a year off in Boston before embarking on a career.

Karen looked out through the landing window. Below lay the quad, across it the stately buildings that had sheltered aspiring students for over five hundred years. Not women, of course – they were a late addition. At one time no females had been permitted beneath the sacred portals of those male-dominated seats of learning.

Just one more night spent there. It was sad, really. Despite her assertions to Jeremy, Karen was nervous of taking up the position she had been offered. She unlocked the door of the college flat. Inside the cosy panelled sitting room she stepped out of her sandals, padded across to the little kitchen and switched on the kettle. While waiting for it to boil, she opened the letter.

Dear Karen,

Am looking forward tremendously to having you join me at Blackwood Towers. You'll like Porthcombe. Miles of beach, a pounding sea and spectacular cliffs. The library is a mess. I really need your help. It's too much for one person. The late marquis neglected it. He was only interested in the farming side of the estate. But Lord Mallory Burnet is different and wants everything in order. There's enough work here to last us years!

See you on the 20th, Exeter Station, Platform 2, at 2.30 p.m.

Yours,

Tony

Tomorrow, Karen though, folding the letter and returning it to the envelope. *By this time tomorrow I'll be there. One door closing and another opening. Dear Tony. He must be keen. We've already settled these arrangements by phone.*

*My old friend and teacher who got me the job. He's a gentleman and won't expect anything in return, though I'd not say no. He's forty-something, I know, but it was he who taught me how to achieve an orgasm. Before his tender tuition, I was a bundle of ignorance and frustration. I wonder why he never married. The typical bachelor, but what a lover! Jeremy could take a few leaves from his book.*

Even remembering those hours spent in Tony Stroud's apartment when, as an unhappy, rebellious teenager she had discovered what sex really meant, made her loins ache and her clitoris pulse. Maybe it, too, remembered its awakening, she thought. The first time it had blossomed and bloomed, rising hard and proud at her teacher's expert caressing. His long fingers, his skilful tongue, her nub sucked and fondled until it reached such a frantic explosion that she had fainted with the shock and pleasure of it, then begged him to do it again – and he had. She recalled achieving nine orgasms during that night with him, a record she had not yet beaten.

The kettle steamed and Karen poured water on to instant coffee granules in a pottery mug and settled down on the shabby cretonne-covered couch, tucking her feet up under her. Her packing was almost done, the evening ahead planned. She had half an hour of rest before she set off – space to herself, a time to get her thoughts in order.

Her books and belongings had been boxed up and awaited collection. Most of them would be dispatched to her parents' home in Wimbledon. The housekeeper would take them in and store them. Karen's father was on a lecture tour of the States and her mother had gone with him. They never liked to be apart, utterly absorbed in each other, still madly in love after twenty-five years, a phenomenon Karen found remarkable, moving and exasperating.

She had always felt surplus to requirements, sure she was an accidental not a planned child. Not that they were ever unkind or neglectful, far from it, but she had been aware, right from the start, that they were so wrapped up in each other that anything or anyone else was considered to be an intrusion. Even a well-loved off-spring. Needless to say, Karen had been an only child.

Such an upbringing had made her independent, a loner, living a great deal in a fantasy world. History, literature, antiquities of any sort, these had become her obsessions. Boarding school had cemented her emotional isolation, then university.

'I'm so sorry we shan't be in London when you finish,' her mother had said on one of her recent visits, drifting about the flat in an elegant navy and white Chanel outfit. 'Unfortunately we're off to America.'

'Don't worry, Mother. I'm going straight to Devon,' Karen had assured her, feeling gauche in the face of such perfection, while Alison had obligingly aimed the camera, capturing the three Heywards for posterity.

Now Karen set down her cup and went into her room to change. She stripped, glad to remove her stained skirt, and thrust it into the linen basket. Naked, she prowled to the bathroom and stepped into the shower cubicle.

The jets gushed, stinging her skin with pleasurable little jabs, pouring down her shoulders, over her breasts, across her belly and between her legs. She soaped herself, breathing in the scent of shower gel, enjoying the sensation of her own hands sliding across her flesh. She circled her nipples, which rose instantly at her touch, travelled down to her navel, made tiny soapy swirls and corkscrews in her pubic hair and gently rinsed between her pouting lips.

Wrapped in a white towel, she padded into her room with its low, sloping ceiling and black beams, chintz curtains and powder-blue carpet. This had been her home for months. She had taken time to settle but having done so had no desire to move. It was inevitable, however, and a part of her was excited by the challenge – fresh fields to conquer, new people to meet, opportunities, even lovers. She had the urge to snort and paw the ground like a warhorse scenting battle.

She let the towel drop and considered herself critically in the long mirror fastened to one wall. It wasn't a bad body, all things considered. Working out and practising martial arts had kept her in trim, and she was streamlined – tall but slender boned, and her breasts were full, her waist slim and her stomach flat. She ran her hands down the long sweep of her thighs, past the shapely knees and rounded calves to the trim ankles. Her body thrilled at the friction of palms of skin.

*Amoral, wanton body*, she addressed it sternly. *You don't care who offers you caresses just as long as you can purr under them. Particularly if they culminate in your clitoris, the epicentre, the key to ecstasy, the only organ in the entire human body designed exclusively for pleasure.*

Why had it been put there? she wondered. Was it to compensate the female for the pain of childbirth? Sensible, really, for had the vagina been the seat of orgasm, then it would have been impossible to endure the passage of a baby through it. As it was, the clitoris was well up out of harm's way.

Her hand wandered involuntarily down to part the freshly washed hair and press on her bud's stem, tracing it back to where it joined her pelvic bone. At once a tremor of excitement stirred in her loins, and her honey-dew commenced to flow. She wriggled her hips against her finger's sweet invasion while, in the glass, she could see her nipples becoming redder, hardening in response.

*Stop it*, she chided herself. *Save it for later*.

Karen controlled the urge to bring herself off,

smoothed body lotion into her skin, and dusted talc over her mound and between her legs. She sprayed deodorant beneath her shaven under-arms and applied a matching haze of Casmir.

She glanced at her watch. Ten to seven. No time to waste. White cotton briefs now concealed her genitals, followed by a black tracksuit bottom. A matching sweat-shirt was pulled over her head. Her hair was piled high and confined by a headband. On her left breast was a badge emblazoned in red and gold which proclaimed 'Shotokan Karate'.

After peeling on white socks and lacing her trainers, Karen picked up a tote bag and left the apartment. In a few moments she was cycling through the streets towards the sports centre. This had been the major back-drop for much of her life at college. Here she had practised karate three times a week, playing badminton, pumped iron and swum. A fitness fanatic? Hardly. One of the prime instigators of her interest had been the man under whose direction she would train tonight – her sensei.

After chaining her bike securely to a stand, Karen pushed through the swing doors into the foyer. The centre was, as always, busy. Young, beautiful people wearing colourful leotards, shorts, legwarmers and T-shirts were chatting as they made their way to the various rooms devoted to their particular sport. Karen walked towards the lofty gym, which had been transformed into a training *dojo* for the evening. She nodded to several students who were already in the changing room, replacing her tracksuit with a white *gi*, the thick cotton unyielding against her skin, the brown belt folded correctly round her waist. Barefoot, she trotted back to the *dojo*, bowing to her master as she entered.

Kan Takeyama was standing by the window, illumined by the sunset glow behind his body. He straightened, returned her bow. 'Good evening, Heyward,' he said, poker-faced. No smile of recognition crossed his impassive features.

'Good evening, *sensei*,' she replied, equally formal, though her nipples tensed under her fighting suit.

His fiercely masculine yet sensual good looks instilled in her a feeling of tranquillity on one hand and awoke her slumbering sexual passion on the other.

His body was perfection. Now, like her, he wore a white *gi*, though his was girded by a black belt, as he was a third dan in the art, but she knew what he looked like naked. Besides being her master in karate, he lectured on oriental history and art. Karen had proved his most promising student. The opportunities for lovemaking had been legion.

In the *dojo*, however, Kan was severe and professional. Twenty novices were put through their paces. First the rigorous warm up, enough to exhaust all but the fighting fit, then from simple groups of techniques the class moved to exacting *kata*, before progressing to sparring.

Karen was paired with a short, stocky opponent, quick and light on his feet but no match for her. She was the star of the dojo. But Kan would not permit anyone to think themselves superior to the rest. He took over, giving her no quarter, an exacting taskmaster, intent on pushing her to the limit, for she was due to grade as a black belt soon.

This was a responsible position, and she would be issued with a licence only if she used her hands in self-defence, not attack. Empty hands – *karate*, the name given to it centuries before when disarmed Okinawa islanders found a subtle way to fight their tyrannical Japanese conquerors.

As Kan her *sensei* and mentor, worked with her, she was aware of the tension growing between them, an electric thrill passing through her every time he touched her in correction or instruction. This always happened, always had, always would – and her need for physical contact with him became almost painful in its intensity.

She was volatile as she fought him, every line of her expressing not only the spiritual warrior but the woman, too – her green eyes, her firm mouth, lithe limbs; she was powerfully aggressive, gloriously female; sexuality incarnate. Kan was conscious and responsive to all these things yet did not betray it with the flicker of an eye.

The session ended. Everyone bowed to everyone else. People trailed off to the changing rooms. Karen sat panting, wiping her face with a towel, aware of an echoing wetness between her thighs.

'You're doing well,' Kan said in his quiet, serious way, never giving praise lightly. 'You'll get your black belt. No problem.'

'I'm moving away,' she replied regretfully.

'You'll keep training, and come to Crystal Palace next May. Grade then. I'll arrange it with the judges. We'll keep in touch.'

As usual after training, they wound up at Kan's cool, light apartment. Karen thought of the opera *Madame Butterfly* every time she set foot in there: there were low tables, low stools, a paper screen, artistically arranged flowers, netsuke in a glass cabinet, a couple of gnarled and ancient bonsai trees on the balcony. Taped music of the *samisen*, a three-stringed lute, tinkled in the background.

'Is this new?' she asked, pointing to a delicately executed print of Mount Fuji with a peaceful river and a pine tree in the foreground.

'Yes. I've started a collection. Japanese wood blocks are known as *ukiyo-e*, which means images of the floating world.'

'How lovely,' she replied, a catch in her throat. Soon she would be without her charming, aesthetic *sensei*.

'I'm glad it pleases you,' Kan said, watching her with wise, slanting eyes.

'Can I take a shower?' Karen needed to be fresh for him, as if trying to recapture her virginity. This was so divine and pure a setting that she wanted nothing to mar her final experience of it, wishing to be fragrant from top to toe, her flesh masked in silk, which she knew would be appreciated by the beauty-loving Kan.

'Be my guest.' He ran his fingers through his straight black hair, every gesture graceful. 'We'll make love and then I'll send out for some sushi.'

The bathroom was immaculate, the shower hot and refreshing. After she had anointed her body with jasmine-scented lotion, she draped herself in the splendid cream kimono Kan reserved especially for her. Padded and lined with crimson silk, it was rich with embroidered chrysanthemums and appliqué birds outlined with gilt thread. The hanging sleeves were wide, and she fastened a magnificent obi round her waist. It was the attire of a court concubine, and Karen could feel herself changing, taking tiny steps, moving modestly, eyes cast down.

'I'm too tall to be a geisha,' she said as she glided back into the room.

'You're beautiful,' he replied earnestly, his eyes darkening with desire.

He was kneeling on the *tatami*, wearing a turquoise silk robe patterned with trees set amid snow-covered foliage. Karen sat on her haunches facing him, fingers linked lightly in her lap, and for a moment he did nothing but gaze at her. Then he took her hands and placed them on his thighs, doing the same to her. Silence descended on them, a deep, meditative silence, healing and cleansing.

He sighed, reached for her, drew her into his arms. His kisses were just right, tongue flickering over her lips before venturing between. And his hands cupped her silk-covered breasts, the nipples rising urgently against the crimson lining. He rewarded them with the merest grazing touch. Lust snaked through her like a white-hot flame.

Kan rose, lifting her with him. He released her for a second and slid the gown from his body. His smooth, silky skin was bronze coloured. It had the sheen and texture of polished marble, every muscle honed, unmarked by a single blemish, free from hair except for the wiry black thicket covering his pubis.

This served to accentuate a formidable penis, long, thick, copper hued, curving above a pair of plump testicles hanging in their scrotal sac. His smouldering eyes, his voluptuous lips, exquisite mouth and magnificent prick promised ecstasy and never failed to deliver.

Kan's eyes continued to hold hers, and what she read in them sent a shiver right down her spine to her clit. He took one of her hands, raised it to his lips and licked the centre of the palm with the tip of his tongue, sealing it with a kiss. She sighed, trembled, his every touch a strong aphrodisiac.

His hands as gentle as a woman's, in odd contrast to his reputation as a warrior, he removed her kimono. Her nipples sprang erect with excitement and sudden chill and, standing before her, he took the weight of her breasts in his hands, then lowered his shining dark head to lick over the tips. She could feel the swollen cap of his phallus nudging intimately against her belly. Leaving her breasts momentarily, he took the band from her hair and let the burnished curls fall across them like a veil.

Karen stood perfectly still, legs pressed together, and Kan stroked her mound of Venus gently, seductively, inserting a finger along the dark fissure which opened like a flower under the knowing caress. He was a master of sensuality, a student of ancient books of all kinds, particularly those that dealt with the language of love. His knowledge of the female body was extensive, and he took pride and delight in playing it like a finely tuned instrument.

Karen closed her eyes, the double action of his lips sucking her nipples and his finger stroking each side of her clitoris, but carefully avoiding the head, lifting her to the brink of orgasm. Kan had no intention of allowing this yet. Her pleasure would be heightened if the tension was built up slowly and gradually.

He lifted her in his arms, and she gripped him round the waist with her legs, her wide open pussy rubbing on the stalk of his cock, her juices glinting against his pubic hair. He carried her across the room and mounted a couple of wide, shallow steps to the area he used as a sleeping place. There she was laid down on a double futon. Pools of soft golden light filtered through the globular paper lampshades, casting a subdued glow.

Kan submitted every inch of her to attention, a man so secure and confident in himself that he could lavish admiration on the woman in his arms. His mouth feasted on hers, while his hands made exciting and passionate love to her breasts, then he kissed between them, his tongue lapping her waist, her belly, dipping into her navel, burrowing lower like a hungry little animal amongst the thick curls protecting her sex.

He paused, his head between her legs, eagerly observing her reaction as he held her labia majora apart with two fingers. The inner ones opened like petals at his stroking, and Karen gasped as he wetted the cleft between with saliva and started to caress her clitoris. Her pleasure was his, it seemed. He didn't hurry, content to have her fondle his cock as he brought her closer and closer to ecstasy.

Karen was hot, slick, the force gathering to roll across

and through her. Kan judged her condition, held off for a second, his fingertip hovering over but not touching her tortured bud, then sliding across it once more, back and forth. He stopped and she groaned in protest, then felt him shift down, felt his tongue sucking her clitoris into his mouth, rolling it, licking it. Her climax flared through her body like an electric current, making her shudder and cry out.

While she was still convulsing, he slid his penis into her depths, yielding to the sexual rhythm of passionate intercourse. She embraced him with her thighs, urged him on, impaling herself on his raging prick, till at last he gave a long groan, his spasms echoed by her throbbing vagina.

It was past midnight when he dropped her off. Jem had shut up his office and gone home.

'What about your bike?' Kan had asked as they left the apartment and headed for the parking lot and his Nissan.

'D'you know someone who'd like it? I shan't be taking it to Devon,' she had replied, feeling sleepy, ripe, languid with sex, her other hunger sated with raw fish, rice and saki.

He promised to find a home for it and kissed her again. Karen clung to him for an instant. 'I'm going to Tokyo for the vacation. Come with me,' he whispered, his hands slipping under her sweatshirt and skimming over her naked back. 'I'll be training with my own *sensei*. He's an eighth dan. You'd like him. He's very wise.'

'No. Thank you all the same.' It was hard to refuse. 'One day, perhaps.'

Shakily, she fled up the stairs and let herself into her rooms. She could tell Alison was home by the creaking of springs and moans of pleasure coming from the second bedroom. Obviously she was entertaining her boyfriend, the good-natured, reliable, boring Gareth.

Karen's suitcase stood open on the floor, ready to receive the last items of clothing. Smiling as she reminisced, she laid in the cream silk kimono Kan had given her as a farewell gift. It still carried the spicy cinnamon smell of his hair, the personal odour of his body. She would never forget him, but her heart was not bleeding because she was leaving him.

*Maybe my critics are right, and I don't have a heart after all*, she thought as she climbed into bed and switched off the light. Drowsily, she listened to the distant night sounds of the college building, car doors slamming occasionally, voices, a dog barking somewhere. Soon they would no longer be the background pattern of her existence.

# Chapter Two

*I don't know about fucking in the hay*, thought Armina Channing as she proceeded to do just that. *It's scratchy – smelly. Bits stick into one's most delicate and private parts – though you could hardly call mine private.*

The brawny young man who was pleasuring her, head burrowed between her spread legs, seemed to have no such reservations. Hidden in a stall at the back of the stable, they were practically invisible. This would have been a great place to do it if it had been less uncomfortable. Armina revelled in the refinements of life – satin sheets, the touch of velvet against her pampered skin, perfumed bath water – exquisite cuisine, fine wines and decadent luxury.

Yet a bit of rough could be stimulating, and Tayte Penwarden was rough all right – Lord Burnet's head groom. And Armina was one of His Lordship's mistresses, the chief odalisque of the seraglio. But while the cat was away the mice would play, and anything Tayte lacked as a sophisticated lover, he made up for in enthusiasm.

Fit and muscular, his olive skin glowed with health, a hearty young stud indeed. Armina, clitoris fired by the caresses of his fleshy wet tongue, buried her hands in his tightly ringleted hair. Tayte was a Cornishman who had slipped over the Tamar into Devon, but was also of gypsy stock if his swarthy colouring and those black-lashed eyes tilting upwards at the outer corners were anything to go by.

Whenever she looked at him, she tingled at the remembrance of the Carlos Saura movie based on *Carmen* and performed by a Spanish dance company. It was one of her favourite adjuncts to masturbation, a rich, sensual feast of a film, overflowing with passionate flamenco, smouldering fire, world-weary languor and desirable dancers of both sexes. She often watched it on the video in her bedroom while she used her dildo or fingered herself to climax. The leading male had a body to die for, gorgeous enough to bring a puritan to orgasm.

A critic had described him as having 'wolf's eyes. Gypsy eyes.'

Just like Tayte's.

Now, sensing her distraction, he stopped nuzzling her sex and moved upwards, fixing her with that lupine gaze. 'What's wrong?' he asked in his guttural voice.

'Nothing,' she answered in her melodious, cultured accent.

She was frustrated because he had stopped, but she savoured the denial, too. Had he continued she would have spilled over by now. As it was she could look forward to further leisurely, lubricious arousal.

She trailed agile fingers up the well-muscled inner surface of his denim-covered thigh. He wore tattered work jeans, faded blue. Through a hole in one knee she glimpsed his coppery, darkly furred skin. Her juices wetted her labia even more as her hand moved nearer to the generous swell at his crotch. It made her dizzy with anticipation simply to look at it. She thought of the thick brown serpent nestling between Tayte's legs and was overwhelmed by a hot surge of lust.

'That's OK then,' he muttered and stared at her

pert breasts. Tiny, like their owner, with wantonly pink nipples, they were as wilfully lascivious as she was, demanding to be fondled, sucked, teased and pinched.

Armina was Tayte's first lady, though not his first woman by any means, and she offered a bewildering wonderland of new delights and wickedly shameless sensations, unbelievable in one so dainty, ladylike and innocent looking.

She had entered the stable that morning on the pretext of an early gallop, wearing a white shirt tucked into the waistband of skin-tight jodhpurs that outlined the division of her rounded buttocks at the back and cut between her plump secret lips at the front. Black riding boots had completed her attire. It had been obvious she was wearing no underwear.

Tayte had been waiting for her, leaning nonchalantly against a manger, chewing a blade of grass. His hands had shot out, seized her with that brutal impetuosity she found so intoxicating and propelled her into the hay. Her jodhpurs had not remained in place for long.

'You know he's abroad,' Armina continued, lazy with desire, watching as he unfastened his belt, then the top button of his old jeans. Long before he had reached a hand into his pants she had visualised his curving, iron-hard phallus emerging from its nest of black curls.

'I do,' he said, taking it out, its smooth, red-brown knob poking from between his fingers as he cradled the shaft and rubbed it, sliding the foreskin up and down, excited by having her watch.

'Then there's nothing to stop us doing it in my house,' she said, eyeing him lecherously.

Lord, what a weapon! Thick as a truncheon, stunningly long. How was it possible she could take all of it? Only just, she recalled. It felt as if it reached right up to her waist when he pumped it almost painfully against her cervix. Her avenue was slippery wet, her mouth too, as she imagined it thrusting into her void which longed to be filled.

'Suppose so,' he agreed, looking down at his cock, fascinated as it swelled even more under the familiar touch of his fingers. 'Suppose we could do that even when he's home.'

'I don't think so.' Armina shook her blonde head and knelt before him, lifted her face to his prick and took the head of it in her mouth.

Tayte groaned, thrust his pelvis forward, pushed in further. Armina could feel the blunt tip pressing into the back of her throat, and was delighted by the salty taste and solid feel of it. She played with him as he stood above her, legs tense and parted, back against a beam. Her hand cupped his taut balls, gently squeezing the full velvety sac. Slipping him from her mouth, she hovered with her lips barely touching his cock head, breathing on it, soft as a whisper, then lowering herself so that it entered between her teeth again, sliding across her palate.

Tayte gasped, his strong, sinewy hands gripping her shoulders. His lids were half closed, his expression that of a tortured saint. Triumph flamed through Armina. There was no greater aid to sex than having control over a man. Would he be able to hold back? Or would he suddenly come, his seed gushing out to fill her mouth and cream her face?

This was the novelty of him – he was as yet untried, a virgin when it came to the voluptuous games at which she was adept, games she had learned from promiscuous people far removed from Tayte's simple ken. She had lived and been brought up among those whose extravagant lifestyle allowed them to experiment with sensuality, refining it, glorifying it: the touch of cruelty, the hint of mystery, the realisation that a shiver of fear could give an adrenalin rush as fierce as a snort of amyl nitrate.

Tayte controlled himself with an effort. He moved away from her and lay flat on his back on the straw. Now it was Armina's turn to be mouthed. He held up his arms and she slipped between them, thighs spread open, a knee each side of his body. She still wore her white shirt. The buttons were undone all the way down, breasts jutting from the opening. Tayte supported her above him, examining those tip-tilted orbs. She was as light as a child, fragile seeming as a fairy, randy as a bitch on heat. He lifted his head, groping for her nipples with his lips, sucking hard on the right one, then the left. Armina squealed her pleasure.

Sitting back, facing him, she could feel his penis prodding the crease between her bare bottom cheeks, blindly seeking entrance to one or other of her openings. She was not in the mood for anal penetration so rose slightly, positioned her hips and impaled herself on him, feeling him drive into the farthest depths of her vagina. Closing her eyes, she pumped furiously on the mighty, glistening organ, creamy now with her juices, while Tayte fastened his hands round her breasts, pinching the rosebud teats with his fingers.

Armina could feel the force gathering in her, tingling along her spine to the small of her back, flooding through her womb. She ground herself down on Tayte's pubis, hoping this friction might bring on her orgasm. But it was too harsh a pressure on the sensitive clitoris, dulling rather than sharpening sensation. She needed the delicate mouthing he had given her before. Her body readied itself as she knelt above him, legs opened wide around his head.

Tayte stared at the depilated area, still an exciting novelty to him, the pussy hair removed in a way he had never before seen in a grown woman, her mound silky smooth to the touch, the delicate pink flesh divided neatly, swollen lips fully exposed, clitoris standing up proud. It expressed Armina's disregard for modesty; this flamboyant display of her womanhood was a statement of her defiant, hedonistic view of life.

His tongue was waiting for her when she lowered herself on his face. It flicked unerringly across her nub, tiny, darting, butterfly-light caresses, tip on tip, till she could feel her control dissolving. She moved her hips backwards and forwards, very carefully so as not to disturb the rising excitement as he sucked her love-button, flicked it with his tongue, ravished it with firm, steady strokes. Armina gasped, her groin heavy with need, a light sheen of sweat dewing her Dresden china complexion. Heat poured through her. The stable span in space. She came in a sudden, merciless rush, yowling like a female cat speared by a tom's spiky probe. Tayte shifted her down, even as she clung to him in ecstasy. He worked the head of his enormous shaft along her sex-lips, slick with saliva and vaginal juice, then sheathed it in her. The spasms still roiling through her, she lunged against him, riding him hard, inner muscles contracting joyfully round his bar of solid flesh.

Molten waves fused them together, till she finally collapsed on his chest, his replete and softening cock slipping from inside her.

It was comforting to be met at a strange station, Karen decided, stepping from the corridor to the platform. She was cramped from sitting too long, drowsy, hair ruffled where she had rested against the back of the seat. In all, she was not feeling her best, thinking, *I'm glad it's Tony and not Lord Burnet who'll be taking me to Blackwood Towers*.

There was nothing remarkable about Exeter Station. It was filled with tourists and students seeking temporary employment, with the usual gaggle of goofy-looking train spotters in hooded anoraks and spectacles, on a mission, clipboards and ballpoints at the ready.

Karen found the atmosphere nostalgic. Too often she had stood on similar platforms when shunted back to school or off to stay with relatives during the vacations, her parents too busy to be bothered with her. Some people found trains exciting, their fumes hinting at adventure, but they only served to depress her.

Once they had been sooty, dirty, littered. Now some bright spark had ordered a clean up. Freshly painted plastic benches; sterile canteens, toilets and newsagents; large notices proclaiming primly that this was a smoke-free zone and would passengers kindly put out their cigarettes. But no one had been able to stop maverick pigeons dropping their white-grey shit with Rabelaisian disregard for rules and regulations.

'Bloody hell,' commented Tony, a rebel himself, ignoring the edict, a Marlboro held defiantly between his fingers as he took her outstretched hand in his free one. 'How doom-laden everything is these days. We users of the weed are persecuted. "Oh, my God! He's turning me into a passive smoker! Off with his head!"' He bent to kiss her cheek. 'You look good enough to eat, Karen. Better still, good enough to fuck. Are you well?'

'Very well, thank you, Tony, and you're looking positively Bohemian. Doesn't Lord Burnet object to his librarian wearing cutoffs?'

Tony's lips curled into a smile, lighting up his sharp hazel eyes and bearded face. 'He doesn't give a toss as long as I do my job without bothering him.'

He picked up her case and put a guiding arm round her. Soon they were outside, brilliant sunshine slicing through the shadows. Tony slung the luggage in the back of a gunmetal-grey Vogue SE Range Rover, singing out, 'All aboard the *Skylark*!'

'Posh,' Karen remarked, for the sturdy vehicle was shiny new.

'That's nothing, love. There are half a dozen cars to choose from. I thought you'd like a ride in this. I enjoy driving it, anyway. Makes me feel like Indiana Jones, or a gentleman farmer, depending on mood and fancy.'

'I was thinking of buying one of my own, something small, you know.' Karen sat back in the passenger seat and fastened the belt as he wheeled recklessly out of the regulation parking area and headed through the streets. They were packed with herds of loitering visitors gazing, mesmerised, at the multitude of gift shops, burger bars and stores.

'Emmets,' Tony sneered disparagingly, jerking his head at them. 'We have to put up with this invasion during the summer. It's far worse at the coast. There we get the others, the caravan clubbers and amateur sailors. Every weekend they come trolling down, towing their mobile homes and boats, cars crammed with children, dogs, grannies. It's enough to drive one back to the Smoke.'

Karen glanced at him from the corner of her eye. He had not changed much, still acerbic, still handsome in a craggy sort of way. His brown beard threaded with grey, long hair pulled back in a pony-tail. He was tall enough to top her, his shoulders were broad beneath a black sleeveless vest. His tanned arms, chest and legs were bare and his supple waist and lean hips were confined in a pair of shorts with frayed hems. These had once been jeans. Tony had simply taken the scissors and performed an above the knee amputation. He wore nothing on his feet.

Karen's clit stirred, warmed by memories. *Once I hero-worshipped him*, she thought. *Hung around after school, just on the off chance of seeing him. Jail bait. But*

*I was sixteen and past the age of consent before I succeeded in persuading him to seduce me.*

The twitch of a smile beside his mouth told her that he was aware and remembering. 'Water under the bridge, Karen,' he remarked.

'Gallons of it.'

'You're not married.' He glanced at the third finger of her left hand, but this told him nothing. She wore large rings on every finger, casual and hippyish in dress, inclining towards flowing Indian cottons, baggy palazzo pants, loose tops and sandals. 'Divorced? Engaged? A regular boyfriend?'

'No. Fancy-free.'

'Good. So am I.'

This could have meant anything or nothing at all, but she was painfully conscious of his bare thigh close to hers on the seat (his shorts really were short) and those sensitive hands with the manicured nails handling the gears with the expertise they had once used on her eager pussy. How sweet it would be to repeat that journey from innocence to awakening, but how impossible.

Karen would have liked to linger in Exeter: the cathedral was reputed to be worth a look. But Tony was hellbent on getting out of the congested traffic. They left the town, skirting a roundabout and driving along the bypass.

'No hurry,' he said. 'We'll take the scenic route. Can't stand motorways.'

The secondary road rose and fell, curved and straightened, presenting an enchanting, picture-postcard vista of valleys sweeping up to rolling hills as graceful and smooth as a young girl's breasts. Their sweet tips were constantly changing from green to blue through to mauve according to the passage of cumulus across the sun.

'It's wonderful,' Karen exclaimed, tiredness forgotten, leaning forward in her seat, waiting eagerly for the next panorama.

'Not been in Devon before?' Tony asked, amused by her enthusiasm and sorely tempted to tackle the button-through skirt of her flower-patterned dress or untie the shoestring straps. The dress was long, flowing between her thighs, pressing against her mound. The skinny girl had been replaced by a queenly woman.

'No, never.' Karen linked her hands in her lap. Beneath them she could feel the ridge of the briefs that barely covered her pubic hair. Already the crotch was wet with her juices, her belly aching for love. This was the effect Tony had always had on her.

'You haven't lived till you've scoffed back a Devonshire tea of home-made scones and strawberry jam obscenely loaded with cream as thick as bulls' spunk. We'll stop when we find a decent café.' He looked at her sideways, grinning puckishly. 'Darling, you haven't changed one bit. Still the wide-eyed ingénue who'd never come till I showed her how.'

Karen could feel a blush heating her face. He had an uncanny knack of reading her thoughts. She darted a glance at him, the tip of her tongue coming out to lick over her coral lips. 'Trust you to remind me of that.'

'Sweetheart, don't try to kid me that you've never thought of it.' He reached across and fondled her knee. 'Maybe you'd care to show your old teach what you've learned since.'

'Maybe I would.' She placed her hand on top of his. His grip tightened, his touch evocative, sending shocks through her nipples and clitoris in unison.

One peaked brow shot up, and his eyes twinkled mischievously as he said, 'Meanwhile, light up a couple of cigarettes and pass one over.'

Now the lanes were narrower, lined by thick hedges. Five-barred gates afforded glimpses of lush meadows polka-dotted with buttercups where *café au lait* Jersey cows with heavy udders stood chewing the cud beneath shady trees. The vehicle careered over little stone hump backed bridges spanning gurgling streams and through picturesque villages where irregularly built thatched cottages leaned against each other like besotted lovers.

Tony braked outside one of them. It had a 'Cream Teas' placard propped against its lobelia-festooned drystone wall. Seated in the garden at a rickety table beneath a big striped sunshade, they smiled at one another, that easy smile born of friendship, good sex and genuine affection.

'You like living down here?' she asked as the apple-cheeked, beaming waitress went off with their order. Tony watched her retreating, her backside swaying tantalisingly beneath a miniskirt.

'Sure I like it here. It's fine. Quiet off season. The villagers consist of well-heeled professionals who can operate their businesses just as easily in the country, with the occasional foray into town.'

'Tasty women?' Karen loved him for his out-and-out admiration of the female of the species. He liked their minds as well as their bodies, finding them much more diverse and interesting than men.

'Sure, though they all seem to be studying

aromatherapy. It's the in thing. Dozens of 'em of all ages, shapes and sizes, eager and willing to practise on one. I think they'd be naughty if they'd only let themselves go. It's also considered groovy to be on the self-sufficiency jag and to join the barter system.'

'What's that?' University had not prepared her for this entirely different culture. She had some vague notion that rural entertainment consisted of baking cakes for church fêtes or helping to run jumble sales in the village hall.

'Everyone offers a skill of some sort, like, "I'll muck out your cesspit if you supply me with organic vegetables." Very quaint, my dear. As fashionable as giving up smoking and risking a coronary on the jogging circuit.' There was a sardonic slant to Tony's mobile, humorous mouth. 'The men are keen – when it comes to saving money on the domestic front, I guess. When I was asked if I'd like to add to the list and contribute something, I wrote "Raw Sex". It went down with the husbands like a pork chop in a synagogue.'

'I'll bet it did. You're incorrigible.'

'I hope so.'

The waitress sashayed across, arch and flirtatious as she placed the tea things in front of Tony and leaned across to arrange them. Her blouse was semi-transparent and her big, jiggling breasts crowned with nipples like organ stops brushed momentarily against his shoulder.

'It's my charisma,' he explained with a wide smile as the girl reluctantly retired.

Karen knew all about that, honeyed fluid seeping from her sex as she longed to have him toy with her. She put a curb on her wayward thoughts. It was no use. She simply had to be more businesslike in her dealings with him. The situation had changed. Hadn't it?

'What's he like?' she asked, deliberately cool as she cut into a floury, dusky-capped scone. A plate heaped with more stood on the white cloth. The cream was clotted, yellow and delectably lumpy; the jam contained whole, succulent strawberries glinting like overblown rubies in a tsar's crown.

'Our boss, the marquis? Some say he's a hero, others that he's an objectionable, arrogant bastard.' Tony shrugged, pantomiming with his expressive hands. 'He's a pig. He's a saint. He seduces and betrays women. He's an honourable gentleman. He cheats. He's overbearing. Abominable. He's a good mate. It depends where you stand, who you are and what you need from him.' He picked up the brown earthenware teapot. 'Shall I be mother?'

'Please,' she nodded. 'I'll keep an open mind.'

'You do that,' he answered solemnly, passing her a cup of tea. 'We needed you down here because Lord Burnet has some fat-cat American businessman interested in the library.'

'He's not selling?' This was a horrible idea. Karen hated to see any part of English heritage disappearing overseas.

'No, no. He talked to me about it some time ago. Seems he met this guy in California and he's an Anglophile, wants to own some of the more valuable works but is content to leave them where they are. Lord Burnet seems to agree with him that it would be a good idea to open the house and library to the public.'

'He can't need the money, can he?' Somehow she had imagined that a marquis would be beyond financial stress.

'Not in the way you and I think of, but he did have to pay the most crippling death duties when he inherited.' Tony's eyes twinkled as he added, 'The American's coming over and the library has to be got into shape pretty damn quick. Hence your involvement.'

He leaned closer. There was a smear of cream on her lips. He carefully removed it, licking the tip of his finger where it had touched her mouth, the cream still warm from contact with her tongue. She felt her womb contract involuntarily, as though wanting to suck him into her. She glanced down. His arousal was obvious.

Legs apart, he had positioned himself in such a way that she could see the top of his penis peeping out through the fringed hem of his cutoffs. A pearly drop glistened at its single eye; the red glans was swollen, bare of foreskin. Was the shining head less sensitive or more without its fleshy sheath? Karen wondered, never able to make up her mind which she preferred – the cut or uncut male?

Tony grinned, mind-reading again. 'Yep, it's ready for you, girl. Ready and raring to go. I'll take you on a guided tour of my humble abode before we go to the big house. You'll love my antique bed.'

Karen did not realise they had entered the Blackwood estate until they were a couple of miles inside. Then the surrounding area became more woody, and there was a noticeable absence of vehicles. No other living person was anywhere in sight.

They drove along a sandy road surrounded on either side by tall pines, stately beeches, oaks and ash with verdant grass carpeting the avenues and ridges between. A dazzling display of rhododendrons, with blue and pink blooms drooping as if worn out by excesses, sheltered in the arms of leathery bottle-green leaves. There was a momentary glimpse of deer heads raised alertly as they paused before vanishing with a quick white flash of their scuts.

All was silent, except for birdsong. Lord Burnet's kingdom.

'Where's the house?' She was eager to view her employer's domain.

'Further on. I've a cottage near the spinney. It goes with the job. You'll get one, too. Convenient. Not far from the pub.' Tony swung the Range Rover down a shady lane at the end of which stood a small dwelling with ivy swarming over its walls.

Tiny dormer windows stared down like curious eyes watching from beneath a fringe of thatch as he drove through the gates and pulled up on the gravel. Karen was surprised by the well-tended garden with its shell-edged path. There were wild flowers in the borders and geraniums in large clay pots on the cobbles outside the front door. Honeysuckle and roses rioted around the door unchecked, forming a scented arch.

Karen felt Tony's touch on her shoulder, then he

unlocked the door and entered first, saying, 'Mind you don't bump your head. The beams are low in some places.'

There was no hall. One simply walked straight into the living-room, and the cosy intimacy of it made her heart thump and her blood quicken. She was a girl again, alone with her teacher. He was forbidden fruit, irresistibly alluring and dangerous.

The cottage was plainly furnished, centuries old with two-foot thick walls and low latticed windows. A fireplace occupied most of one side. Inside it were seats and the pitted cast-iron door of a bread oven.

'I don't use it,' Tony said, moving to the sideboard and picking up a bottle. 'The supermarket does a marvellously unhealthy white sliced loaf. I buy half a dozen at a time and bung 'em in the freezer. Thank God for progress. D'you want a drink?'

'Yes, please.' Tension was coiling tightly in her loins. She could almost see it flowering, a pulsing, throbbing crimson. *My chakra*, she thought. *The core of my being. My sex*.

'The bedroom's upstairs.' He lifted a salver containing glasses, the gin, mixers and a freshly filled ice tub.

Karen nodded and followed him up a winding flight

of stairs leading from a doorway next to the fireplace. There was no landing. A few steps, and she was standing beneath the low attic ceiling. The windows were on a level with the uneven floor. They were open. The smell of roses crept in.

It was a strictly masculine room: a mirror supported on a dressing table, a built-in wardrobe, a chest of drawers and a wide mahogany bed, neatly made, the duvet pulled straight.

'You keep your house very tidy,' she commented, remembering vividly the chaos of his flat, the floor strewn with books and papers, the dilapidated settee where she had lost her cherry.

'I've a woman who "does".' He put the tray on the bedside table. Gin and tonic splashed into the glasses, topped with shaved ice and a twist of lemon.

'Here's to my assistant librarian,' Tony said, smiling into her eyes as he toasted her. 'I recommended you for your abilities, not because I expected to screw you, though I'll admit that wasn't far from my thoughts.'

'Wicked, wicked tutor,' she murmured, leaning into him, nipples aching to feel his fingers rotating on their tender tips.

'I am. An unabashed scoundrel.'

He put down his glass, took hers away and nestled her in his arms. His fingers roamed her face, tracing the line of her neck to the lobe of her ear, setting the dangling hoop swinging. Karen sighed and tingled, the caress awakening a pleasurable echo in her epicentre.

'You smell yummy, like patchouli and *chypre*,' he whispered in that husky, totally captivating way of his. Then he tongued the rim of her ear and kissed the lobe. Karen moaned. She could feel the warmth and quickness of his breath, her increasing wetness dampening her knickers.

He was becoming as excited as her, the solid rod of his penis pressing against her pubis through the censoring denim and her cotton skirt. His mouth was soft, working its way across her cheek to the corner of her lips and resting there. She relished the gentle, seductive warmth, then opened her mouth to him, her tongue like a fiery arrow winging to meet his.

'Ummm,' he sighed appreciatively, removing his lips from hers. 'You always were my star pupil.'

It was Tony's habit to make love with words as well as caresses, and this was one of the most exciting things about him. Karen was warmed right through by his kisses, feeling relaxed and languid. He guided her to the bed, laid her on the pillows, hands hovering over her breasts as if they were ripe fruit about to be plucked from a tree. Karen arched her back, thrusting them up to meet his touch, the chafing of her bodice excitingly acute against the pink, needy crests.

Then Tony proceeded to do what he had wanted to do since seeing her at Exeter Station. Fingers on the front of her dress, he started to open the buttons slowly until her naked breasts were exposed to his admiring gaze.

He cupped one, his thumbnail scratching across the tip. Karen jerked, writhed her hips, strained to meet that tormenting arousal, labia thickening, but thrumming in response, pleasure gathering in her vagina. Not content with having her bare to the waist, he continued with the unbuttoning until the dress fell open either side of her long, slim legs, exposing her narrow waist, flat belly and wisps of chestnut bush showing above the triangle of white cotton hiding her mound. Karen held her breath as he leaned above her, filling his eyes with the sight of her and his nostrils with the aroma of her salty, piscine lubrication.

'You're beautiful,' he whispered, voice thick with desire. 'Very, very beautiful.'

He bent to suck hard at one nipple, his fingers busy

with the other, a double feast of pleasure augmented by the tingling rush of blood hardening her clitoris. Concentrating on each breast in turn, he sucked and nibbled, using his tongue, and her nipples seemed to grow larger, as if trying to fill his whole mouth. Karen's hand slid down, pushing aside her panties, unable to resist dipping into her slippery cleft, wetting a finger and fondling her nub that strained out of its tiny cowl.

'Let me,' he said, and she felt his finger fluttering over her pussy, stroking her through the panties, tracing the deep line that scored the centre, then lowering his head and nibbling at it through the fabric.

She surrendered to his hungry mouth, feeling the warm, wet drag of his lips and the delicious frisson of the thin material over her clit head, the brush of his beard against her skin. Her lower lips swelled with blood, the humid heat in her vagina turning to hot lava.

'Do it like you did that first time,' she begged.

She could feel his chuckle vibrating through her and he raised himself on his arms, staring at her from between her legs, chin resting lightly on her mons. 'All this time, and you've remembered? I had an idea you might.'

'A woman never forgets the man who took her virginity,' she assured him, her breathing jerky.

'So the pundits say,' he replied. He moved round to the side of the bed and lay beside her.

Karen turned to him, held him tightly, her open-mouthed kisses leaving beads of moisture on his beard. He smelled of her juices, tasted of the nectar soaking her knickers. He bit her lower lip, drew it into his mouth, his tongue sliding inside, skimming along the roof to tickle the back of her throat.

'Oh, yes. That's how you began.'

She was feeling playful, as she had done on that occasion in his flat, playful and fearful all at the same time. Her hands skimmed over his shoulders, dipped into the opening at the top of his vest, teased his crisp brown chest hair, tweaked his small male nipples.

'But you didn't do that,' he gasped.

'Didn't I?' She wriggled against him, tugging at his belt.

He helped her, swiftly stripping away his clothes. His body was lean, sun browned, the body of a mature man; wiry, strong, with hard muscles and firm flesh trimmed by walking and riding rather than faddy exercise routines.

Her hand closed round his erect penis, thrusting from the thick hair coating his underbelly. She was fascinated by its shaft, brown skinned, corded with bluish veins, supporting the massive, gleaming naked head. Her hand moved to cradle his testicles, testing their weight. These were not boyish cods, but solid orbs dangling in their hairy net, ripe with the promise of fulfilment; the balls of an older man who has made love to many women.

Tony laughed with the joy of the moment, tipping her face to his mouth, feeding on her lips. 'You've learned a lot.'

'I have. Now I want to share it with you, but first let's pretend we're back in your flat. Treat me as you did that day.'

Tony smiled tenderly and began to weave his magic. He settled her comfortably on the bed. First her toes were caressed and licked, each one receiving attention, then her ankles, his lips coasting up her calves, across her knees, the insides of her thighs. She quivered, her ultra sensitive skin stippled with goose-bumps, responding to every touch.

When he reached the barrier of her panties he parted her legs slightly and squeezed the prominent swell of the hidden mound, then slipped a finger round one side and rubbed the furry bush. He watched her face, seeing her rapt expression, carefully judging every move.

'Oh, Tony,' she whimpered, clutching him round the neck, burying her face in his unbound hair.

'Hush, darling. Wait – that's right.'

He pushed down her briefs and she helped him, squirming out of them. He trailed a finger back and forth across her sex-lips and kissed her, his tongue relishing hers, till it seemed there was nothing but tongues and tasting. She shivered in the grip of passion, wanted to draw him into her very centre, but more than that she needed him to bring her to orgasm.

Then she felt the compelling combination of tongue and hand as he gently opened her labia, stroking the damp aisle, then sliding a finger into her vagina while keeping his thumb on her pulsing clit, never stopping that enticing friction. She could feel the pre-orgasm tremors flowing along her thighs, and he too was as aware as if they were his own. His fingers sunk in further and she moaned loudly, beginning the ascent, reaching that perilous plateau where it was possible to stick if disturbed. No disturbance or frustration today, however. She was in the hands of a master.

He paid homage to that glorious bud of flesh, tenderly caressing its stem, fondling it on each side to prolong the sensation, and the head ached and swelled, shiny like a gem amidst its plump hood and guardian pink lips. He had positioned himself so that he could look at it, flick it, tease it, have it almost speak its need. They worked together, he and Karen's clitoris, and his timing was perfect. Never for a moment did he allow her to become bored, varying his touch, sometimes feather-light and slow, sometimes fierce and rapid, but always holding off when she began to peak.

'I want it,' she implored, trembling.

'In a while.'

'Now, please!'

'Now? You really want it now?'

'Yes, yes.' Her climax was hovering, waiting for the next slow slide of his finger over her clitoris which would bring her to the peak.

He smiled, kissing the tips of her stone-hard nipples, hearing her short, sharp cries and rewarding her eagerness with a steady, unstoppable friction. Karen felt the heat surging up, dying back, surging higher. Nothing could prevent her coming, and the spasms poured through her, bringing joyous relief.

As her body shook with pleasure, Tony slipped his eager penis into her, and she heard herself laughing joyfully at the unadulterated perfection of their coupling, a roller-coaster of delight.

# Chapter Three

Tony led Karen up the meandering, hollyhock-bordered path to a house not far from his own. The whitewashed walls were dappled with ochre lichen and cushiony green moss. He produced a key and opened the oak front door, standing back with a flourish so she might enter.

'*Voilà, madame!* Your very own country retreat.'

'The marquis has given this to me?' It was more than she had expected.

'Not exactly, dear. It's a tied cottage. Part of your wages. If you stop working for him you're out, lock, stock and barrel. Nothing is for nothing. These were designed especially to quarter the lord of the manor's peons – field hands, groundsmen and foresters. Slavery wasn't invented by the Americans.'

It was a carbon copy of Tony's cottage. A basic one up, one down, with the later addition of a kitchen and bathroom built on at the back.

'There's not much room.' Karen humped her holdall up the stairs and set it down on the patchwork quilt spread over the double bed.

Tony followed her, a suitcase in either hand. 'I'm told it wasn't unusual for the serfs to raise upwards of twenty children in one of these. In the summer the older kids were sent out to sleep on the common.'

Karen shuddered. 'And they call them the good old days?'

'Oh, they were – for the upper crust. Still are, my dear. You'll see when you've been here a few days and learnt about Lord Burnet's habits.'

'I can't wait,' Karen said ironically, beginning to resent this high and mighty personage who had not yet deigned to meet her.

The kitchen had every amenity: blue Delftware tiles, a washing machine, tumble dryer, cathedral-style light-oak units and matching leaded-glass wall cupboards. The fridge-freezer was stocked with essentials: milk with a two-inch layer of gold-tinted cream, primrose butter, a wedge of tongue-tingling Cheddar cheese. A farmhouse loaf with a mouth-watering crusty brown top sheltered in the bread bin. There were reliable stand-bys in the larder – baked beans, tuna fish and plum tomatoes – and cleaning materials in the under sink unit.

The bathroom was decorated with whimsical old-world charm. A floral-patterned ceramic washbasin, a free-standing bath on brass claw feet, a matching bidet and a lavatory with a polished wood seat. 'Thank heavens, it's been modernised!' Karen exclaimed, growing ever more delighted with her residence.

'All these new-fangled gizmos,' Tony remarked, leaning a broad shoulder against the tiled shower stall. 'What's wrong with using a communal crapper in the back-yard and having a swill under the pump?'

'Shut up! I hadn't noticed you were averse to mod cons.' She went to brush past him, but his arm snaked out and clipped her round the waist.

'What about having a shower together?' he suggested, hands sliding down to fondle her buttocks, a finger slipping between to trace the tight nether orifice.

'What about showing me the big house?' *I mustn't get too dependent on him*, she thought, though unable to resist grinding her pubis against the swell of his prick. *One fuck with him is enough for today. He may start getting possessive, and I want to be free to explore every possibility.*

'Tonight suit you? Then we'll go down to the harbour for a drink.'

'Give me half an hour to change.'

When he had gone, she took a quick shower, then carried out Kan's meditation technique while making up her face. Dreamily she studied her reflection in the dressing-table mirror as she applied brownish-black mascara to her curling lashes. Not too much make-up; pencil-thin grey eyeliner where the socket deepened, a touch of white powder on the lids, a smear of bronze at the outer corners blended with the tip of her little finger. This served to make her eyes larger, brighter, greener. Carefully she brushed over her lips with rose blusher. She had no intention of going out looking tarty, just in case Lord Burnet had returned from his wanderings.

What to wear? The scarlet-edged evening cast long shadows over the trees, sculpting sepia spaces between them. It was cooler, so she opted for baggy cream and brown patterned trousers in cotton crepe that enhanced rather than concealed the length of her legs, a beige

T-shirt plunging in a deep V beneath her breasts and a loose nutmeg waistcoat in fine crochet.

Images drifted through her mind, too formless to be called thoughts. She was determined to get that black belt and intended to seek out a local *dojo*, if such a thing existed. If not, what was to stop her opening one of her own? She knew enough about the art. This would give her an excuse for getting in contact with Kan. The thought of his bronzed body and lusty, uplifted cock made her cunt ache with hunger, juice seeping out to bedew her freshly shampooed pubic floss.

Gritting her teeth against this forceful spasm of desire, she centred her mind on her career. This was of prime importance. Her parents expected her to be an achiever, but she was ambitious on her own account – impatient to get started, wanting to meet her employer.

Where was it Tony said he had gone? To India? To the Seychelles? Feathery palms, white sand, a clear blue ocean lapping a tropical beach floated before her inner vision, and a mysterious man, his back turned towards her.

She asked Tony again when he picked her up half an hour later. 'Where's the boss vacationing?'

'First Goa, then the States.'

He also had changed; a lawn shirt covered his muscular torso, and he wore loosely cut linen pants that fitted his trim waist snugly and seemed to emphasise the fullness behind the fly. Able to afford the best, he wore the latest line in leather thong sandals designed by Gucci.

'Have the mistresses gone too?' She picked up her canvas shoulder bag ever so casually, as if His Lordship's amours were of no possible interest to her.

'The mistresses? How sweetly old-fashioned.' His quirky smile lifted those bearded lips, and she knew he saw through her pretence. 'I presume you're referring to his strumpets? Dear me, I didn't think you'd stoop to reading the gutter press.'

'I developed a taste for the gossip columns when I knew I was to be working here. Didn't you always teach me that forewarned is forearmed? Isn't it true he keeps a dozen women?'

'No. He keeps four at present. The paparazzi have got it wrong again.'

'Ha! Only four? Poor deprived man!'

Tony was finding her reaction highly entertaining. Ever since he had known her she had been a romantic, harbouring dreams of chivalrous knights on white chargers, though she would have denied it with every last breath in her gorgeous body. Presumably she had some-how slotted Lord Burnet into this category and wasn't taking kindly to being disillusioned.

'He hasn't taken them on holiday,' he supplied as they walked to the Range Rover. 'Never does. Goes into retreat at times. An unpredictable person who likes his own company. He has the makings of a recluse, though you'll find that hard to believe.'

The evening was glorious, pouring over the parched land like *après-soleil* milk on a sunbather's skin, sooth-ing away the heat of the day. The fosse-like lane enfolded them in secretive green.

Noisy conclaves of rooks gyrated over the tops of the trees, seeking night-time roosts.

Karen was on the edge of her seat, straining against the belt that crossed and divided her breasts, eager for her first glimpse of Blackwood Towers. The road descended into a broad valley of parkland, and then she saw the house, dozing there as it had done for centuries. It was surrounded by hills and hanging woods. The sunset was reflected in a mass of bayed, mullioned win-dows, turning them to fire. Blackwood Towers fulfilled all her hopes, blending with the sky, the landscape and the country around it as if it had stuck down roots and grown from the soil rather than owing its creation to man.

Karen fell in love with it immediately, and for ever.

'I've never seen anything like it,' she breathed, enraptured.

'It began as a priory in the sixteenth century, then the land was acquired by the Burnet founding-father, through skulduggery, no doubt,' Tony said as they cruised down the long, gradual slope leading to the front of the house.

'Was he dishonest?' Karen was intrigued, bewitched, already falling under the manor's powerful spell.

'Probably. Descended from Norman robber barons like most of England's aristocracy. Anyhow, he knocked down the ecclesiastical buildings and erected this massive pile in the Italianate style. It's way over the top.'

They circled the stone basin of the fountain, where a mighty bronze Titan, flaunting a phallus nearby as big as his trident, sported with adoring Junoesque water nymphs. Gravel sprayed out from under the Range Rover's wheels, and the vehicle rocked to a halt at the bottom of a flight of wide steps. The façade of the house was even more impressive close up. There were larger than life statues of Greek gods and Roman heroes in niches between the windows, and a long balustraded and pinnacled enclosure with domed pavilions at the corners. The front door was huge, set back under a towering portico resembling that of a mausoleum.

'We'll use the tradesmen's entrance,' Tony said. 'The indoor staff aren't here at present. Just a caretaker to tend the burglar alarms.'

He was exaggerating as usual, and the door he used to admit them led to a private stair to the library. 'I'll give you a duplicate key,' he promised. 'You'll be working here without me sometimes. You won't be scared, will you? Not afraid of ghosts?'

'I've yet to be convinced they exist,' she replied, overawed by the magnificence surrounding her. The library was as long and wide as a ballroom, wainscotted in oak, every surface richly carved and inlaid, with an elaborate chimneypiece and pedimented doors.

The tall, recessed casements were hung with damask drapes held back by cords with long tassels. The windows overlooked the formal knot garden laid out like a complicated embroidery, and a sweeping green lawn guarded by sentinel trees.

There were books everywhere, lurking on tables, piled on the floor, snoozing behind the glass doors of specially constructed shelves; old books, rare books, first editions, folios.

'Some are worth the proverbial king's ransom.' There was a touch of pride in Tony's voice, as if he was some-how personally responsible for garnering such a collection. 'So valuable that no insurance company will risk taking them on. It's the only place where I agree with non smoking.'

'Do we have to sort them?' She wandered round, run-ning a caressing finger over the bookcases, craning her neck to look up at the ceiling with its overpowering design of wreaths and straps. As far as she was con-cerned, this was paradise.

'Are you computer friendly?' He answered her ques-tion with one of his own.

'Sure. No graphics, but I can handle a mouse and a key board, data base, spreadsheets and word process-ing.'

In an adjoining office was state of the art equipment, more advanced even than that which she had used at Oxford. It was odd to see the latest technology standing on a desk that had once belonged to the Emperor Napoleon, in a room hung with Flemish tapestries.

Tony patted the machine fondly. 'I'm tempted to call

it Hal – though I hope it'll never take it upon itself to be rebellious.'

'Computers can't think. They're only as good as their programmers,' Karen reminded him sedately, seating herself in the operator's chair, which was upholstered in chocolate-brown leather. It had hydraulic lift and swivelled at a touch.

'Nice,' she added, feeling the upholstery squish beneath her bottom and drag the seam of her pants tightly between her pouting pussy lips. She savoured the piquant smell of the top-quality animal hide.

'We're on the Net.' Tony perched on a corner of the desk, one leg swinging lazily, the other braced on the Turkish carpet. 'And we can link up with any library or university in the world.'

'Useful. Have you entered any data yet?'

'Some.' He was looking at her speculatively. The rich light falling from the stained glass of an oriel window complemented her colouring. It gave a fierce lustre of her burnished chestnut hair and flushed her skin as he had seen it flush during the little death of orgasm.

Tony's penis rose and hardened in response to Karen's beauty and hot recollections of the afternoon's coupling. He focused on her lips, so sensually perfect. Was it only an hour or so ago she had used her mouth on his cock, lipping, sucking, tasting it? A mouth that had mastered the art of fellatio.

He had never lacked sexual partners, but the memory of his clever, ardent, passionately eager pupil had remained with him down the years. The reality of shafting her again had exceeded his wildest dreams. Now the thought of having her with him day after day was wildly exhilarating, sending the blood pulsing through his stiff organ.

'My God, Karen, just feel what you do to me,' he whispered. Instinctively she curled her fingers around his turgid prick, the heat of it burning tantalisingly through his trousers.

He reached out and touched the tip of her breast. At once it bunched, the taut cone pressing against her T-shirt. He moved closer and, still fondling his bulge, Karen sat back in the chair, one leg thrown over the other, squeezing her thighs together to bring pressure to bear on her clitoris.

There was something powerfully erotic about the glorious interior of Blackwood Towers. Generations of Burnets had fucked there – not only husbands and wives but, no doubt, a multitude of illicit lovers as well. It was as if the tumescence, liquid arousal and violent pleasure of these people from the past had impregnated the walls. She could almost see them dressed in period costume, ruffles and lace, hooped skirts and powdered wigs. Her mind slipped notches, filled with swirling coloured lights and images of fornicating couples.

*How on earth am I going to work here?* she wondered. *I shall be in a permanent state of excitation.*

'I've something to show you.' Tony's voice brought her back to herself. 'It's the pride of the library. Only the privileged are permitted a viewing. I've orders to take extra special care of such a rarity, particularly in light of the Yankee millionaire's interest.'

He had the key to an inner sanctum, hidden by a door cunningly constructed to look like a bookcase. It was even lined with fake volumes, their spines meticulously engraved and painted. The small room was simply furnished, its only ornamentation a gilt-framed mirror. Tony unlocked a walnut cabinet with a further set of keys. It contained several large, shallow drawers, and from the top one he lifted a sheaf of yellowing cartridge paper covered with black and white drawings. Karen, tingling with anticipation and curiosity, watched as he spread them out on the surface of a mahogany table of Georgian vintage.

She glanced down at the first and then stared harder, arrested by the subject. 'My God!' she breathed in a husky whisper.

Tony gave a slow smile, his eyes bright. 'I thought you'd appreciate them. They're much more inventive than even Giulio Romano's illustrations of Pietro Aretino's smutty poems, *Sonetti Lussuriosi*.'

'Aren't they just!' She had seen copies of the pornographic Renaissance pictures representing the various 'postures' of sexual intercourse. 'Much later, of course.'

'Eighteenth century.'

'By Hogarth, or James Gillray, Thomas Rowlandson – George Cruikshank?' Her throat felt dry. It was hard to speak. Try as she might to be sensible, lust washed through her in gigantic waves.

'No,' he said, and she knew by his tone he was picking up on her feelings. 'An unknown artist produced these cartoons. He used the pseudonym of Dick Bedwell. No one is sure of his true identity. This leads to much heated debate among connoisseurs, which is strange, considering how few have actually seen the originals.'

The drawings were beautifully executed, explicit and detailed, the nearest thing to photography produced at that time. The first example, coyly titled *The*

*Morning Toilette*, was of a lady reclining on a four-poster bed, skirts hitched high, exposing the dark wisps coating her mons veneris. Her legs were wide apart and her maid knelt between them, while another servant leaned across, fingers toying with her mistress's large bare nipples.

Their costumes were typical of the era in which they had been immortalised; mob caps, low necklines, tightly laced corsets pushing breasts high, crested teats protruding over the tops of bodices, flounced petticoats, stockings rolled below the knee and fastened with lacy garters, Louis-heeled shoes with paste buckles. And, most important of all, they were pantiless, this having been an age when it was considered immodest to wear drawers, which were considered male garments.

The faces of Bedwell's sitters had been captured for all time, lasciviously curved Cupid's-bow lips, heavy eyelids, the kneeling girl ecstatic as she held back the fleshy hood and licked the tip of the recumbent woman's clitoris. This vital little organ was drawn with amazing accuracy, as if the artist had spent much time closely studying how it poked from the embrace of the furled and thickened lips, glistening with droplets of love juice. A handsome young dandy in a queue wig and frilled shirt, his breeches agape, was half hidden by the curtains, stroking himself to erection as he watched them with a lecherous smile.

Despite herself Karen could feel heat spreading between her thighs, her pussy moistening even more. Most cartoons of that period were crudely done, the lowest kind of rude representation intended for the masses, but these were brilliant and subtle. It was as much as she could do to keep her hand away from her pubis, the warmth doubled by the knowledge that Tony was sharing the same almost uncontrollable emotions.

He brought out the rest, one after the other, an exotic feast of sensual delights, each more daring and innovative than the last. There was one of a woman wearing vaguely Eastern dress suggestive of a harem. She was on all fours, bending over so that her pudendum was in full view: the shadowed area between her legs, the plump wet labia fringed with hair. Her mouth encompassed the turgid prick of the youth beneath her. An older man straddled her, about to thrust a truly spectacular twelve-inch cock into the depths of her forbidden rear entrance. A beautiful slave girl lay beside them, fingering the woman's enlarged clit.

Tony watched slyly as Karen's tongue passed over her

lips rapaciously and her hands crept up to cup her breasts, cheeks pink as she scrutinised each picture avidly.

There were idyllic gardens with girls on swings, skirts flying high, showing sturdy thighs and the peach-like bloom of dewy pubes amid a froth of white petticoats. Their gallants stood below, admiring the heavenly view while rubbing one another's cocks.

In contrast to the country landscapes of the period, Bedwell had sketched London's gambling dens, squalid dives with card-strewn tables, bottles standing on their sticky surfaces along with half empty glasses. The bawdy gamesters, pricks jutting out of their unfastened breeks, dropped chips down the cleavages of giggling girls. A naked whore, trussed like a chicken, lay on a trestle while they vied with one another, lobbing coins into her wide exposed cleft.

A sketch labelled *Symptoms of Sanctity* showed the interior of a monastery. A bald and very ugly monk was leering obscenely at a lovely young virgin standing before him, head bowed in prayer. The holy man's hand was resting on her bare breast while he fondled his balls with the other. They were surrounded by a rutting crowd of nuns and priests, clothing in disarray, black robes pulled up over nude backsides, each linked with another sexually by mouth, cunt, prick or anus.

The artist's imagination had known no bounds. He had drawn grand ladies entertaining swaggering grenadiers in their boudoirs, where dildoes stood in vases in place of flowers and randy maids and valets watched through window, fondling sex lips and penises. Or coaching inns where female passengers took time out to romp in the stables with well-endowed grooms. A masked highwayman pressed a lady against a carriage, her skirts whipped high as he penetrated her with a weapon longer and thicker than his pistol.

The study seemed to vibrate with the heat and grind of passion as Karen viewed the hump backed beast, transvestites, flagellation; dirty old men with grotesque, distended members and huge sagging testicles; beautiful youths with sprightly cocks springing eagerly from thick pubic hair, their balls firm and taut. No aspect of physical congress was left unexplored. Women with women, men with men, women with men, every variation under the sun depicted – a seething bacchanalia.

'You see how wonderful they are,' Tony said unsteadily, hand working up and down the outside of his trousers, distended and dampened by his urgent cock-head. 'It's great to look at them with you here. You, of all people, who understand and appreciate them.'

Karen's nipples and honey-pot were burning; the entire surface of her skin had become unbearably sensitive. She struggled for control. This was absurd and most unprofessional, throwing her into an ethical tizzy. She should be able to give a cool, unbiased assessment of the artistic merits of Dick Bedwell's work.

'I can see why they're so valuable,' was all she managed to gasp.

Tony pushed the drawings to the far side of the table. 'Lie down, Karen,' he said in a dark, persuasive tone.

There was no way she could deny him or herself as he pressed her back, the hard table edge cutting into her thighs. He possessed her lips hungrily, and she sighed with satisfaction at the feel of his tongue moving insidiously in the wetness of her mouth. He insinuated a hand into her T-shirt, fingers caressing her bare breasts with exquisite tenderness, then moving down to the elasticated waistband of her palazzo pants. Beneath he found the fragment of saturated cotton covering her mound.

'I'm surprised you're wearing knickers,' he whispered thickly, and wormed his way inside and teased her intimate lips with his fingers, opening the flood-gates of desire for her.

Twilight filled the quiet room. Blackwood Towers enfolded them. Guardian angel of lovers, or demon of desire? Karen gave a whimpering sob of longing. 'Touch me. Touch me there,' she begged, her hand reaching down to guide his finger to her pleasure centre.

He pressed on it hard, a fiery current shooting right through her. It was too much, so she took his hand in hers, lifted it to her mouth and wetted his finger with spittle, catching the fragrance of her juices on it, tasting it, rich and fruity. Tony's eyelids closed and he grunted with pure enjoyment as her lips closed around his finger, warmly, wetly, mimicking her lower lips. She guided his hand back down, dropping her pants, the thin material whispering down to tangle round her ankles.

His saliva-coated finger stroked her clitoris softly while she supplemented her pleasure by touching the crests of her nipples, circling them, pinching and rolling them, adding to that desperate need pounding through her veins. Her climax was on its way. She grew quiet as if in a trance, and Tony lifted her by the hips so that she could slide into position on the table, spread legs bent at the knees. He pressed between them, adoring her cleft, paying homage to the jewel in the crown – her gem-hard, pink, hungry clitoris.

His fingers and tongue encouraged it to swell even more, ready to take her higher. With a long moan she reached the summit. She was rising, swirling, tossed into an intense whirlpool of sensation, screaming with delight and release.

Then Tony was on top of her. She was aware of the mahogany against her bare back as he entered her in a single stroke, plunging deep, filling her with his big, powerful dick. She knew his crisis was upon him, feeling him thrust faster, hearing his laboured breathing, seeing his long, strong neck strained backwards, the tendons bulging.

She drew up her legs, folding them round his waist, feeling his furious ride towards completion. Her inner muscles held him, adding to his pleasure as, with a loud cry, he suddenly reached his goal.

Behind the two-way mirror in the priest-hole hidden in the thickness of the wall, Armina lay back in a wing-chair. She had a leg hooked over either arm, every part of her smooth, shiny wet quim exposed. With a hand slipped between her avenue, she worked her clitoris to a furious climax. Waves of molten heat gushed over her as she watched the scene in the next room where Tony and his lovely assistant thrashed on the table in the last throes of ecstasy.

They slumped. So did she, closing her eyes to appreciate fully the violent muscular contractions of her vagina sucking greedily at her fingers. When she opened them again, it was to see him lifting himself away from the relaxed body of the girl, his softening cock anointed by her juices. He wiped it on a tissue before sliding it back into his trousers and fastening up.

Armina grinned to herself, desire beginning to claw at her loins again. She had not realised Mallory's historical archivist had such a magnificent tool. Up till then she had not seriously considered cultivating him, but today's performance changed her mind.

As for the new girl? She was beautiful. Armina's clit twitched as she replayed the image of Tony bringing her to climax. A handsome young savage with the hips of a boy and the breasts of an Amazon, she had bucked and arched against the finger frigging her, moans escaping from her full lips. Did she swing both ways? It would not be difficult to find out. *Fun and games*, thought Lord

Burnet's most influential mistress. And there was no time like the present.

She had spied on them from a lookout post on the roof when they had arrived at the house, having learned from Tayte earlier that Tony Stroud had fetched his assistant from the railway station. Mallory, in the first flush of their affair, had introduced Armina to some of the manor's underground passages, and she had used one that connected the folly, a mock Greek temple built near the lake, with the priest-hole.

She liked it when Mallory was away, leaving her free to explore the house, poke into corners, rape bedrooms, ransack drawers and help herself to items she was certain he would never miss. She had the instinct of a magpie, unable to resist acquiring bright, sparkling objects that belonged by rights to others.

Armina never saw herself as a thief, more an opportunist. With a private income of her own, she had no need to shoplift but did it for kicks. It excited her as much as sex – the thrill of getting away with it, the powerful rush of excitement as she tripped nonchalantly out of a store with unpaid-for goods in her bag or about her person. She couldn't wait to find somewhere private after one of these adventures, the need to masturbate so extreme that she could have done it in the street with an audience of pedestrians.

Mallory, who had introduced her to the observation room, had told her how it had come into existence. Once a place to conceal priests during the days of religious persecution, it had been shut up for years. Then his roisterous ancestor, the notorious Regency rakehell Marmaduke Burnet, had won the Bedwell cartoons in a wager. Of fertile, lickerish imagination, he had at once seen the potential: open up the secret nook, install a mirror such as he had used to view the whores at work in Mother Baggot's brothel, where he was a frequent client, and bingo! Not only would he have a source of entertainment for his lecherous self, but a profitable sideline, too, charging fellow voyeurs for the privilege of watching those in the sanctum driven to a frenzy of lust, uncontrollably aroused by the drawings.

The whereabouts of this window on sin had been revealed to Mallory when he had inherited, the knowledge handed down to each successive heir to the title and estate. He was circumspect in his choice of intimates with whom to share the secret. Armina, to whom intrigue was the stuff of life, was one of the select few.

A mischief maker, with an eye on the main chance, she

could see that it would be a useful aid to blackmail, if circumstances arose. But just for now it provided a fillip for her rampant appetite and helped to keep Mallory's interest in her alive. He was fickle – cunt-struck for about a month after meeting someone new, then needing fresh stimulation.

Many a time he and Armina had amused themselves by standing in the dim, warm confines of the recess, viewing the action taking place on the other side of the mirror and reproducing it. The occupants of the cartoon room had been blissfully unaware that their activities reflected so excitingly in the beautiful antique Venetian glass were being relayed, slavered over and emulated.

He's as wicked as I am, Armina concluded smugly. My lover, my Lord Burnet, my Marquis of Ainsworth.

The library door opened on well-oiled hinges. Karen turned from helping Tony put the precious drawings away and stared at the woman who strolled in as if she owned the house and everything in it.

She was petite, her white-blonde hair cut short, forming cherubic curls round her shapely head, little fronds caressing the nape of her slender neck. Her face was gamine, elfin – big blue eyes, a retroussé nose, bull red lips.

There was hardly anything of her dress but Karen recognised it as being couturier designed and ferociously expensive. It was made of pale-blue chiffon and velvet with a scooped neck and a sequinned hem, which at its longest point reached halfway down her thighs and at its shortest was slit almost to the waist. Her clear, typically English skin was tanned to pale gold. Her naked legs were exquisitely formed and her feet pushed into high-heeled white satin mules, absurdly laced across the instep.

'Good evening, Armina,' Tony said, with a lift of his brow. 'How did you get in? I thought the house was out of bounds.'

She shimmied towards them, a feline smile dimpling her cheeks as she answered a shade defiantly, 'Mallory gives me the run of the place.' Her voice was low, husky, thrillingly modulated.

There was a self-satisfied air about her that suggested she had been up to something. Tony wondered what. He knew about Tayte. Who in and around the estate didn't? But he sensed an element of deeper mischief than her rogering the head groom.

'May I introduce my assistant, Karen Heyward? Karen this is Armina Channing, one of Lord Burnet's friends.'

'Hi,' Armina murmured, extending a perfectly manicured hand.

'Hello.' Karen was disconcerted as she took it, aware of the cling of those cool, slim fingers. By 'friend' did Tony mean 'mistress'? There was no doubt that Armina looked like someone's costly toy.

'She's not been here long. I met her at Exeter Station this afternoon,' Tony replied, considering the two lovely women who fitted so perfectly into the library's ornate splendour, both elegant, both infinitely desirable in entirely different ways.

'Has Mallory put her in one of the cottages? Armina asked, seating herself on a brocade-covered couch. As she sank into the deeply feathered cushions, her skirt rode up.

Karen quickly looked away, but not before she had caught a flash of a fascinatingly pale, hairless triangle. Armina's smile broadened. Karen knew without doubt that His Lordship's friend had done this on purpose.

A new, exciting feeling quivered along her nerves and centred in her sex. Curiosity, certainly; a burning desire to touch that depilated mound, to ask Armina why she had removed her down and what it felt like to do so, to probe between the chubby lips, to finger a clit other than her own. She swallowed hard, paced to the window and looked out at the darkening garden. Bats made swooping, noiseless rushes across the lawn and an owl screeched in the woods. Karen could see Armina's dark reflection in the panes, the glow from a reading lamp forming an undeserved halo round her flaxen head.

'She's staying in the one next to mine,' Tony said steadily. Somehow he was always wary when in Armina's presence, choosing his words with care. He followed his intuition and wouldn't trust her further than he could throw her.

'How neighbourly,' Armina cooed. 'So handy if she wants anything in the night.'

'Like what?' Tony was almost sure she knew he and Karen had been screwing. How she knew, he couldn't tell, but there was a darkening of her blue eyes as she looked at him, and invitation in the way in which the tip of her luscious rosy tongue played over her lips.

She lifted her bare shoulders in a shrug, the action raising her nipples above the chiffon, bright and shiny as cherries. 'Who knows? Maybe she'll be frightened? Have you lived in the country before, Karen?'

It was the first time she had addressed her directly, apart from the formal greeting, and Karen felt her voice brushing her ear like a kiss. She shivered as she heard her name, and felt the tender opening of her sex quiver, felt that voice like fingers trailing over her naked skin, touching her nipples and then dipping down to familiarise themselves with her labia ands ever-eager nub.

She straightened, drew herself up to her full, graceful height. 'No, Armina,' she replied levelly. 'One can hardly call Oxford University the country. I'm pleased to be here, and am looking forward to meeting Lord Burnet.'

'An, I see. You've not actually met him? Well, I can do something about that. Come with me.' She uncoiled her limbs and rose. Karen felt the soft yet firm touch of her hand. It sent fiery shocks up her arm, across her shoulders and down her spine.

They left the library, Tony following behind, walking through seemingly endless corridors until reaching a T-shaped intersection dominated by a large window. Armina nodded towards the passage on the right, pausing to run a hand over the thick crimson silk cord barring the way.

'That leads to the West Wing and Lord Burnet's private apartment,' she said. 'Strictly taboo. No one goes there unless he invites them. We go left. Don't worry. I know it seems like a rabbit warren but you'll get the hang of the place eventually.'

More lengthy corridors with vast doorways and tall windows, and then Armina opened a pair of doors and announced, 'The Long Gallery.'

'It's the finest room in the house, baroque in the extreme,' Tony said, as they stepped inside. 'Sixty feet long and forty wide, a perfect example of the Elizabethan penchant for grandeur, but with a practical application as well. On wet days, members of the family would have played carpet bowls here for exercise.

Karen stared round her, overwhelmed by the magnificence. Portraits of every Burnet from the sixteenth century to the twentieth lined the walls: bewigged statesmen, dashing admirals, generals in full dress uniform, red-robed judges and dandified gentlemen of fashion.

Their faces all bore the same stamp of strength, pride and confidence in their God-given right to ride rough-shod over lesser mortals. They were flanked by portraits of other members of their élite family – their wives and numerous offspring, even their favourite hounds and horses.

It was a wonderland of costumes and history, and Karen wandered down its length in a happy daze. She was distinctly aware of Armina at her side. It was as if sexuality emanated from the woman's pores, coiling round Karen, reaching out to her. Karen knew with absolute certainty there was unfinished business between them.

Tony was somewhere behind, paling into insignificance against the silken thread binding her ever closer in Armina's web. She was finding it hard to hide her arousal, and could tell by the brightness of Armina's eyes that she was aware and sharing the same feeling.

The mystery of the softly lit gallery wrapped itself round Karen like a feathery quilt. Its atmosphere was redolent of beeswax and pot pourri, of the wind blowing in from the sea, of old, far-off events, both grave and gay.

This house had seen sons ride off to war, had welcomed them home in triumph or received their coffins to stand in state in the Great Hall before interment in the family fault. It had been the venue for marriages – many brides must have yielded their maidenheads under this roof. Karen hoped they had done so willingly. There had been births, parties and great, costly occasions like a visit from a monarch during a royal progress.

'There he is,' a voice murmured in her ear, scented breath skimming lightly over the sensitive lobe. 'It was painted last winter. Isn't he drop-dead gorgeous? I helped him choose his outfit. The gold velvet slacks are by Van Noten, the black velvet jacket and damask waistcoat created especially for him by Moschino. And the long windcoat came from the Miyake workrooms.'

It was a shockingly arresting portrait, hanging incandescent on the wall, a visionary glow of paint. Karen's heart missed a beat, then rushed on again. Every nerve in her body tingled. Her sex ached emptily and her breasts hungered for a touch. Not anyone's touch. His.

It was as if he stared straight at her, was there in the flesh. He was magnificent. Perhaps the most magnificently handsome man she had ever seen. Long dark hair brushed his shoulders, his funky elegant clothes as modern as tomorrow, yet his features could have graced a Roman coin, classical, timeless: aquiline nose, high cheekbones, tawny eyes and a mouth with a ruthless slant, the upper lip hinting at impatience, the lower full and sensual. He was tall, with good shoulders and strong hands, the arrogant master of Blackwood Towers.

This was depicted in the background, glimpsed through dark, shrouding trees. Two hounds lay at his feet, gazing up at him as if hypnotised, and a hooded falcon rested on his raised right wrist, talons gripping the leather glove, as fierce and dangerous as her handler.

Karen reached out blindly, completely disoriented. Her fingers were met by and enmeshed in Armina's, who pressed against her side, whispering, 'Isn't he lovely? Can you see his bulge? Doesn't the very sight of him make your tits tingle and set your cunt on fire? Come back to my place tonight and I'll tell you about him.'

# Chapter Four

The Ainsworth Arms had merited a mention in every good-food guide covering Devon. Though its restaurant was fully booked, the landlord always kept a table in reserve for Lord Burnet or his friends.

The pub occupied a prime position at the top of the main street winding down to the crescent-shaped bay, an ancient hostelry which had opened its doors to travellers since the Middle Ages. That night was no exception. Every room had been taken, the holiday season being in full spate.

Karen was charmed by this fine example of a traditional coaching inn, a place of sooted beams hung with polished horse brasses, and open fireplaces that would blaze with logs in cold weather. Gleaming copper warming-pans adorned the panelled walls, and a collection of willow-pattern china, ships in bottles, enamelled signs and a hundred and one curios.

Their table was in the wide semi-circular window looking out over the harbour. The dying sun spread a dazzling copper path across the sea, and masts reared into the gathering night sky, not fishing boats but private yachts bobbing at anchor near the quayside.

The port relied on the tourist trade. Each hotel and house carrying a bed and breakfast sign was chock-a-block, chalets were booked from one year to the next, the caravan park was full and they would be turning away campers on every farm leading to Porthcombe. The boarding-house proprietors, shop keepers and publicans worked like galley slaves, sacrificing their own beds if need be. The season was short, money tight, and a long hard winter lay ahead.

'I'm famished,' Tony announced, scanning the menu. 'What d'you fancy, girls?'

Armina beckoned to the wine waiter. 'I want a Pimms, long and cool and fruity. I drove here, so it's only fair that one of you takes us back, then I can get rat-arsed.'

Tony shrugged good-naturedly. 'OK. I'll do it. Order

me a lager, and that'll be my lot.' Earlier he had returned the Range Rover to the garage of Blackwood Towers and Armina had commandeered the vintage Alfa Romeo Sprite she regarded as her own.

The fragrance of cooking wafted from the kitchens. Karen's mouth watered. She had eaten nothing but a sandwich all day, and a buffet-car one at that. There had been no time to think about food, Tony sweeping her away with his enthusiasms and his passion, but now she was ravenous.

A darkly smouldering Italian waiter sauntered across, smiling down at Armina then checking Karen out.

'Two Pimms and a Pils lager, please, Mario,' Armina purred, laying a hand on his arm with lazy intimacy. 'How are you, sweetie? Haven't seen you for ages. We must meet. When's your next evening off?'

Karen could not hear his murmured reply. She felt surprise crossed with resentment at Armina's familiarity with him, especially after the way she had drooled over the portrait of her lover, Lord Burnet. They were screened from the rest of the diners by a trough loaded with flamboyant hothouse plants, but Karen could see Armina running a crimson fingernail across the baton of Mario's cock as it sloped against his inner left thigh, underscored by the close fit of his black trousers.

Yet there was something wickedly attractive about Armina that made Karen forgive her peccadilloes. She defied convention with her skimpy dress clinging seductively to her body, naked beneath the sensual fabric, her breasts pert, nipples poking through the chiffon. Her precious little peach of a bottom tempted and teased with every movement she made.

Mario disappeared to be replaced by an older, plainer waiter who served their order. This was better. Karen was able to marshal her confused thoughts and concentrate on the food. She ate voraciously, though not blind to the way in which Armina's serpentine tongue sipped and tasted with the avidity of a lover sampling her partner's juices. Her every action had a sexual connotation.

The Ainsworth Arms lived up to its reputation: ravioli mixed with lobster and scallops and creamy fish sauce, followed by wafer-thin slices of veal cooked in wine and covered in mushrooms, mange tout and tiny puffs of deep fried potatoes that melted in the mouth. After this came pudding: glass dishes of magnificent ice cream, a symphony of raspberries, toffee fudge and whipped cream lavishly sprinkled with grated chocolate and almonds.

'Have you known each other long?' Armina directed her question at Tony as she licked a morsel from her lips.

He grinned at Karen, his beard giving him a raffish appearance. With his yoked cotton shirt and full, putty-coloured pants, he might have been an artist or man of letters fresh from Paris.

'I taught her how delightful sex could be and brought her to orgasm for the first time,' he replied, his gaze wandering over Armina's lips and throat and coming to rest on her breasts.

'Very old and close friends,' she murmured with a sultry smile.

She extended a foot in its fashionable mule and nudged him gently between the legs under cover of the table. Her intelligent yet decadently sensuous eyes were fixed on Karen's face with an absorption embarrassing yet stimulating in the light of her contact with Tony's testicles.

'Until him, sex for me had been all clumsy boys, a lot of heavy breathing, inexperienced penises, premature ejaculation and crushed breasts,' Karen said, her inner core tingling and moistening as she watched this brazen foreplay.

Had Tony and Armina been lovers? Hot images of

them fucking right there in the middle of the restaurant ripped through her mind. Or in the sanctum, perhaps? Maybe he had shown Armina the cartoons, sharing an upsurge of excitement leading to coition?

'I know. Been there. Done that. It's enough to turn a girl lesbian.' Armina, cool as a mountain stream, wriggled her toes against Tony's cock and then withdrew them.

'Even if she wasn't already inclined that way,' Tony purred sarcastically, his voice soft as silk.

Later, coming out of the lavatory in the ladies' room, Karen found Armina gone. She had left her powdering her nose and promising to wait. Where was she? Making a date with Mario? Bonking him against the garden wall? What would he be like in the sack? She had never done a field trial, but they did say Latins were lousy lovers.

She washed her hands, staring at herself in the mirror as she held them to the dryer, tired now, full of food and a tad too much alcohol. She wanted to go back to her little house, tuck under the duvet and sleep. Laurel Cottage. Such a pretty name, such a pretty place, and she must send cards to her mother and Alison, let them know she had arrived in one piece. Jeremy? Maybe. Or perhaps she'd wait till she received one postmarked Greece.

The corridor connecting the toilets with the restaurant was deserted. She moved in the direction of the bar, lost in thought and not looking where she was going. A man stepped in front of her. They collided. Clothed entirely in black leather, he carried a crash helmet under one arm.

'Sorry,' he said, steadying her with a large hand. Blue eyes contacted hers and held. 'Didn't mean to send you flying, miss.'

Her heart jumped. 'That's all right,' she replied automatically.

He was roughly six-two, with broad shoulders under a fringed, metal-studded biker's jacket. Thick, dark-blond hair straggled over the collar, a neatly braided plait behind each ear. Gold sleepers bearing tiny ankhs pierced the lobes. He had a wide-planed face and short nose. *If he'd been American*, Karen thought, *I'd have said he came from the Mid-West – a Hollander, like Brad Pitt whom he rather resembles. What a hunk!*

She could not resist glancing down, checking his equipment.

Yes, sure enough, there between his muscular leather-covered thighs lay the prominently thick finger of his phallus. Leather! There wasn't a smell like it anywhere on God's earth. Animal. Feral. Totally sex oriented.

She melted inside, loose and moist as she relived the moment in the library when she had sat in the operator's chair and rubbed her pussy against the seat. Leather combined with male sweat, male aftershave, the strong tang of male sex organs. Wonderful! Juices seeped from her vulva, soaking her panty gusset.

There was a certain rough charm about him, a combination of virile masculinity and innocent boyishness. He looked too wholesome to be a Hell's Angel. How old? She wondered during that long moment when they took each other's measure. Twenty?

'Can I buy you a drink?' His shyness was masked by a veneer of brash self-assurance, his accent West Country, but no country clod with straw in his hair.

'No, thank you. I'd like to but I've friends waiting. Another time, perhaps.'

*Damn*, she fretted. *I would have liked to get to know him, in the biblical sense, of course. Nothing serious. I've never pictured myself as a biker's old lady.*

'I haven't seen you around before,' he said, with an ingenuous smile.

'I only arrived today.'

'Where are you staying? I'll call for you, take you for a spin on the Harley. I've got another lid.'

A Harley-Davidson. He hadn't taken long to drop that into the conversation. Obviously it helped him pull.

'Laurel Cottage.' She wondered if this was wise but was unable to resist the lure of the huge basket in his leather trousers.

'Up on the estate?'

'Yes. Now, I really must go.'

'I'll call sometime. My name's Spike.'

*Get a life!* she thought sardonically. *I'll bet it's not; probably something plebeian – Michael or Alan, even Bill. Spike? How priapic, like motorbikes themselves.* She hoped the theory of big bike, small dick didn't apply to him. From what she'd seen, it looked far from small.

He did not move and she pushed past him, hotly aware of their bodies touching as she squeezed through the narrow doorway. She felt a responsive quiver deep inside her, the smell of him irresistibly provocative.

Armina lay on the chesterfield in a circle of lamp light. 'I'm pissed,' she announced. 'Not very pissed, just enough to make me feel horny as hell.'

'You should have brought Mario or Tony along.'

Karen lounged in the chintz-covered chair opposite, too indolent to stir a muscle, idly watching the television screen. *The Twilight Zone* was showing, the sound turned down, Vivaldi's *Four Seasons* drifting from the elegantly slender stereo speakers.

'Mario's working till two. Then he'll be bushed. That's no bloody use to me. I'd rather have a vibrator. Wouldn't you rather have a vibrator?' She propped herself up, staring at Karen owlishly. 'Great invention, vibrators. D'you realise there's no longer any need for men? They've outgrown their usefulness. We've enough semen in sperm banks to last for years – and have always had more pleasure from wanking or bringing each other off than having them poke us.'

'I thought you liked men?'

Karen wondered how she was going to get home. Tony had dropped them at the Dower House before driving back to his cottage. He had told her it was within walking distance, but it was dark outside, quiet and eerie. She had not come to terms with the country yet.

'I do,' Armina vowed earnestly. 'I love the brutes, but I love women, too. Variety, change, the element of risk the surprise, the unexpected – these make life worth living.' She uncurled with the ease and sinuousness of a cat. Karen could see her nipples, pink through blue silk. She wanted to stroke them, to feel them bunch under her fingertips.

Restless and desirous, she was haunted by visions of the fat, leather-wrapped package nestling in Spike's crotch. Had he been cut or was he *au naturel*? An intriguing puzzle, which she intended to solve at the earliest possible moment.

Armina's presence encouraged prurience, and Karen was experiencing actual discomfort in her pussy, a tormenting, pulsing need. With a tremendous effort of will, she concentrated on her surroundings.

The Dower House was a delight, pseudo-Gothic and wildly eccentric, furnished in a variety of styles and periods, mostly overblown Victorian, reflecting the period in which it had been refurbished. Once it had sheltered widowed marchionesses, now it housed a marquis's whore.

'You said you'd tell me about Lord Burnet,' she said, quashing her libidinous feelings.

'What d'you want to know? The size of his tool? If he lets a woman leave his bed unsatisfied? Things like that?' As she spoke, Armina rose and slowly, almost absentmindedly, slid down the nylon zip at the side of her dress, treating Karen to an enflaming glimpse of a perfect breast, a supple bare waist and hip, a fragile thigh, and a tiny, svelte bottom cheek.

She stepped out of the puddle of velvet. Nude, apart from her stilt-heeled shoes, she swayed across to where Karen sat. Standing in front of her, legs apart, she lifted her hands to her own breasts, her long lacquered nails lightly tracing over the nipples. They hardened, turning from pale to rose red, their tips on a level with Karen's mouth.

'I don't want intimate details about him,' Karen lied, resisting the frantic urge to tongue them. 'Just day to day things. For example, what's he like as a boss?'

She was becoming unbearably aroused. The combination of Armina's words, the nearness of that lovely flesh and the aroma wafting from the other woman's labia caused mayhem in her own wet and needy places.

It was incredible how someone so dainty could exude such unrestrained carnality. Karen could not tear her eyes away as Armina, obsessed with herself, cupped those tip-tilted breasts, lifted them, loved them and brushed her thumbs over the hard teats. Like a doll made by a master craftsman, her narrow shoulders dipped down to a handspan waist, concave belly and a pubis as naked as a prepubescent girl's.

'Why isn't it hairy?' Karen whispered, on the edge of the chair, drawn by the magical, alluring cleft stripped of its protective fuzz.

Armina was breathing deeply. 'I think my quim looks sexier bare. Men like it, too. It's a novelty. Sometimes I let it grow bushy when I feel like a change.' She became serious, tipping her pelvis forward so that her mons was even closer to Karen. As she moved her legs, opening them wider, the smell of her love-juices became more pungent.

'Tell me about Lord Burnet,' Karen gasped, hovering on the brink, desperate to come.

'He's a bastard to work for, I should imagine, if his behaviour elsewhere is anything to go by,' Armina murmured dreamily, and now one of her hands crept down to her pubis. Her sex-lips pouted between her fingers, swollen and flushed, glistening with nectar. 'But there's nothing more exciting than an arrogant bastard, providing he looks like Mallory. He's hung like a stallion. His cock is a good nine inches long when he has a hard-on. Thick as a flag pole, and, boy, does he know how to use it!'

Karen was no longer listening, her mind spinning as she watched Armina playing with herself, ripples of lust coursing down her spine to centre on her pulsating clitoris. When Armina moaned, eyes half closed with longing, the urge to help her achieve orgasm was the most powerful thing Karen had ever experienced. Without realising what she was doing, she touched the velvet-smooth mound and inserted a finger alongside Armina's, deep within the hot, wet crease.

'Do you still have your maidenhair, Karen? Is it chestnut or a lighter shade. May I see?' Armina's voice rang with excitement.

'I've never – I'm no dyke. I like men,' Karen began, tripping over the words.

'That makes no difference.' The elfin eyes smiled encouragingly. 'If you've never tried, how can you tell? You may find you prefer women. Why restrict yourself? Enjoy the best of all possible worlds.'

'I'm not sure I want to.'

Armina moved away, scooped her dress from the floor and held out her hand. 'Let's continue this conversation upstairs. No one will disturb us. It's late, dark; we're quite alone. What happens between us can be forgotten or dismissed as a dream – or maybe remembered and repeated.'

With the scent of Armina on her fingers, Karen was

unable to do other than trail after her, bewitched by the slender back and the perfect spheres of her buttocks, thighs elongated, calves clenched to keep her balance against the unnatural cant of high heels. Moonlight notched through the tiny panes of the first landing window, adding its blue-white frosting to the peachy glow of wall lamps.

There was deep-pile carpet underfoot, William Morris wallpaper on either side, lithographs of Edwardian subjects – sentimental, sensual – of an era when nudity was permissible as long as the subject was artistic and classical. An arched cedarwood door, and Karen stepped over the threshold of Armina's lair.

A sweet, spicy odour filled her nostrils, as of smouldering joss sticks. It took a moment for her eyes to adjust. Candles dipped and wavered as the breeze stirred the muslin curtains. A cool room – white carpet, white walls – a brass bedstead with misty lace cascading around it.

Armina leaned against an inner door, a tulip-shaped wine glass in her hand. 'I'm taking a bath. Will you join me?'

More candlelight, silver holders ringing the sunken black marble tub, the flames reflected in mirror tiles alternating with shocking pink. The incense mingled with other exotic odours – saffron and frangipani, carnation and attar of roses. Steam drifted over the dark water like mist on a bayou.

Karen's fingers shook as she unfastened her top. She had never been shy in exposing her breasts to male eyes, but now she wanted to fold her arms across them.

Armina stretched, ribs lifting, raising her tits high, then kicked off her mules and walked down the steps circling the bath. Her feet were immersed, then her legs and lower thighs. The perfumed, oily water, shining like onyx, cut across the lower point of her triangle, brushing the avenue dividing her pubis before diving impudently between her legs.

Karen was bemused by wine and a surfeit of beauty. 'You remind me of Leighton's *The Bath of Psyche*.'

Armina chuckled, patting her pudenda. 'Dirty old buggers, the Victorians.'

'I thought they were passionately obsessed with art.'

'Obsessed by their cocks, like all men.' After firing this volley Armina slipped into the tub, floating with her head supported on the rim, body and legs outstretched. Her skin shone like alabaster in contrast to the Stygian gloom, nipples crimson buds.

She sat up a shower of flashing droplets, reached out and grabbed Karen by the ankle. Her hand was wet, and warm trickles coursed between Karen's toes to puddle the shaggy black carpet. Slowly, luxuriously, her fingers walked up the wide trouser leg, a creeping heat radiating from them towards the fulcrum of Karen's pleasure.

Armina released her, sitting back, bright-eyed. 'Well?' she asked challengingly.

Karen gasped, flung open her arms, the heat growing as Armina's eyes roamed over her breasts. In one swift movement she dropped her pants and peeled down her briefs. 'There,' she cried defiantly. 'You wanted to see it.'

'Ah ...' Armina's sigh was one of deep satisfaction. 'What a marvellous muff! It needs stroking, petting, bathing.'

Karen capitulated, sex the only imperative within her. Dreams were about to be realised – soft hands rousing her clit, soft thighs entwined with hers, the feel of soft skin, the embrace of a lover who knew exactly where she wanted to be touched and why; a twin soul, another woman who shared the same requirements to bring her to sexual completion. She could feel her body tightening, the heavy drag of desire warming the base of her belly.

Caressed by the water as its sly fingers insinuated themselves into her love hole, Karen welcomed the feel of cool moisture on her heated skin. Armina's hands brushed through her hair, loosening it, spreading it across her shoulders.

Now there was music, swelling from concealed speakers. She recognised Debussy's *Prélude à l'après-midi d'un faune*. Mysterious, evocative. It was one of her favourite pieces. She had read how Vaslav Nijinsky – that tormented genius loved by the impresario Diaghilev – had choreographed the ballet. Against her closed eyelids, Karen experienced the sensual dreams cunningly provoked by the tone poem. A steamy, languorous afternoon in mythical Greece; the faun, half man, half beast, beautiful, passionate, lustful, a voyeur watching naked nymphs disporting themselves.

'I adore this piece,' she began, then gave a sharp, distressed cry as Armina's clever fingers dipped down, performing a measured dance over the wet brown floss of Karen's mons. The tiny sensitive hairs created electric shocks, spreading along her thighs, into her epicentre, tingling up to force her nipples erect.

'So do I, darling.' Armina lathered her hands with creamy soap heavily scented with ylangylang. 'Did you know Nijinsky caused a scandal on the first night by wanking on stage during the finale?'

'Yes, I knew. It makes it all the more thrilling.'

'Music to jerk off to. Why d'you think I'm playing it?'

Karen shut her eyes and opened wide the doorway of her senses, imagined sunshine pouring on to her body and the smell of wild garlic, fresh grass, pines. The music soared higher, reaching a crescendo.

Armina gently massaged Karen's sex with soapy fingers, parting the fringed outer lips. Her finger was slickly wet over the furrow between, circling the vaginal opening, finding the mouth of her anus, dipping a finger in, then concentrating on the seat of power. The miniature foreskin was gently drawn back, the naked head of the clitoris bared in order to be thoroughly stimulated.

Karen's lids became heavy, the scent of the soap, the feel of those busy fingers on her bud lulling her into a trance-like state. She could feel the glorious glow of orgasm building up inside her. Then Armina's finger hovered, tapped the aching head lightly, stopped, was withdrawn.

She drew Karen close, nipples pressed to nipples, her mouth closing over hers, tongue tip darting between her lips. The kiss deepened, lengthened, and Karen was kissed as she had never been kissed before, every recess of her mouth explored.

Caught up in an anguished paroxysm of excitement, she lifted her hands, stroked Armina's shoulders, then moved down to touch those little breasts, marvelling at their firmness in her palm, enchanted by the tremor running through her lover's body. She gently disengaged herself from Armina's mouth and leaned forward, licking the tight teats, nipping them with her teeth, teasing them with her tongue. She slid down against the bath and gripped one of Armina's thighs between hers, hardly aware of what she was doing, beginning to rub her mound against it with a lithe movement of her hips. Her clitoris was erect and thrumming, overloaded with passion, ripe and ready to burst.

'Not quite yet. Lie back,' Armina whispered, smiling into her eyes, then taking the shower head in her hand.

This was bliss, the cool touch of the marble, the warm, stinging jets of the spray. It moved slowly, starting at her shoulders and then disappearing under the water, a miniature whirlpool betraying its presence, the feel of it swirling over her pubis, playing with her labia, toying with her clit. She moved her pelvis, thrust her shameless little organ towards that teasing fount.

With delicate precision, Armina lifted the shower to direct its humming stream to Karen's breasts, each nipple subjected to exquisite torture. Then she allowed the fanning tide to swirl over the swollen nether lips and wash the hard, greedy pearl so desperate for relief.

'Please,' Karen whimpered, gripping Armina's hand in an attempt to keep the force on her clit head, frustrated beyond belief.

'Only if you masturbate me after you've come.'

'I promise.' The idea roused her to even greater excitement. Let her only receive the bounty of orgasm and she'd willingly carry out Armina's every fantasy.

The jet died, and the women rested in the water while beneath Armina's skilled fingers Karen's roused clit bloomed. She began a soft circular motion around its sensitive hood. Karen heard a mewling sound and realised it was coming from her own throat. Armina's instinctive awareness of her body's needs was breathtaking. It was almost as if she was bringing herself to climax.

Tense, mad for release she worked herself against that artful digit, the water sloshing around them as Armina responded with a frenzied rubbing. Karen's need was basic – she didn't want gentleness now. Gasping, clinging to Armina's shoulders, she abandoned herself, coming in a thrashing, screaming frenzy, a surge of sharp, almost painful pleasure unlike anything she had ever known.

Armina's fingers plunged into the convulsing vagina, taking the tight spasms as wave after wave rolled over Karen. She did not withdraw them right away, allowing her time for them to subside – allowing her space to fall down from the stars.

With glowing eyes, she gently left her, rising from the bath, water streaming down her limbs. 'Come to bed,' she whispered, and as Karen joined her on the black carpet, she tenderly wrapped them both in an enveloping towel.

Karen felt like a virgin, shattered by the experience Armina had taken her through, anxious to please her. The satin bed sheets embraced them as they sank into the depths of the vast couch. Now Armina was the willing victim of pleasure, and Karen knew for the first time the delight of rousing a woman, every caress, each tender embrace she lavished on her echoed in her own secret parts.

Honeyed kisses, long and deep, the taste of scented flesh – smooth as silk, not hard and hairy like a man's, nipples that sprang alert at the merest brushing of fingers, satisfying nipples swelling against the tongue, the gasps of delight, the moans of want – an uninhibited creature writhing under her caresses, emotional, expressive, all soft, ensorcelled delight.

And then the final exploration. Armina spread her legs, and Karen went down to enjoy the heart of her flower, labia like petals moist with honeydew. No stiff phallus with its hard ridges and aggressive thrusting – just delicate flesh with the bloom, scent and colour of a wild rose. Karen worshipped at the alter of Armina's sex, fingers adoring the clitoris enthroned at the top of the delicious avenue.

Armina moaned, rubbing her nipples in time to Karen's gentle friction on the treasured gem. 'Faster,' she begged. 'Don't hold back! Make me come! Bring me off!'

'I will. Oh, yes … I want you to come. I want to watch you do it. It's me giving it to you – and I love it!' Karen cried eagerly, forgetting any other lover she'd ever had, driven by this need to satisfy Armina.

She used a light, rhythmical stroke, feeling the clit stalk thickening, the head swelling even more, feeling the shivers gathering in Armina's limbs, smelling the fresh juices welling from the mouth of her vagina. It was heady stuff, making her own nub burn and quiver in response.

Armina bucked and yelled and forced herself up against Karen's finger, long shudders convulsing through her. Then she collapsed and lay prone, head to one side, eyes closed, at peace. Her breasts rose and fell with the quickness of her breathing, then gradually subsided.

After a while she stirred, opened her eyes, smiled at Karen and drew her into her arms. Cradled together the two women slept, the misty curtains enfolding them as in an enchanted arbour.

Dreams, half formed, fragmentary. Karen rose through layers of sleep into consciousness. Somewhere she could hear the thud of a horse's hooves. It was not important enough to awake her fully. She fell back into the velvet blackness of oblivion.

A door opened and closed. She felt the draught on her face. Then silence and darkness. There seemed to be a disturbance around her, the bed moving, no longer a bed but a raft floating on a spangled crimson sea. She heard Armina saying,

'I wasn't expecting you.'

A voice answering her, a deep, masculine voice threaded with amusement. 'So I see.'

Karen opened her eyes. Dawn was poking inquisitive

fingers through the drapes, and she stared full into the face of the man leaning against the bedpost. Still part enmeshed in dreams, it was as if the portrait had climbed off the wall in the Long Gallery and walked to the Dower House.

He lounged there, legs crossed at the ankles, arms folded over his chest, audacious, beautiful, regarding her lazily through a masked expression, a coiled alertness in his indolent stance.

His stare shocked through her to the heartland of her being. In his eyes she read his awareness of her loving with Armina. His lips curled into a sardonic smile. His down-sweeping glance went over her nakedness, slowly, speculatively. It was like flame and frost, making her nipples rise and her sphincter clench. She pulled the sheet up to her chin.

'Who are you?' he asked.

'Karen Heyward.' She felt at a complete disadvantage, anger rising in a turbulent flood.

The bar of his black brows swooped down. 'I don't know you, do I?'

Karen swung her legs over the side of the bed, keeping her body covered. 'You know of me. I'm Tony Stroud's assistant.'

The silk was slippery, difficult to control. It slid away from her shoulders with consummate ease, its weight pulling it to the ground, leaving her nude. She grabbed at it, the fresh morning air invading her crease like a cold finger as she inadvertently raised her bottom. Her face flamed and she turned away from Lord Burnet, clutching the rebellious folds about her.

He moved, graceful as a panther, taking her place beside Armina, sprawling on the bed, relaxed and unconcerned. 'I remember. Tony told me about you. When did you arrive?'

'Yesterday,' she mumbled, cursing him, Tony, Armina and, most of all, herself. This was a lamentable start to her career. What must he think of her?

Armina smiled at him sleepily, secure in her position, one hand coming over to smooth the corded material covering the solid baton of his cock resting along one thigh. Karen had never been more embarrassed in her life, bedevilled by odd thoughts and alien emotions that disturbed and infuriated her. Mallory was enough to unsettle the most self-confident of women. To her horror, she found she could not stop looking at him. He possessed that fatal combination of high-powered personality and aristocratic breeding well nigh impossible to resist.

He was too devastatingly handsome, a lock of night-black hair falling across his forehead. The glitter in his amber eyes caused a tremor of primitive fear and desire to bolt through her. The white linen shirt he wore fitted his arms and shoulders superbly; the tight buff riding breeches revealed the hard, muscular strength of his legs and the superb fullness of his genitals. Love-fluid eased from her vulva as Karen remembered Armina's assurance that his penis was formidable when aroused.

She watched as the long, thick rod in his breeches began to stir under Armina's ministrations. He lay supine as his mistress lipped his chest through the gap in the unbuttoned shirt, then opened it further. The skin was deeply tanned. Ebony hair grew in swirls around the nut-brown nipples, thinned out to a narrow line dipping to his navel, then vanished behind the silver buckle of his belt.

Karen knew he was observing her beneath lowered eyelids. She wanted to leave but her feet were rooted to the spot. Armina's deft fingers undid the belt and the top button of his breeches. Karen's throat was parched, her sex soaked, and Mallory's eyes were smoky, never leaving hers – daring her, challenging her.

*I won't yield!* she vowed. *I won't become just another of his women!*

Armina coiled herself round him, then sat astride his thighs, her cleft spread wide, pink lips thickening, the round head of her clitoris bulging shamelessly. Her fingers nimbly unzipped him. His penis reared from the restricting jodhpurs. Karen shivered and ached to have that cock buried inside her. It was everything Armina had promised – long and thick, the mauve glans rising from the retracted foreskin. Pearly moisture bedewed the tip, and Karen longed to sip it with her lips, savour it with her tongue, take every last inch of him into her throat.

Armina looked up with an I-told-you-so expression.

Karen stood there like stone. No movement, no expression betrayed the torment she was enduring. Her whole body throbbed while she grappled with desire. Instead of going away, it got stronger. Arms held straight at her sides, fists clenched into white-knuckled balls, she refused to beg for release as she endured the frustration of seeing Armina pleasuring Mallory.

She watched her go down on him, taking that rock-hard phallus between her lips, teasing the cock tip, then absorbing it into her mouth, slowly, gingerly, as if unable to take it all in one swoop.

His eyes remained fixed on Karen's face, the bright,

predatory eyes of a hawk. Up and down Armina went on the thick engorged bough of his phallus. His fingers were like talons in her hair, forcing her to go faster, thrusting mercilessly till his black pubic hair was against her lips. He gasped, eyes still spearing Karen's. She saw the sudden jerk of his body as he came, spurting his creamy load into Armina's throat. She coughed, spluttered, come streaming from her mouth.

Karen burned with frustration and fury. *He knows how much I want him, the arrogant devil!* she raged. *I'll teach him he isn't the only man worth fucking!* Deliberately she turned her back on him and stalked out of the door.

# Chapter Five

'What a job!' Karen exclaimed from her perch on the library steps. 'I shouldn't think anyone's been up here for a decade.' Hot, dusty, she had already spent three days at it but so far had only scratched the surface of the monumental task of correlating the vast amount of undocumented material.

'Take a break,' Tony advised, looking up at her legs, bared to the tops of her thighs by her cotton shorts. A divine vista from where he stood – the shaded area under her buttocks, the seam running between them drawn tight against the rounded swell of her closed sex-lips.

'You're too darn conscientious,' he continued, hands sunk deep in his pockets, the left one surreptitiously scratching his balls. 'There's no desperate rush. It's taken a couple of generations to get in this mess and you can't expect to put it right in five minutes.'

Karen climbed down carefully, a pile of books in her arms. Placing them on the only available corner of the table, she brushed the back of her hand over her sticky forehead. Her spine and calf muscles ached. She had hardly stopped since the day after she arrived, driven by a force far stronger than interest or ambition. Pride was the spur – the desire to show the high-handed individual who paid her wages that she was a competent, hard-headed historian, not one of his mistress's play-fellows who would fall over herself to provide him with an additional lay.

She had seen neither hide nor hair of him since that unfortunate introduction at the Dower House and told herself she was glad. The less contact they had with one another the better. Tony had carte blanche to catalogue the library as he saw fit, already putting his plans into operation. All Karen had to do was follow instructions, arrange the volumes by title, author and subject, and add fresh data to that already on file.

Dick Bedwell's masterpieces had been described and itemised before she came. Tony had not taken them out again, but she knew he was seeking an opportunity to do so. Lust stirred in her belly as she visualised looking at them. Work, however, came before pleasure, and she had much to do, not only in the library but also at Laurel Cottage.

She had spent time arranging the interior to her liking. More of her possessions had been delivered by carrier and it was beginning to look like home. A Volkswagen Golf had been placed at her disposal, and she'd driven down to Porthcombe to familiarise herself with the layout, and to stock up on provisions. Everything was to hand there – hypermarkets, hair stylists, several antique emporiums, a halfway decent record shop where she discovered a couple of CDs she had been seeking, even a cinema.

So far she had not met many members of staff, though they had returned when the master had arrived. *Far too many to cater for the wants of one man*, she thought scathingly. *It's immoral, almost obscene in this day and age*.

Seated on a bench on the terrace where luncheon was served, she leaned her head against sun-baked stone and raised her face to the cloudless cobalt sky. Her legs were tanned, arms bare as she soaked up the sunshine, radical views on the fair division of wealth fading. Gracious living was undeniably good. Servants to do the chores and bring trays of food, gardeners to keep the grounds in order. The staff were unobtrusive, going about their tasks with quiet efficiency.

'I could get used to this,' she confessed, running her hands down the length of her smooth brown thighs, stretching luxuriously as a cat will when taking its ease on a sunny windowsill.

Tony poured her a tumbler of iced orange juice. 'I already have.' Then he shot her a shrewd glance. 'You haven't told me much about your meeting with Lord Burnet.'

Her eyes darkened. 'I don't want to talk about it.'

'He talked to me about you. Seems he was impressed.'

'Really?'

'Oh, yes,' Tony said with a lopsided grin, and passed her the salad bowl. 'I think you're in with a chance there, girl.'

Karen took up the servers and helped herself. Each day they had eaten thus, every item beautifully prepared and presented. A cold collation with a continental touch. Lush beef tomatoes and wafer-thin slivers of onion saturated in tasty olive oil and spiced vinaigrette, to which had been added a whisper of garlic; a cheese board with Brie, Gruyère, Edam, Stilton and Leicestershire; a platter of sliced smoked sausage; a basket of crusty fresh rolls. The citron hue of lemon juice, the fiery blaze of orange, the purple velvet of grapes waited in cut-glass jugs, blended and iced and delicious, to be followed by dark coffee as bittersweet as love.

She lifted her fork and pushed the food about her plate, saying slowly, 'Let's get one thing straight. I don't much care what he thinks of me personally, as long as he's satisfied with my work.'

'Of course,' Tony replied solemnly.

'I'm not joking.'

He spread his hands wide and lifted his shoulders. 'Did I say you were? Perish the thought.'

'I mean it, Tony. Don't get any ideas. I've no intention of taking part in a cosy little threesome with him and Armina.'

His look was wide-eyed and innocent, but he reached out and ran a seeking finger along the low oval of the crop-top struggling to contain her full breasts. Her nipples immediately stiffened, two sharp points lifting the thin fabric. Tony tweaked them gently. She moved away, sliding along the bench, the action dragging her shorts across her secret lips. Like her nipples, they responded to the friction, perturbation starting in her core, juices welling to dampen her panties.

'Shall we make it a short lunch-time?' he murmured, and she could not fail to be aware of the high, taut line of his prick under the cotton trousers. 'I fancy working on the cartoons this afternoon. Don't you?'

The priest-hole was drenched in the somnolence of summer. The scent of newly mown grass drifted in through the arrow-slit window, along with the drowsy sound of bees hovering over heavy, pollen-coated stamens. A single ray of light, grainy with dust and circling flies, formed an aura round Mallory Burnet's head.

Lounging in a comfortable chair placed opposite the double mirror, he became alert as Tony and Karen entered the sanctum. Desire coursed through him. The archivist was carrying out his request.

Karen had the kind of looks that turned him on – tall without being gawky, graceful as a ballerina, slender but strong bodied, with hips wide enough to accommodate the largest of male members. Independent and feisty, too. This added to her attraction. As he remembered her naked in Armina's bedroom, his penis stirred like an awakening serpent and he felt a heavy ache in the spunk-loaded balls loosely cushioned by his black jogging pants.

He saw Tony glance in the mirror, a half smile on his lips as he deliberately turned the unsuspecting Karen to face it. She leaned back languidly, wriggling her backside into the hardness of his groin. Tony kissed her neck, then freed himself and went to the cabinet, taking out the drawings. Karen followed him, moistening her lips with the tip of her tongue as she bent over to look at them. Tony draped an arm round her shoulders as he also scrutinised the drawings.

Mallory's excitement burgeoned as he watched the historian's hand wander down to cradle her left breast, thumb circling the pointed hidden nipple. Her face flushed as she responded to the pleasure and at the same time absorbed the rich sexual feast spread before her.

This was too much for Mallory's self-control, the ache in his cods needing relief. He loosened the cord of his pants, relaxed his thighs and slid a hand under the waistband. A shiver passed through him as his fingers made contact with the naked flesh of his belly, touched the wiry pubic hair and cupped the full globes resting between his legs under his sky-pointing penis.

Before him, framed in the mirror, was the disturbing sight of Tony removing Karen's top and then her shorts. He positioned her to give Mallory an uninterrupted view of her furry wedge, his fingers holding her sex lips open, the outer ones bordered with hair, the inner pink and smooth. Angled against him, her pubis was thrust forward as he began to massage her clitoris till it protruded like a miniature dick, hard and shiny, betraying its need for orgasm.

Ignorant of her audience, she watched in the mirror as Tony's fingers worked her bud, following the movement with her eyes. Mallory could almost feel the silken lips and smell the fragrance seeping from her, almost share Tony's excitement as he opened his fly, grasped her firmly by the hips and thrust his cock into her from the rear.

Slowly Mallory stroked the thick shaft of his phallus until it dribbled, aching for release. Karen's head rested back against Tony's shoulder, her long throat arched, hips gyrating sensuously against the double pleasure of a slick, wet prick driving into her and a finger frigging her love-button.

Mallory stifled a groan, the scalding heat of lust greater than he had ever known it, his cock-head slippery, his fingers curled round the trunk, pleasuring it with long, smooth strokes. It was as if he held Karen in his arms, thrusting his spear into her hot wet sheath, her tangled mane of hair flowed over them both, a perfumed curtain in which a man might hide himself and his fears. This mental image transcended the reality of the couple screwing in the sanctum and him masturbating as he watched them in a trick looking-glass.

Tony's movements were becoming frenzied and Karen ground her clit against his hand, eyes closed, an ecstatic expression on her face. Mallory drew his foreskin down over his glans then pushed it up, repeating the motion, sensation pouring through him as the frisson brought him painfully close to climax.

Karen's eyes were aflame, her skin flushed and glowing as Tony heaved and lunged, panting heavily. The fierce heat of Mallory's release thundered through his body, forcibly ejecting a spurt of liquid from his balls with such violence that it spattered the mirror with milky drops.

The phone was ringing as Karen opened the door of Laurel Cottage. She dropped her bag on the floor and reached for the receiver. 'Hello,' she said.

'Armina here,' a breathy voice answered. 'What're you doing tonight?'

'Not a lot. I'm about to take a shower—'

'Wish I was there—'

Crimson-tinted visions of spicy-scented female organs made a coil tighten in her womb, but Karen continued calmly, 'Then I'm going to cook myself something to eat and watch telly.'

'Come round to my place.' The mellifluous voice was temptation itself. 'The girls will be here.'

'The girls?'

'Celine and Patty and Jo. You've not met the rest of our happy band of pilgrims, have you? Mallory's tarts.'

OK, so the mistresses were turning up in full force. Karen could cope with that, but, 'Will he be there?' she asked tersely.

'No,' Armina replied and gave a silvery chuckle. 'This is strictly one for the girls. Nothing formal, just a few drinks and nibbles. A bitch session, if you like.'

It was one of those enchanted, balmy English summer evenings and Karen was restless. She could think of no plausible excuse to avoid accepting the invitation. In fact she was curious to see the ladies who had intimate knowledge of Mallory's body. Time to grasp the nettle, prepare herself for battle and meet the opposition.

She showered, deliberated, discarded one ensemble

after another, then settled for a burnt-sienna skirt in cotton crepe, flowing, button fronted, semi transparent. It undulated about her legs, sometimes opaque, at other times displaying the misty outline of the gap between her thighs and the minute scrap of matching silk covering her full, rounded triangle of freshly washed pussy hair.

*Good*, she thought, turning this way and that before the mirror. *I'm not prepared to sacrifice my individuality. This looks unusual, very French Riviera, and cost a bomb, for all its throw-away chic.* The top was short, low necked, sleeveless and coffee beige, which showed off her tan. A chunky African necklace, big dangling earrings, an ivory and brass bangle of great width and thickness, gold strap sandals, and her outfit was complete.

Karen was never quite satisfied with her appearance, and had always regretted having curly hair, dreaming of locks as straight as pump water, but now those thick, scrunch-dried ringlets pleased her. They added to the image she was trying to project – of someone bold and fearless, who knew her own mind and followed her star, striding confidently through the world, disregarding the opinions of others.

She decided to walk, taking the woodland path

towards the Dower House. And it was there she came upon Spike, leaning against a gleaming electric blue and chrome monster propped on its stand near the trunk of an oak tree.

He looked bigger than ever, loosened yellow curls brushing his shoulders, chest bare beneath a black leather waistcoat. His arms rippled with muscle; the skin was tanned a solid brown sprinkled with gold fur and ornamented with tattoos. A wolf snarled from his left bicep, a wild-haired Harpy from the right. Engraved bracelets of Celtic design coiled round his forearms. He was smoking a hand-rolled cigarette and registered no surprise on seeing her.

Karen stopped, acutely aware of her skirt lightly tangling between her bare thighs and skimming over her plump mound. Lingering rays of sunlight struck through the trees, lending the glade a copper tone. The arching branches met overhead, enclosing them in an Arcadian grove. A damp smell rose from the warm soil, redolent of growth and fertility, almost the smell of sex. And there stood that flaxen-haired young man, an Adonis in leather. The blood began to gather in her loins, thickening her labia, galvanising her sentinel clit into action. It never slept, always alert and hungry for sensations.

'Want to try out the hog?' he asked, and it was as if they were carrying on the conversation started in the pub.

'OK.'

He put on his helmet, dark visored, making him look sinister, blank faced, like Darth Vader. He could have been an alien or a knight errant – he was no longer quite human. Karen thrilled to this strangeness, every nerve sending urgent messages to her skin surface. He straddled the machine like a lover possessing the body of his mistress, his bulging tackle supported by the seat. He manoeuvred the bike's sleek bulk on to the footpath, his thigh muscles straining against his black leather trousers.

Taking its weight, one booted foot braced on the earth, he kick-started the engine and let it idle as he handed Karen a helmet from his pannier. It felt foreign, heavy, hot. The visor darkened the forest, making it greenish, like being under water.

The action of spreading her legs astride the passenger seat sent a charge through Karen's cunt. This intimate contact with the Harley's leashed power quickened her desire. Legs clasped round the warm leather, knees open, skirt rucked up, her pudenda rested against smoothness underpinned with the edge of steel. Anus and pussy were pressed down into that surging force by her own weight, and she felt herself growing wetter, fragile panties soaking with the lubrication engendered by desire.

'You OK?' he glanced back to ask, a man with no face.

'Yes.' She nodded vigorously and slid her arms round his waist, clinging tightly as the bike roared into motion.

Bumping, skidding, it careered down the uneven path, then met the crossroad at the bottom and took the lanes at speed. Out in the open now, Spike let out the throttle. An arrow-straight Roman road lay before them, cutting a swathe through the countryside.

The wind tore at Karen's hair. It flowed from under her helmet, made her skirt stream back, the air stinging her legs, forcing itself between them, plundering her sex. Her inner lips were alternately exposed and covered, crushed by the leather seat, abruptly released. She inhaled the hot smell of tarmac and the scent of Spike's body, his broad shoulders bent under the shiny leather, broad hands gripping the handlebars. She clung to him frantically, maddened by the speed and her own lust, terrified yet exultant.

She was no longer Karen but a wild warrior woman, a Valkyrie riding the storm clouds to gather up the bodies of dead heroes from the battlefield and carry them to Valhalla on the back of her warhorse. And Spike was Siegfried, super hero, about to claim her as his bride. The majestic chords of Richard Wagner's The Ring thundered through her brain, and she found herself singing aloud.

Spike had absolute control over the brute: 1300 ccs it might be, but he was master. They purred along at seventy, accelerated to do a ton in a fierce rush of speed, then dropped back to a steady eighty. The miles flashed under the wheels. Karen was aware that he had slowed, turning back towards the woods, cruising now, seeking a place to pull over.

He killed the engine and free-wheeled to a stop. They sat there for an instant, Karen's face buried against his shoulder, her breasts crushed into his back, nipples erect with cold and excitement. He dismounted, kicked down the stand and supported her as she climbed off. Her knees felt like jelly. Her sex was on fire. He unfastened his helmet and took it off, his tawny hair matted with sweat. She removed hers and went straight into his arms.

They did not speak. Words were superfluous. He wedged her against the bike. His hands came up to hold her head steady and his mouth fastened on hers. This is how she wanted it, no tenderness, no pause, just sheer, unbridled animal lust. She felt intoxicated with it. Gasping with pleasure, she was desperate to feel him come inside her. Spike's tongue darted between her lips, exploring her mouth, and she savoured the taste of his saliva spiced with tobacco. She pushed open his waist-coat, running her hands over his crisp, light chest hair. Her questing fingertips encountered something else..

Each of his nipples was pierced by a small gold ring. This discovery roused her to fever pitch. Where else might he be pierced?

Spike's hands were under her top, pushing it up, exploring her breasts. Karen moaned; big though they were, they seemed lost in his enormous paws. They firmed to his touch, the tips taut. She could feel the hard-ness of metal at her back and the hardness of his stiff rod grinding against her front, twin pressure points of delight. Eyes half closed, she breathed in rhythm with Spike's finger kneading and rolling her nipples.

He lipped over her face and neck, his mouth finally closing on a rosy teat, sucking it with the avidity of an infant. One of his hands pushed up her skirt, fondling her buttocks, while the other made a beeline for her mound, fingering the damp cotton covering it, then working under one side, finding the margin of her swollen labia. Karen wriggled out of her knickers, the scrap of material abandoned on the earth between their feet, and slid her legs further apart to give him ease of access to her hot, hard centre. She could see his cock swollen behind its leather covering and yielded to the longing to undo his wide belt, lingering over the brass buckle.

He groaned, watching as she started to release him. His cock was big, long and uncut. It shot out, causing the zipper to descend on its own, not only delighting her with its size and stiffness but offering a surprise: a gold ring pierced the flesh, passing through the foreskin. Karen stared, smiled, opened her legs wider.

Spike placed his hands under her backside, stretching the cheeks apart as he lifted her, supported her weight against the bike and lowered her on to his upright shaft. She was so wet that he entered her in one swift stroke. She gasped as she did her best to accommodate him, hanging on to him round the shoulders as he moved her up and down on that length of rigid, slippery flesh, the blunt glans bumping against her cervix at every upward thrust, the ring a strange and pleasurable invasion.

She could feel him growing bigger, felt his cock twitch

and knew he would come at any moment. She held herself still, her fingers buried in his bush, pressing firmly at the base of his penis, preventing the spending of his abundant seed.

He got the message, pulled his prick from her, and she sat sideways on the saddle, legs spread wide, holding her sex-lips apart, her pearl glistening between them, pouting and steeped in honeydew. Spike knelt before her, his phallus at a ninety-degree angle as he bent to kiss her clitoris, lapping greedily round the stem, taking it between his lips.

She shuddered, arched her pelvis to meet him as her body tensed, rushing her towards orgasm till she peaked, her vagina spasming again and again. Then Spike swept her high, her legs clasping him round the waist as he impaled her on his cock. His hips moved savagely, once, twice, thrice, then his convulsions matched hers as he poured out his load.

When he withdrew, he kept his arms round her, his wet cock cooling against her belly. 'You're OK,' he murmured, his face radiant.

'You're not so bad yourself.' With a smile, Karen moved so that his softening prick slipped away from her. She bent and retrieved her panties, stepping into them and then smoothed down her creased skirt.

He tucked his penis away and zipped up. 'I'd like to see you again,' he said, with a disarming grin.

'I'm not looking for commitment,' she warned, pushed her fingers upwards through her hair, fluffing it out.

'And I'm not offering it.' He mounted the Harley. 'Can I give you a lift anywhere?'

'I was on my way to Dower House.' She got up behind him.

'One of Lord Burnet's women?'

She could not read his expression through the visor. 'No. I'm working in the Blackwood library.'

'Good.'

'D'you know him?' Karen fastened the chin strap of her helmet.

'Yep. My dad owns Cassey's Garage and we service his cars.'

'And the women? D'you know them, too?'

He nodded. No more talk; the bike was too noisy, the throbbing of its engine too enveloping. They reached the gates of the Dower House in a few seconds. Karen got off and gave him back the helmet. She felt a certain reluctance to leave, not that she intended to get involved, but she would have liked to have continued riding, experiencing the buzz of speed, the throb of power penetrating her core.

The front door was open but the house seemed deserted. After knocking, Karen waited for a moment, then walked round to the rear. Soon she head the sound of voices, feminine laughter, the splashing of water, and inhaled the odour of smouldering charcoal, charred meat and fried onions.

She rounded a corner and came out on a patio paved with terracotta Spanish tiles surrounding a pool lined with blue and white mosaic. The shallow end had wide steps leading down into the water, and seated on the middle one were a pair of beautiful women, one black, one white, both superb.

Armina was by the barbecue, using tongs to turn the steaks and chicken portions browning on a grid above glowing red coals.

'Glad you made it,' she cried. 'Make yourself at home. Meet Patty,' and she indicated the girl who was slicing baps on the pine table. She nodded at Karen and continued cutting. The women in the pool looked on curiously.

Karen felt overdressed. Everyone else was clad in next to nothing. Armina, water trickling down her body, had obviously been swimming. She was topless, her tiny breasts crowned with cold puckered nipples. Her silver Lurex G-string clung to her pussy like a wet stamp, and the straight line of her crease could easily be seen through the damp material.

Patty, a plump brunette, wore a pair of cut-down jeans with the legs hacked so high that only a thin strip of denim was left between them. She had nothing on underneath, and had pulled them up into the crotch so tightly that the two separate halves of her sexual fruit were openly on display, the seam only just visible as it emerged from between her lower lips. The fact that she had carefully removed every trace of pubic hair made it all the more intriguing.

'Meet Jo and Celine,' Armina said, slipping her arm round Karen's waist and leading her to the poolside. 'Girls, this is Tony Stroud's assistant.'

They smiled and stood up, women who gloried in their bodies and the power such beauty bestowed on them. Celine was tall and sleek, with broad shoulders and tight-muscled buttocks. Her jutting breasts were crowned with huge nipples. She stalked up the steps, her hips and lean legs moving rhythmically under the single layer of thigh-length chiffon shirt moulding itself wetly to every curve and hollow. Her chocolate-coloured skin, her pitch-black hair braided into a hundred tiny plaits tipped with gold wire and bright beads, gave her the aspect of an exotic tribal queen. Her abundant bush formed a thicket from her lower belly to the apex of her triangle, the fronds curling between her legs.

Jo was small by comparison, yet not as petite as Armina and of athletic build. She was honey-skinned from sunbathing, with ash-blonde hair falling to her waist in one log sweep. Her eyes were deep violet-blue with thick curling lashes, dark at the base and gold at the tips. Given to a certain eccentricity of dress, her narrow waist was made even tinier by a red satin basque trimmed with black lace. The half-cups pushed her breasts high, the nipples two pebbles standing out proud. The tightly laced garment ended at the hip bone, and her lower torso was bare, drawing the eye to a part-depilated quim. An individualist, she had left a narrow line of hair sprouting each side of her deep amber-coloured cleft.

*These, then, are Lord Mallory's concubines*, Karen thought, fire coursing through her veins to settle and burn in her centre as she thought of him. She appreciated the freedom of this place where the women flaunted their nakedness with total unconcern. It was getting dark, but lights sprang on to illuminate the patio softly, under-water bulbs striking upwards from within the pool. All the scents of evening stole from the bushes and orna-mental hanging baskets to seduce the senses.

'D'you want a drink, honey?' asked Celine, in a deep, husky American accent. She held out a champagne flute in her long, brown fingers. The filbert-shaped nails were painted strawberry pink.

Karen took it, and also accepted steak and salad, touched by how the ladies were taking care of her, each seeming concerned she should feel at ease.

'Did you have many lovers at university? Was there much talent?' Patty asked. 'I went for a while, studying sociology. Couldn't concentrate on work, though; too many distractions. I met my first husband there. He was a dork but I wanted to get away from my parents.'

'I'm a singer, between gigs at the moment,' Celine sup-plied.

'And I'm a model, darling,' added Jo, fingering the nipples that lifted above her boned corset, teasing them into even stiffer points.

'D'you live in the village?' The wine was going to Karen's head and she needed to sit.

'Celine stays here when she's down,' Armina replied.

'I have a penthouse in London and another in New York,' Celine informed her, and Karen could not keep her eyes off those up-thrusting brown breasts, longing to open her mouth over the big dark nipples surrounded by even darker areolas. Her experience with Armina needed to be repeated.

'Jo and I have a cottage along the lane,' Patty put in, seated on a low wall, the fold of her shorts deeply trapped between the lips of her labia The denim was darkly stained from her quim juices. 'I like gardening, and it's great to be able to do what I want when I want without being bullied by a bossy husband.'

'How many have you had?' Karen warmed to the pretty, good-natured girl. Not too bright, perhaps, but of a friendly disposition.

Patty pulled a face. 'Three.'

'A glutton for punishment.' Armina laughed from her place on a wide padded lounger, bare legs elegantly posed, bare cleft exposed, the pink outer lips protruding. She patted the space beside her. 'Come and sit by me, Karen darling.'

'So, you're Lord Burnet's entertainment committee. He keeps you, does he? The ladies of his harem,' Karen said as she obeyed, her head spinning as the girls came closer, draping themselves on big, square tapestry-covered cushions circling the lounger.

They laughed, long throats stretched back, wide red lips opening on perfect teeth, scents escaping from their skins, exotic products from French perfumeries – jasmine, verbena, musk – overlaid with spices. This mingled with their individual body odours, fragrant hair and strong vaginal emanations. They were women who were sexually active and aware, joyously embracing every aspect of bodily sensation.

'Not exactly. We're too independent. Each of us met him through the social scene, but we come and go as we like. Has he made a pass at you yet?' asked Jo, looking Karen over with the eye of an expert, then putting out a soft hand and gently touching her ankle.

Karen's skin tingled, goose-bumps stippling her limbs, yet her anger against Mallory remained. 'No, he hasn't, and I don't wish him to,' she snapped.

This provoked more laughter. 'That's what we all thought, in the beginning,' Jo said, with a shake of her long blonde hair. 'He can be a bastard, but he has much to offer. It's a buzz to be able to say that you sleep with a lord. Good for the image.'

'He's OK.' Celine flexed her limbs, reminding Karen of a tigress. 'He plays the hard guy, but I guess he got that way when his wife walked out on him.'

'He's been married? I didn't know.' This was a shock. Was there no end to the hidden depths of this man? Even as this occurred to Karen, she was very conscious of Armina stroking her upper arm, slowly, languorously, making her melt inside.

'Oh, yes, when he was twenty. Too young, of course. And she was a bitch by all accounts, after him for his title and money. Did well out of the divorce settlement, went back to the States and took their son with her.' Armina was watching her closely, a smile deepening the dimples each side of her mouth.

'A son?' Somehow Karen could not imagine him as a father.

'An heir, my dear. It's essential for some one in his position. The boy will go to an English public school when he's older. Mallory visits him. Has just come back from LA, as a matter of fact. He's always in a bad mood for a while after.'

'Understandably.' Celine seemed more sympathetic towards him than the others. 'He'd like the kid with him full time.'

'Would he?' Patty murmured. 'I'm not sure about that. It would put a stop to his parties. He'd have to behave more responsibly.'

'Have you been invited to the one he's planning for next weekend?' Jo's hand slid higher, stroking the inside of Karen's thigh under cover of the flowing cotton skirt.

'No. I've not spoken to him since that morning when he turned up here.' Karen managed to answer in a steady voce, though her clit was jumping in eager anticipation of Jo's further exploration.

'He'll ask you. It's up to you whether you accept or not,' Armina said slowly, the touch of her fingers on Karen's arm echoing those of Jo's on her thigh. 'But don't turn it down out of hand. You might find it entertaining. He's an exceptional man and has some interesting friends. She stirred, swung her legs over the side of the lounger and rose to her feet in a graceful movement. 'It's getting chilly. Shall we go inside?'

Karen wanted to say it was time she was leaving, but her tongue seemed too big for her mouth and it was hard to speak. She wasn't sure how it happened but her glass always seemed to be brimming, no matter how often she drained it. They went through the French doors connecting the reception room with the terrace. It was a beautiful room filled with deep armchairs and couches, but this was not where Armina intended to spend the evening. After fetching further bottles, she led the way upstairs.

Karen followed, the stairs dipping and swaying, arms supporting her to the boudoir where she had been seduced by Armina and met Mallory. It was familiar yet strange tonight, wavering unsteadily. *No more champagne*, she thought, and tried to stand alone. She succeeded momentarily, leaning against the mullioned window embrasure. Behind her she could hear the girls laughing and Armina saying, 'Switch on the video, Celine. I want to see a porn movie.'

'Can't I watch *Salome*?' the American asked. 'You know I'm studying the role. It turns me on more than dirties.'

'It's too blood-thirsty,' Patty complained, plumping down on the four-poster, elbows resting on her humped knees.

'It's great!' Celine protested. 'John the Baptist spurns Salome. He's King Herod's prisoner, and she's the dirty old guy's step-daughter. He's got the hots for her. She does a striptease to give him a hard-on and demands John's severed head on a silver platter. Then she makes love to it.'

Karen turned to her, daylight dawning. 'I know the opera. It is wonderful. You said you were a singer. I thought you meant pop.'

Celine's smile was wide and warm. 'No, honey. I sing opera. I know I'm black, but that doesn't matter. I can play Tosca and Carmen and certainly Salome. Other parts, too. With all these avant-garde directors no one minds about colour these days, just as long as there's a big voice. And mine's certainly big.'

'As big as your fanny,' put in Armina, smiling at her lovingly.

The screen lit up and Strauss's seductive, decadent music permeated the bedroom. Celine had fast-forwarded the tape to the *Dance of the Seven Veils*. The fine down rose on Karen's limbs. It was spine-chilling stuff. Savage, sweet – demonic, divine; expressive of yearning, of the longing for the unattainable that torments the human heart. With every musical phrase, each dynamic chord, the beautiful diva coiled and twisted in sensual dance, removing drape after diaphanous drape, slowly, lasciviously, until she was stark naked.

'Get her nerve!' Celine whispered, awe-struck. 'Showing her bush at Covent Garden Opera House!'

'She's marvellous!' Karen enthused, high on watching

the singer portraying the obsessional madness of Salome, adoring the bloody head, kissing the dead lips, writhing on stage with it in her arms as if about to achieve orgasm.

Unified by their mutual love for this art form, Celine drew closer where they sat at the end of the bed, then slipped the T-shirt from Karen's shoulders, running her slender fingers over each bone and muscle. Karen drew in a sharp breath as Celine traced a line down between her breasts then, bending forward, opened her mouth to a nipple, not caressing it, simply warming it with her breath.

Karen braced herself, rejoicing in this intimacy, needing more, pushing upwards against that torment- ing mouth, till Celine relented and closed her lips over the taut, needful teat, sucking it strongly. Karen straightened, gripped Celine and hugged her. Armina took an ornamental box from the bedside cabinet, opened the lid and lifted out several dildoes, handing them to Patty and Jo.

'D'you want one?' she asked Karen, and offered a selection.

'Not yet,' she whispered. 'I'm happy as I am.'

Excitement shivered through her as the opera reached its dramatic conclusion. Celine reached over to switch off the machine, then concentrated on Karen again. She felt those brown fingers brush over her upper thigh. Her legs opened involuntarily and Celine pushed down the little triangle of cotton concealing the feathery mons. Her finger slipped lower and slid effortlessly between the folds of the outer lips while her thumb flicked lightly across the eager clitoris.

'You're wet,' Celine murmured in that resonant voice, her face pressed in Karen's neck, lips moving against her soft flesh. 'It's almost as if you'd had sex recently. Have you?'

'Yes. On the way here,' Karen confessed, while those artful finger continued to rouse her bud. 'He's a biker called Spike.'

'Spike? He's a good lay, isn't he?'

'You know him?' Karen no longer cared who had screwed who, when or how. All she wanted was for that smooth, perfectly timed caressing of her love-bud to continue till she erupted.

'We all know him, don't we, girls?' Celine looked up to say.

'We do,' they chorused.

Armina was seated on a chair, legs spread wide, running a huge black dildo across her slick-wet avenue, dallying to circle the head of her clit. It was a perfect model of a penis; veins running up its stem, knotted and realistic and a rounded, bulging cock-head. It hummed persistently, and she flicked a switch to make it move faster.

Patty, naked now, was kneeling over Jo who lay on her back on the bed. Patty's pussy was level with Jo's mouth and Jo's tongue was lapping at her juices and licking her bud. At the same time, Jo held a vibrator in her hand, pushing it between Patty's thighs and working it along her crack, touching her puckered nether hole and letting it idle over her plump button.

Armina squirmed and yelled, carried beyond the edge. She joined Celine and Karen on the bed and, as Celine slowly continued to move her fingers in a slow slick arc over Karen's aching bud, Armina inserted a thick pink rubber dildo into the singer's vagina, forcing a moan from her lips. When it was well moistened, Armina drew it out slowly and rubbed it over Celine's opened pussy, concentrating on her large red clitoris.

Karen lay there quietly, relishing every movement of Celine's fingertip – so wet now, slippery with that clear, fragrant juice seeping from Karen's aching vagina. Celine had settled down into a steady rubbing motion, the friction sending agonising need through Karen's entire body. It was gathering, centring, hot waves washing over her, the feeling tingling up from her toes, rushing down from her brain to explode in rainbow prisms of light and feeling.

While the ripples were still shuddering through her, she heard Jo and Patty cry out and felt Celine's spasm as she, too, climaxed.

# Chapter Six

Karen and Armina cantered across the wide stretch of land joining the cliff tops. The wind was fresh, blowing from the sea, which rolled in remorselessly, pounding and crashing on the rocks far below. Huge clouds threw swiftly moving shadows over the mighty expanse of green water. Patches of sunlight broke through to cast a radiance on the curling white breakers.

It was Saturday, and Karen had escaped the stuffy library, accepting Armina's invitation to ride. She had brought equestrian kit with her, and Tayte Penwarden had fixed her up with a lively mare. Now she turned in the saddle and shouted to Armina, 'I'll race you.'

Armina grinned, leaning over to slap her impatient

mount's finely arched neck gently. 'All right. Where's the finishing line?'

Karen pointed to a clump of stunted trees. 'Over there!' Her mare fidgeted restlessly, sensing a gallop.

They shot off, two speeding arrows, one piebald, the other grey. Karen loved being in the saddle again. She had ridden since she was a girl and understood horses, respecting their moods, their big hearts and courage. Now she rejoiced to feel the broad back between her legs, the skin-tight jodhpurs pressing hard against her cleft, stimulating her clitoris, but most of all she enjoyed the speed, the control, her mastery of the animal.

Armina was an expert, but Karen's pride insisted that she beat her. Head down, face flicked by the flowing mane, she dug her heels into the mare's sides, urging her to even greater effort. The animal stretched her graceful limbs in the air, touching the short springy turf only to leave it again with a single strike of her hooves. Armina was gaining, her wild, exultant shout carried on the wind. Her horse whinnied, his coat flecked with foam.

Karen felt her body lacked substance. She became one with the mare, wanting nothing but to fly like this for ever, the stormy sky, the fertile, spongy earth, the tumult of the sea mixing and melding with her own passionate being.

The trees were coming nearer. With one final burst of speed she reached them first. She slowed the mare to a walk, lovingly patting her streaming neck. Armina drew up alongside. She removed her hard hat, a gloved hand ruffling her springy curls.

'Well done, you.' There was genuine pleasure in her voice. 'You'd better join the hunt and enter the local gymkhanas. Ride for Blackwood Towers. Mallory's the champion at the moment, but we could do with a female challenger.'

Pink with exertion and Armina's praise, Karen dismounted, petting the mare, who was recovering her wind. The animal's warm breath wafted over her skin; the big noble head nuzzled gently into her shoulder. Karen knew a moment of pure happiness. It was as if she had passed through an initiation rite and been accepted by the ancient manor and its environs.

Tayte was waiting for them in the stable and Karen, blood running hot from the exhilaration of the race, was sharply aware of him. As he helped her down his hand lingered for longer than was necessary, black eyes boring into hers. He was ruggedly handsome; ebony curls, a good body, long legs with a promising swelling in the fly area. She caught the strong, evocative smell of him, comprised of hay and horses, fresh sweat and the underlying odour of masculine genitals. Her pussy clenched and her clitoris rose.

They stood there for a heartbeat no more and then he jumped back at the clatter of hooves on cobbles and ran out to assist Mallory. Karen strolled after him, leaning against the lintel, her heart contracting despite herself in appreciation of the picture presented to her bedazzled eyes. It could have been in any century, any country – man, horse and dogs returning from the kill.

Mallory was easy in the saddle, seated like an emperor on a black beast of enormous height, power and magnificence, two hounds panting at its side. His head was bare, the sudden sunlight striking ebony stars from his hair. A thonged jerkin in a natural shade of leather covered his wide shoulders, the full sleeves of his white shirt ballooning to band round his strong wrists. On his left wrist perched a hooded hawk, bells jingling on the jesses bound to each of its legs, just as in the Long Gallery portrait.

Several carcasses dangled from the back of his saddle, grey fur streaked with crimson. As Tayte held the horse steady, Mallory swung down, the raptor still balanced on his gauntlet, the tired dogs panting at his heels.

His eyes met Karen's. An electrifying jolt darted straight down her spine into her root. He nodded coolly. 'Miss Heyward.'

'Good morning, sir.'

'Hello, Mallory.' Armina sauntered out, hands on her hips, a diminutive horsewoman in elasticated breeches that boldly emphasised her sex-lips and rump. 'Caught some bunnies?'

He gave a narrow smile, and his right hand caressed the bird's brown speckled feathers. 'Leila has done well. Haven't you, my beauty?'

Karen had never before heard that caressing, tender note in his voice, and the hawk responded to it, quiet under his sure touch. An entirely new and astonishing facet of his personality had been revealed. She felt her resolve weakening, moved by this show of affection to a dumb creature and bewitched by his extraordinary good looks and animal magnetism.

'She's lovely,' she ventured, putting out a hand to touch Leila in lieu of touching him. All she could think about was the reptile slumbering in the warmth of and darkness of his crotch.

He swung away.

'Don't even try,' he warned grimly. 'The hawk is a wild thing, not some domesticated canary. She'll peck you as soon as look at you. She's nervous, highly strung. Leila's a true peregrine falcon. See her long sickle wings? If she wasn't hooded, I could show you her dark-brown eyes and the notch on either side of her beak.'

'I'd like that,' Karen answered, refusing to be intimidated. 'And I'd like to learn hawking.'

'I doubt you'd have the patience,' he said, with a scornful lift of his brow. 'Each bird is an individual, and all are difficult to train. They learn to obey one master and one only. I spent ten days and nights in the mews with Leila until she learned to accept me. We were alone the whole time.'

Karen's head spun as she visualised being alone with him in similar circumstances: the dimness of the mews, the soft rustle of feathers and the tinkle of jess bells, the isolation, with only this man beside her. Her sex ached, the lips swelling, the jodhpurs riding up her wet pussy, but she exerted her will power and did not betray this overwhelming longing, ice cool as she turned back into the stable.

'I'm sure I'd be able to do it,' she said levelly. 'I can do most things, if I set my mind to then. I've studied karate; that helps develop self-control.'

'Have you indeed?' He strode past her towards the adjoining mews.

'She's just beaten me in a race,' Armina called after him. 'I've said she ought to enter the horse trials.'

He paused, looked back over his shoulder, tall and lean and haughty. 'How d'you feel about that, Miss Heyward? Will you have time, or is there too much work for you to do in the library?'

Karen could feel her face flushing scarlet. 'Don't worry, sir. I won't neglect my duties,' she retorted, furious with him for suggesting she might be incompetent or lazy.

He smiled, that slow smile that never quite reached his eyes. 'I've no doubt you're a superwoman,' he said, his sarcasm cutting like a lash. 'We'll talk about it.'

'We won't!' she snarled, her breasts tingling, nipples aching for his mouth, brain refusing to admit it.

'I'm holding a dinner party tonight. You're invited.' He threw this casually over his shoulder as he disappeared into the shadowy mews.

'He approves of you,' Armina said, about to go after him. 'You'll have to excuse me. He likes me to give him head after he's been hunting. Catch you later.'

*Damnation!* Karen swore inwardly, disgruntled, disappointed and livid with herself for her reaction. *I won't go to his bloody dinner party!* But she knew she was lying. Curiosity would drive her there, if nothing else.

Her skin prickled as she became conscious of someone watching her. It was Tayte, leaning with his arms folded on the edge of a stall, his peaty, unsmiling eyes fixed on her breasts. Karen's breath shortened and her heart began to beat in slow, steady thumps. That uncomfortable feeling in her crotch refused to go away, the material chafing the moist, hair-fringed outer labia. She needed attention, needed it badly, and now, made desirous by the ride, the sudden appearance of Mallory and the strong emotions he provoked in her.

Tayte came round the stall and stood near her, not attempting to touch, simply looking, but his faded jeans were distorted by the erection stretching the denim. Karen wanted to free it, to see it spring out, to rub it until it paid her milky tribute.

'I've a room close by,' he said at last, and his calloused hand opened her riding jacket and rasped over the silk shirt she wore beneath, pausing when the nipple of one breast stiffened against his palm.

'Have you?' Her voice was unsteady, but she stood

there rigid, only her wanton teat betraying the tumult raging inside her.

'Why don't I show you?' His thumb revolved on the excited tip, then he lowered his head and she felt his mouth fasten round it, the silk damp now, his tongue wetting it as he slowly teased the hard little peak.

'I'd like that,' she whispered.

Tayte kissed her fingers, clasped in his for guidance. The gloom was full of obstacles, old chains, saddles, tackle and empty crates. The building had once been a tower, one of a pair from which the manor had taken its name. Used for stabling cattle during sieges in the old days, it now formed the mews, housed horses and acted as a storeroom for harnesses and fodder.

Karen stumbled on the uneven treads of the stair and Tayte's arm steadied her. He had, it seemed, the entire loft at his disposal, not a single room but a well-appointed flat, with a kitchen, bathroom, living-room and bedroom, it was all lime-washed walls and knotty, blackened beams, with a wood-burning stove set back in the thickness of a brick fireplace. A perfect venue for an amorous bachelor. Soon they were standing on opposite sides of his big old-fashioned bed.

Karen was thinking of Mallory and Armina in the

mews, imagining her taking his cock in her mouth and sucking it till he came. At the same time she remembered her nights in the Dower House when first Armina and then Celine had awakened her to the wonders of lesbian sex. She was burning, steamy, nectar escaping from her love-hole to make a wet patch on her breeches.

Tayte unbuttoned his check shirt while she watched, agitation rising at the sight of that gypsy-tinted flesh, his chest broad and hairless, the pectorals honed through breaking and training horses. His arms were coated with dark fuzz, his waist slim, clinched by the leather belt supporting his Levi's. He came round to her side of the bed, then reached for her, his wide mouth hovering about hers for an instant.

Karen reached up to meet his lips with a fire of her own, her tongue touching his. He held her firmly against the stirring mass of his cock, and her arms crept up round his sinewy neck. He explored her mouth deeply, his tongue working round her gums and teeth, tangling with her own tongue, sucking it between his lips. He released her and she helped him take off her jacket, then the silk shirt. It slithered to the floor, her breasts bared, round and firm, the nipples hard and rosy, arching upwards to be fondled.

Karen fell back on the bed, arms outstretched towards him. He left her momentarily, tugging at her boots and peeling down the riding breeches. She wore no panties, liking the feel of the rough fabric chafing her skin.

'I want to see your cock,' she demanded imperiously.

She sat up and worked at his fly buttons, taking his steel-hard rod into her hand while he stood there looking at her. It was large, red-capped, thrusting up from its crisp black bush. Karen ran a fingertip over the slit in its bulbous glans, then leaned closer, her tongue tasting the juice smearing it. Salty, sharp, its flavour stung but she took the shaft into her mouth, while Tayte arched his hips, pressing it in till the slippery head touched the back of her throat.

Spreading the opening of his breeches wide, she felt for his balls. The blood pulsed in those pendulous globes as she ran a finger over the ligament dividing them, weighing them, playing with the hardening pair in their velvet pouch. Tayte groaned and grasped her by the hair, pushing hard till she felt herself gagging. His creamy spunk ejected in a hot gush, filling her mouth, running from the corners of her lips to bedew her face.

He pulled away, his still erect prick covered in fluid.

'Don't worry, darling,' he gasped, 'there's plenty left for you.'

He lay on the bed and drew her on top of him. Karen, crazy for relief, moved upwards till her avid pussy was over his face. As his tongue met her engorged clitoris, she ground herself down and rubbed it over him frantically, coming in a welter of pleasure. Her spasms pouring through her, she felt Tayte slide her down till his stiff penis stabbed into her centre. Her legs started to tremble, the ridged sides of her vagina pulsing from her orgasm. It was as if it had a life of its own, grabbing and pulling on his cock, milking him of the rest of his juices.

It just kept coming, as if they were welded together. Karen almost fainted. Finally the convulsions subsided. His relaxed shaft slid from her and she lay across his chest, her face buried in his neck.

The loft righted itself and normal sounds penetrated the misty sex haze. She wriggled off Tayte and nestled beside him, her hand stroking his chest hair.

'God, you're great,' he said and kissed her temple. 'Armina told me you were a good screw, but I didn't realise just how good.'

'Armina?' It was disconcerting to realise they had been

discussing her, but perversely exciting, too. No doubt they would now compare notes. 'Do you fuck Armina?'

'Everyone fucks Armina,' he chuckled. 'You'll see tonight, at the party.'

Karen raised her hands and pushed her hair back from her forehead, and the shower cascaded over her upturned face like a tropical rainstorm. She reduced the jets a little, allowing the water to penetrate every nook and cranny of her body, relaxing under its warm caress. It ran down her breasts in rivulets and trickled slowly over her bunched nipples, the gently friction stimulating those votaries of Eros.

She reached for the shower gel and squeezed a generous puddle into her cupped palm. Vanilla essence spiced the steamy air as she spread it over her shoulders and breasts – milky, viscous, reminding her of jism. Rendered languorous by memories of her session with Tayte earlier on, she smoothed the lather around her nipples, circling the pink peaks, flicking them, lightly pinching them, wondering if she could come by her tits alone. Certainly, everything that happened to her nipples went hot-line to her vagina. She could feel herself getting juicy, and ran her hands down her body to her pussy.

The luxurious feel of the scented lather mingling with the streaming water coursing over her belly and thighs awakened new depths of desire that even Tayte's energetic fucking had failed to satisfy.

Mallory's face appeared in her inner eye, and her fingers slid down towards the water-matted curls of her pubis. In an hour or two she would see him again. Slowly, she opened the pink wings of her labia and pushed back the tiny foreskin, shuddering as she made contact with her precious pearl.

Pictures of her lovers flickered against the screen of her brain: Kan and Jeremy, Tony and Spike and Tayte; most of all, the one who she had not yet had – the enigmatic Mallory. She circled her clit, teasing it, patting it, her finger poised above it without granting the frig it craved.

Which of those men would she like with her now, bringing her to the edge, filling her cunt with their cocks? Their faces faded. She was conscious only of her rapacious centre. The middle finger of her right hand descended on it with a deliberate force that made her squirm.

Of all physical pleasure, she enjoyed masturbation most, relishing the sensation of her fingertip unfurling the petals of desire, finding the bud within, enjoying the sensation of her own finger against her own clit. There was sorcery in the way she could manipulate it, dam the cataract, think of something else, read a book while caressing herself, always aware but playing a game. She could make it last for an hour sometimes, delay the leap into heaven, that high, tumultuous moment of release.

It was a duel between her finger and her trigger button, and now it seemed that rampant protagonist was winning. The first spasm began, and she looked down, legs apart, holding back the labia with her free hand, so excited by the sight of that pearly pleasure point poking from its cowl that other spasms followed, one tumbling over the next.

Karen moaned, wanted to delay it, couldn't, thrusting her pubis forward as a final huge surge swept through her carrying her to an orgasm so intense it left her shuddering and gasping. She put out a hand to steady herself as the convulsions died away, the ripe sexual lubricant mingling with the lathery water flowing down to her feet, washing round them, gurgling towards the outlet.

Refreshed and energised, she stepped from the shower and reached for a large fluffy white towel, draping it round her as she wandered into the bedroom. Dry now, she dropped her covering, staring at her naked body in the pier glass, running her hands down her sleek, damp sides, amazed as always because nothing showed in her face. No one looking at her would guess she had been indulging in a secret vice. She selected body lotion from among the bottles on the dressing table and massaged it into her skin. The pungent aroma of *Samsara* rose above the lingering odour of vanilla.

Dinner was set for eight. She had half an hour to get ready. What to wear? It was a constant problem now, whereas at Oxford it had rarely bothered her. Undergarments or no? The weather was muggy, a storm threatening overhead. She thought no, but then again had not yet had the opportunity to try out the black satin underwired bra and matching girdle she had purchased on impulse in an Anne Summers shop.

The act of unwrapping the lingerie was thrilling in itself; such provocative, sexy scraps of nonsense. First she hooked the brassière at the back. It was only just big enough, her tanned flesh rising above the half-cups, nipples peeking saucily over the black lace. Next came the girdle, a narrow, restrictive strip that gripped her waist and left her lower belly and mons exposed, drawing the eye to it. Seated on a stool, Karen rolled black stockings up her legs, so sheer they resembled pewter mist, and clipped the suspenders to the tops, thighs responding as her fingers brushed them.

Standing again, she thrust her feet into high-heeled sandals and pirouetted before the mirror, enthralled by the sight of herself. She looked like a hooker. The black satin bonded her breasts and waist, cutting into her flesh. Greyish black encased her legs in startling contrast to the pale area of her buttocks and furry pubic triangle with its fascinating furrow.

Eager for more, she stepped into a minuscule thong. It seemed a crime to cover that fragrant slit, so pink and hairy and mysterious; but it was the first time she had worn crotchless knickers. She could not resist pulling them tightly over her crack, enthralled to see the plump lips pouting through the lacy gap. Her nub jutted forth, and she gave it a quick stroke but resisted masturbating again, promising herself she would do it later.

Flinging open the door of the walk-in wardrobe, she scanned the rows of clothes. Which should it be? This was, after all, an important occasion. She pulled out a green crushed-velvet number from an exclusive fashion house, a wickedly expensive extravaganza, consisting of a long-sleeved bodice with a plunging cleavage. This fastened at the back with tiny ball buttons and had a slinky ankle-length skirt which opened to her stocking tops on one side.

Karen wriggled into it and surveyed herself critically. It was daring but suitable for a dinner party at a baronial hall – though from Tayte's hints, she gathered this bash was hardly likely to be a formal affair. She felt good in the dress, and the colour was just right for her.

After moisturising her face and adding a touch of blusher, she brushed her lashes with greenish mascara, added moss eye shadow, then carefully outlined her mouth with carmine. She switched on the hair drier and bent her head, letting her hair fall forward as she subjected it to the diffuser's hot blast, scrunching and tousling, then tossing it back into an untamed mane of curls.

A string of emerald beads, swinging drop earrings and she was ready for anything, even the infuriating man whose very name made her feel unbearably randy – Lord Mallory Burnet.

In a mood of defiance she drove to the house, parked the Golf alongside several newly arrived vehicles and headed for the front door. The butler ushered her in after consulting the guest list and had a footman conduct her to His Lordship's apartment. Tony had offered to escort her, but on this occasion Karen had been determined to go it alone. Timidity had never been her way, and she certainly had no intention of starting now.

The red cord barring the entrance to the holy of holies had been removed. 'Just go down the corridor and turn right at the bottom, miss,' the young manservant said, his blue eyes twinkling, undisguised lust flickering across his pleasant features.

Karen had noticed him before on her daily visits to the library, had registered that he was stocky but well-built, had a thick mop of sandy hair and eyes that spoke volumes. She had already decided that maybe she would find out which pub he frequented and engineer a meeting.

'Thank you.' She gave him her most dazzling smile.

'You're welcome, miss.' His reply was prompt, his answering grin cheeky and too familiar. Karen left him with a spring in her step, fully aware he was sizing up her tush and probably wondering if she was wearing panties.

Long mirrors in gilded frames set at intervals along the panelled walls added to her confidence, throwing back reassuring reflections. Her gown was a perfect choice. She congratulated herself for being on the ball. Lord Burnet and his guests had better beware.

She reached the end of the corridor and stopped in her tracks. A pair of inlaid doors framed a glittering scene. The grandeur of the salon took her breath away. Her historian's eye noted the Carolean architecture and furnishings, carvings from the school of, if not actually executed by, Grinling Gibbons, Charles II's favourite interior designer, noted for his florid style.

Karen passed beneath the elaborate architrave featuring rams' heads and acanthus leaves, her feet encountering the plush pile of an Aubusson carpet, original and priceless, still perfect after maybe two hundred years of usage. Light radiated from three cut glass chandeliers positioned down the length of the ceiling between plaster swirls and medallions, interspersed with paintings depicting the travels of Odysseus.

Her ears pricked up. In the distance someone was playing the piano, a dreamy Chopin étude filling the night in perfect harmony with the setting and company. She did a double take. Mallory was giving as talented and polished a recital as any professional musician.

The men wore dinner jackets, the women evening gowns. There were a dozen couples, plus Patty, Jo and

Celine. And Tony was there, his beard neatly trimmed, wearing a white shirt and black bow tie, bowing to convention except for his midnight-blue velvet coat. He saw her and waved.

'Karen!' Armina trilled, breaking away from a group near the marble fireplace. 'You must meet Sinclair.'

She floated over to Karen, a cross between a pantomime fairy and a debutante clad in an apricot silk-satin bustier and a full tulle crinoline skirt, satin court shoes, and carrying a satin and diamanté bag. She wore no jewels except a pair of steel and gold earrings. Karen guessed the gown was probably by Kristensen and, added to the other pricy items, there couldn't have been much change out of £6000. Had Mallory footed the bill?

Armina linked arms with her and propelled her across to where a stranger leaned an elbow on the overmantel. He looked up as Armina cried, 'Here she is – the postgrad I've been telling you about, Karen Heyward. Karen, this is Sinclair, Mallory's brother.'

For a confused instant Karen thought it was Mallory, and then knew her mistake. He was the same height and build, had the same overpronounced good looks, but his hair was a shade lighter and his eyes were grey not golden sherry-brown. Like Mallory he possessed a powerful carnal attraction, but whereas his brother was aloof, stern, almost austere, Sinclair was a conquistador, an adventurer, with all the charisma of a man of that kind.

He bowed with a touch of irony, took her hand and raised it to his lips, hovering above it. 'Hello, Karen – if I may. So you're the one who has been dealing with those dusty tomes? Have you seen the Bedwell cartoons yet?'

He moved a shade closer, his sensual grey eyes questioning. Karen caught herself fantasising about how it would be to have him fuck her. She was certain it wouldn't be gentle; it would be more likely to contain elements of the jungle. A savage mating.

She struggled to keep her cool, realising she ought to say something, make polite, banal conversation. 'I have seen them, and think they're quite remarkable. Exquisitely drawn, not crude as such works often are.'

'Do you find them a turn on? Most people do, myself included,' he said, then boxed her in between an angle of the wall and his broad shoulders, lowering his voice and adding, 'I learned about sex through them. When I was a kid, I'd steal the keys, hide in the little room and wank my budding prick as I looked at them. My first come was over the one featuring the lady in the boudoir. I can even remember what it was called – *Morning Toilette*. I was frightened I'd stained it with spunk, but I'd managed to catch most of it in my handkerchief.'

Karen almost swayed towards him, tossed by a variety of emotions, uppermost of which was an intensity of attraction. Like Mallory? No. In reality they were as dissimilar as chalk and cheese. This man was unprincipled, not to be trusted, yet her body ached to have him penetrate it. She was wet between the thighs, mesmerised by his cynical smile and worldly eyes, that slim body under the tailored tuxedo, that narrow waist and a pelvis that seemed to throw into relief the solid bar of his cock beneath the narrow black barathea trousers.

Mallory rose from the piano when dinner was announced, resplendent in evening dress. 'You've not forgotten how to play,' Sinclair said. 'I suppose it's rather like riding a bike.'

Mallory's eyes switched from Sinclair's face to Karen's, then back to his brother. 'Why are you here'? he said, glacier cool. 'I don't recall inviting you.'

'Do I need an invitation to visit my old home?' Sinclair replied quietly, but with a sarcastic edge.

'I thought you were in Rio.'

'I flew into Heathrow today.'

'This has upset the seating arrangements.'

'Sorry, but my first thought was to drive down and see how you were getting on, old boy.'

What a smoothy, Karen concluded as she walked into the dining room with a Burnet brother on either side. And what a liar!

On the oval, lyre-legged Regency table, the light of a seven-branched candelabra was mirrored in Georgian silver and sparkled on Waterford crystal glasses. The Spode dinnerware was worth a fortune. Karen had been placed next to Tony, with a dapper, middle-aged stranger on her other hand, who seemed totally absorbed with his beautiful companion, a tall angular redhead in a fabulous Vivienne Westwood creation consisting of emerald-green satin stays and a bustle.

Further down Karen could see Armina next to Mallory, and Celine, looking like an exotic Brazilian orchid, draped in purple silk with a huge turban covering her locks. The unrepentant Sinclair was flirting outrageously with her, running a finger along the edge of her décolletage, causing the big nipples to stand out even more.

Amid light, inconsequential smalltalk, poker-faced

footmen served one fabulous dish after another, worthy of Le Manoir aux Quat' Saisons: wines of Bordeaux and Burgundy, both red and white, were poured with royal extravagance. Foreheads were beginning to flush, faces lighting up, eyes shining, reserve melting. And Mallory lounged at the head of the table, easy, gracious, regarding his guests from under hooded lids, though anger flashed in his eyes each time he glanced at Sinclair.

Karen leaned closer to Tony. 'Come on. Dish the dirt. What's the scandal scam? Why this vendetta?'

'Don't ask.' His lips twisted into a crooked smile. 'They've always resented each other, so the gossip goes. Sibling rivalry and all that. Then Caroline, that's Mallory ex, got the hots for Sinclair – before she was the ex, that is. It was almost a case of pistols at dawn.'

'But Mallory had other women,' Karen reminded him, while a strapping footman in formal gear leaned over her shoulder to remove her plate. He smelt good, a combination of fresh linen and aftershave on young skin.

'That's neither here nor there. Don't be so prissy, my dear.'

'I'm not being prissy. It's just that I've never been able to hack the "What's sauce for the goose isn't sauce for the gander" attitude.'

'Feminist!' Tony smiled and let his hand idle across her silk-stockinged knee under the cover of the damask tablecloth.

'I am, and proud of it.' She remained outwardly composed, though anticipation quivered along her nerves at that persuasive, expert touch and the whisper of his hand moving over silk.

It went higher, circling the top of her stocking and bare thigh, then plunging into the narrow gap between her legs, landing unerringly on the open crotch of her panties.

'Sinclair's jealous because he happened to be born twelve months after Mallory, missing out on the inheritance. As for Caroline – well, I don't think Mallory was unfaithful until she started screwing around. Rumour has it that he was mad about her.' As he talked, Tony's finger insinuated itself between her secret lips, applying a delicious, warming friction to her rapidly engorging love-bud.

'Claret, sir?' the footman enquired blandly.

Tony nodded and Mouton Rothschild gleamed in a fresh glass.

Carefully Tony disentangled his hand from her wet avenue and, as he raised the wine to his lips, passed his fingers under his nose, inhaling her fragrance, murmuring, 'What bliss! The bouquet of a splendid vintage, and your glorious female perfume.'

Desserts were served as if by magic, magnificent concoctions to tempt the most finicky gourmet: sorbet, ice cream, gateaux fecund with juicy strawberries, dusky indigo grapes nestling seductively on beds of sugared vine leaves, luscious peaches, their downy skins flushed like a woman's breasts immediately after orgasm. This luxurious abundance was enhanced by the gleam of porcelain tipped with a green as light and delicate as sea foam, and the openwork of gilt-edged Sèvres dishes decorated with copies of Watteau landscapes.

Mallory made sure that his guests were properly stimulated, the butler ordered to produce the finest contents of the wine cellar. The voices grew thicker, louder. It was no longer possible to hear anything clearly, riotous laughter exploding like fireworks.

Champagne corks popped, and Karen knew she was more than a little tipsy. Celine was singing, accompanied by Mallory, her vibrant voice and forceful personality assuring her of operatic stardom in the near future. The scene wavered, shifted. Karen shifted, too. Everyone was dancing; soul echoed from elongated speakers like miniature skyscrapers. Any sign of formality had vanished. So had Mallory.

The huge doors connecting the various rooms stood wide. A pornographic video was playing, erotic images appearing on the massive television scene, blown up and exaggerated. The size of the actors' penises was unbelievable, gargantuan appendages rearing from matted undergrowth above balls like hairy coconuts. The so-called actresses were notable for their outsized tits, which they used vigorously, wrapping their lovers' cocks in them, rubbing them up and down. There were close-up shots of their pussies, looming larger than life – great dark caverns that might intimidate a nervous man.

'Look at her cunt!' Tony exclaimed in amazement, staring up at one particularly large lady. '*Vagina dentata*. A toothed vagina. Bloody hell! That one looks as if it really might have teeth hidden inside to bite off a bloke's dick!'

The couples on screen were moaning, entering each others' bodies every which way, and Karen's bud was itching, hotly roused in spite of herself. She could feel juices wetting her vulva, and her nipples were painfully sensitive as they rubbed against the inside of her bodice.

The guests stopped dancing, staring at the brash, uninhibited display taking place on the video, inspired to follow suit. One man opened his trousers and brought out his cock, and his partner, ripping off her dress, took it in her mouth and started to suck it madly. Another stood behind the woman he was escorting, hauling up her skirt and sticking his cock into the deep division of her bottom while she played with her nipples. A third, hand raising his lady's gown, was stroking her pussy in a leisurely manner, while she reached round and grabbed his sturdy weapon.

The screen lovers were now showering each other with streams of golden rain. The guests whooped their approval, their activity frenzied. Each couch was occupied by couples straining in ecstasy. The lovely person who had sat near Karen during dinner began to remove her bustle dress. Her breasts were small, her waist slender, but as the gown slid lower, a small penis emerged from the folds. The transvestite stroked it fondly, spread its dew up his arse crack and bent over. The man who had been with him all evening whipped out his stumpy, broad-headed cock and thrust it into the pursed anus.

Tony put an arm round Karen and dipped a hand in her cleavage. White-hot desire snaked through her as he stroked a nipple with one finger. Where was Mallory? Her eyes sought him in the crowd, but she kept getting distracted, thinking, *I suppose this is an orgy. I've never been to an orgy before.*

'You want him? He's in the bedroom.' Tony was attuned to her desires.

They passed under a horseshoe-shaped Moorish arch, guarded on each side by two enormous statues of voluptuous naked slave girls. The ambience of this retreat from reality was Oriental. Persian rugs were strewn on the floor, the fireplace decorated with Islamic tiles, and a narghile with a snakelike tube protruding from its squat brass side stood on an inlaid Damascus table. Subdued light glowed from Art Nouveau lamps with Tiffany shades, each moulded in sensuous flowing lines representing water, trailing vines or women's tresses. The pungent, sickly sweet odour of joss-sticks played on Karen's already quivering senses.

It took her a moment to take in the whole scene, eyes adjusting to the dusk, then she saw movements in the dimness and a vast seigneurial bed – oak wreathed with carvings, elaborate tenting, heavy drapes. Mallory lay within, part covered by a brocade robe. Celine was poised over him, dreadlocks swinging forward, legs wound round his body, working her hips rapidly as she rode his cock, sliding it in and out of her generous, juicy opening.

Armina had shed her dress somewhere along the way. Patty and Jo were nude, writhing in sinuous dance to atonal Eastern music, the lilt of a sitar, the throb of drums, graceful houris for the master's entertainment, adjuncts to his lust – assistants in heightening his pleasure. They caressed one another as they danced, hands fondling breasts, nipples, fingers playing with rosebud nether regions and spreading scented oil and love-fluid over ripe labia and prominent clits.

Karen stared down at Mallory and his eyes opened, meeting hers, mockery in their golden depths. Celine worked harder, and his expression changed to the intense look of a man about to come. He gasped, reared against her pubis, gave a loud groan and spent himself inside her. On cue, the other girls entered the bed, wrapping their limbs round him till his body was buried in silken, aromatic flesh.

Still those magnetic eyes bored into Karen's, making her blood thicken with anger and thwarted desire. He hadn't suggested that she join him. What was wrong? Didn't he find her attractive? She was tormented with need, nipples and lips hot, a rising tide of tears threatening to overwhelm her.

She felt cool air on her legs as Tony pushed her skirt to one side. His erection was stirring against her thigh. She wanted to feel the long hard length of it plunged deep inside her, comforting, soothing her. In a moment she knew he would do it, and she didn't care – let Mallory watch – let him know his rejection meant nothing to her.

She opened her legs, and Tony's fingers penetrated her vagina, widening it, rousing it, his thumb coaxing her bud from its cowl. She reached out and clamped her hand round the stiff rod poking from the slit in his silk boxer shorts.

Suddenly, brutally and without warning, she was seized by the wrist and rushed across the room before she had time to draw breath or protest.

'Come with me, darling,' Sinclair said, smiling wickedly.

'Where?' She was half angry, half amused, totally intrigued.

'To my lair,' he countered dramatically as he steered her away from Mallory's apartment and paused in an angle of the stairs. 'You don't know the secrets of

Blackwood Towers. There are passages – hidden rooms we can turn into jungles. The bower of Aphrodite, the cave of Dionysus, Olympus or Hades? Which shall it be? Dare you enter them with me?'

'Yes!' she cried, possessed of savage recklessness, her heart beating wildly.

Let the brother Mallory hated show her undreamed of depths of depravity. Let him use her while she used him – and just maybe Mallory would get to hear of it, and be hurt.

# Chapter Seven

*It's not exactly fear I'm experiencing*, Karen thought as she allowed Sinclair to guide her through a little door hidden in the shadow of the stairs. *Slight apprehension perhaps. No one can hurt me, Kan made sure of that. I'd react automatically. Even an assailant brandishing a knife would be floored in a couple of swift moves, with a broken arm.*

The blood was singing in her veins, alert for further sensations. The buzz was tremendous – lust, wounded pride, even the stirrings of an emotion as yet unnamed regarding Mallory. No, it wasn't he who led her along so subtly, hand touching her shoulder, fingers skimming across her bare arm, then alighting at the small of her back. But it was a man who resembled him yet possessed a magnetism of his own.

Karen's every nerve directed itself towards him. She could smell his expensive aftershave and tingled to the brief caressing of his fingers. She loosened, moistened. Something exciting loomed ahead. Whatever it was, she would never be quite the same again.

The way was narrow, twisting into the maw of the house, and the thin beam of Sinclair's pencil torch gave little illumination. The air was musty, and Karen's feet encountered steps that turned at a dangerous angle, ending in another, even dustier passage. Here the lighting was powered by electricity, but antiquated and dim – lamps with dingy glass shades, panelled walls black with age, stone flooring on which their footsteps resounded.

'It's a disused wing of the house,' Sinclair explained. 'I always stay here when I'm home. It's supposed to be haunted and no one bothers me, not even the servants.'

It was utterly deserted, a place of hollow, empty corridors and vast echoing galleries. There were reception rooms of sombre magnificence, rich with gilt, damask and drapes, and unsuspected mirrors throwing back at Karen sudden ghostly images of her passing face. In other rooms the furniture was shrouded in dust covers and there were empty spaces on the walls where once paintings had hung. The mirrors were fly spotted, the gilt tarnished, the brocaded chairs frayed, the couches sagging and threadbare. Repositories for unneeded items too valuable to be thrown away, these rooms had a sad atmosphere, keeping their secrets in dusky silence.

Sinclair, hand cupping her elbow, led her to another room, reached by a short flight of stairs. Lamps glowed on sumptuous velvets, on treasures he had siphoned off from other parts of Blackwood Towers or acquired on his travels. The figures on the tapestries appeared to dance, huntsmen and hounds, deer and harbourers – shimmering, lifelike; foam-flecked horses, the fierce faces, the terrified eyes of prey with scarlet gouts of blood staining their hides.

The night was dense black outside, rain lashing the panes of unshuttered windows, adding to the chill that permeated the bones. The room reminded Karen of the interior of a church, with icons and statues and the swirling smoke of incense rising to the fan-vaulted rafters. In fact it was more like a temple. The black basalt figurine of a jackal-headed god stood on an ebony table supported by writhing serpents.

'This is your bedroom?' she asked, and shivered with

desire and anticipation, skin prickling, that persistent, unsatisfied ache gnawing at the pit of her stomach, the unfamiliar feel of the open-crotched thong pressing against her sex lips.

'It is. D'you like it?' He watched her closely, eyes narrowed as he ran an impudent forefinger across the tips of her breasts. 'The bed belonged to the first marquis. Rumour has it that Queen Elizabeth slept in it, but isn't that what they all say?'

It was a truly spectacular couch, more like something from a Hollywood movie set, ornamented with beaten gold and hung with embossed velvet drapes, four bunches of plaster ostrich plumes decorating its foot and head posts.

'It's a monstrosity!' Karen said half in horror, half in grudging admiration, her hand coming to rest on top of his, pressing it closer, her nipples like iron. She revered old furniture, but this was beyond belief. It was the most ostentatious bed she had ever seen, wide enough for six people, a positive battleground for two combatants in the anguished, sweaty, passion-ridden field of sexual congress.

'You think so?' Sinclair grinned and led her towards it. 'It makes me feel like a monarch – omnipotent and horny, ready to spread my seed and service a hundred women.'

'You might find one would be enough,' she suggested breathlessly, her feet dragging unwillingly, her randy clitoris urging her on.

Senses raw, she looked at his dark curls, the elegant lines of his body, and imagined him naked, bending over her, his lips kissing her bud, visualised his cock, a solid bar filling her with its size. Would it be as big as his brother's? Did this characteristic run in families, like the structure of the nose or colour of the hair?

'I doubt I'd be satisfied with one woman, though it would rather depend on who she happened to be.' He stepped away, did not touch her as he spoke, his eyes like molten steel, full of questions. 'Are you Mallory's mistress? Armina says not, but I'd like to hear it from you.'

'Why d'you want to know?'

*Keep talking*, she told herself, find out more about him. *He's used to women capitulating. Make him wait.* But she was trembling with want, indecision crippling her will. She lusted for him, was certain he felt the same, was aware of that unspoken current flowing between them, a stream of mutual need, purely physical in content.

They stood looking at each other till the silence became awkward, then, 'I don't like being second-best to Mallory,' he growled, and his eyes were as bleak as the storm-racked sea battering the cliffs not more than a mile away.

'I'm sure that's not the case,' she prompted, holding his gaze with an effort.

The friction between the brothers heightened the tension. It was as if Mallory was in the room, standing on her other side with herself squashed between them. The heated passions of hatred, of revenge and flawed love seethed like a savage ocean. Sinclair's fists clenched and a muscle quivered by the side of his jaw.

'You don't know the first thing about it,' he snapped abrasively. 'But tell me he hasn't shafted you, and I'll believe it.'

'I don't care whether you believe it or not. I don't owe you anything.' Her anger was rising in time to the powerful throb in the secret depths of her loins. 'Take me back to the party.'

Sinclair's lips quirked, one eyebrow lifting. 'You don't really want me to do that.'

Taking her off guard, he hauled her against him, moulding her to his body, deliberately flaunting the length and hardness of his phallus. She didn't struggle, simply freed herself with an agile twist and fell into a forward stance, slit skirt opening on her long, shapely legs.

Her blow was blocked by his arm. A superb, seemingly effortless but technically correct deflection. *He's an expert!* The astonished thought pierced her like a spear.

'*Kiai!*' she shouted to concentrate her energies, the warrior within her accepting the challenge.

A crescent kick, a backfist strike, a lunging punch – all were blocked. Sinclair scarcely moved, yet turned her every attack into one of defence, redirecting and parrying her blows.

Defeated, she stepped back and bowed with all the etiquette of the East.

'I underestimated you. I had no idea you knew the martial arts,' she panted.

'I'm rusty – out of training,' he replied with a smile and a formal returning bow. 'I admire your *mawashi geri*, and I'd like to see you do it barefoot.' His grey eyes darkened to onyx and he added, 'You're used to being in control, aren't you, Karen?'

She threw back her tangled hair, scrutinising him, not quite trusting him, but kept seeing Kan's face superimposed over his. The warm blood of recollection made her almost sick with longing for the exotic hours spent in her *sensei*'s apartment.

'I guess so. Why?'

Sinclair's voice was low, seductive. 'Haven't you ever wanted to hand your will over to someone else?'

Deep within Karen something awoke, a dark, forbidden seam of eroticism. To yield her will, to give herself into someone else's keeping to do with as he chose – the idea was powerfully attractive, obeying atavistic laws beyond civilisation and reason, directly opposed to her strongly held views on independence. *Yes, yes, yes!* her body screamed, but, 'That isn't the way of the warrior,' the coolly urbane woman answered. 'I like to be in control.'

He chuckled, wound his fingers in her mane, used it as a halter to bind her closely to him. Her face was pressed against his chest. She could smell the odour of *Jazz*, smell his own personal body scent, feel the smoothness of his dinner jacket under her cheek. Her bones seemed to crumble, the strength gone, overpowered by the heat laving her core, making her vagina spasm and send out a warm flood of elixir.

'So you can be, darling,' he murmured in a dusky drawl. 'I won't do anything you don't like. I promise.'

Before she realised his intention, he swung her up, one arm under her shoulders, the other beneath her buttocks. With lithe grace he stretched her on the bed. Karen protested, but he placed cool fingers over her lips, gazing down into her wide, angry eyes.

'No, Karen. Do as I say. Lie still – that's right.'

There was magic in the way his fingers stroked across her mouth, thumb caressing the full bottom lip in a way that made her unable to resist licking it, tasting the salty flavour of his skin.

With measured deliberation he rolled her over, undid the buttons at the back of her bodice, then slipped it down to her waist. She heard his quick intake of breath at the sight of her breasts barely contained by the black satin. She glanced down at them, seeing the astonishing surprise of the nipples protruding over the half-cups.

Still holding her arms spread wide, hands clamped round her wrists, Sinclair bent closer. Her nipples crimped as he breathed on them. She arched her back to raise those ardent teats to his lips, but he teasingly withdrew, wringing an exasperated groan from her.

'Poor darling,' he whispered and straddled her, pressing down to make her aware of the fullness and rock hardness of his cock swelling against the tight evening trousers. 'D'you want me to lick them so very badly? Tell me. Say it. Then maybe I will.'

'You bastard,' Karen hissed, ineffectively, attempting to tear herself from his grip. She half raised a knee, threatening to jab him in the crotch.

'Dear me, how unchivalrous!' he chided softly. 'Besides which, you'll lose out on a lot of fun if you damage my goolies.'

Before she realised exactly what was happening, he had fastened a silk cord round each of her wrists and tethered her to the bed posts like a crucified prisoner.

His eyes were bright and animalistic, his sensual lips parted, the lower one rolled out. For an instant he hovered there, just above her breasts, then lowered his head. Karen cried out as his tongue flicked over the little peaks poking like ripe raspberries above the satin and lace brassiere. Pleasure saturated her body, pooling in her sex, the honeydew dripping, the hem of her G-string cutting into the ridge of her clitoris, almost, but not quite bringing her to climax.

Sinclair held off, barely grazing the aching points with the tip of his fleshy tongue, moving between them, but using the ball of his thumb to repeat the motion on the one his mouth had momentarily abandoned. Karen's legs trembled and her love bud quivered. She yearned to be sucked, nipples and clit, and squirmed to let him know her need.

With consummate artistry he drew a rosy teat between his lips, nipping playfully but almost painfully before relenting and mouthing it hard, Karen sighed, lay still, relished the sensation, as centred on that pleasure-filled spot as when focusing the force in her knuckles as she fought him. Pre-orgasm waves rippled down her spine, suffused her loins and coiled in her womb, but it was still not enough to bring her off.

She yelled with shock and frustration when Sinclair rose, leaving her hungry breasts. With a thin, triumphant smile he muttered, 'Not yet, darling – not for a long while yet.'

He pulled her dress down over her hips and cast it to one side. He stood by the bed watching her in a detached sort of way as a doctor might look at his half-naked patient. Karen was conscious of her bare flesh below her girdle, the tiny wedge of satin with pussy hair showing through the slit, the sight of her shapely black-stockinged legs. She raised one, admiring the curves: delicate ankle, rounded knee, calf muscles exaggerated by the high-heeled shoe. She wanted to run a hand down her leg, but was his captive. After what seemed like years, he took more cords and, nudging her legs wide apart, secured her ankles to the foot posts of the bed.

She was conscious of how ripe she looked, how exposed and vulnerable. A wave of pure excitement washed through her body. She was entirely at Sinclair's mercy. He started to massage her breasts, one in each hand, pinching the nipples between his finger and thumb. Karen gasped with delight, desperate to feel him inside her.

'Fuck me now,' she whispered. 'Please, I need it now.'

He laughed and replied, 'I know you do.'

As if she was of no consequence, a thing existing solely for his amusement, he unzipped his fly and exposed a swollen dick every bit as magnificent as his brother's. As she watched, he rubbed it slowly, caressing the thick dark-veined shaft and smearing the cap with the cock-tears oozing from its single eye. Leaving it supported by its own stiffness, he shrugged his shoulders out of his jacket, waistcoat and shirt, the smooth bronzed skin contrasting with the pristine whiteness of linen.

Now he was naked to below the waist, his trousers sliding down, that impressive phallus swinging from side to side as he moved, jutting above the twin jewels of his impressive balls encased in their hairy sac. Karen's tongue came out to wet her dry lips and her clit spasmed as she imagined taking that mighty weapon in her mouth, milking him till he yielded his seminal libation.

Kneeling over her, Sinclair wielded it expertly, rubbing the tip up and down the division in the thong, making contact with her erect nub till it was slippery with fragrant juices. Shifting up, he circled the creased pit of her navel, then went higher, each nipple in turn caressed and wetted by his cock-head.

'Ah … ahhh!' Karen whimpered, but knew by now that it was useless to beg for the beneficence of its hardness plunging into her vagina. Resting his weighty penis against her, Sinclair's mouth found hers, his tongue diving between her lips, sucking as he had sucked her nipples, probing, darting, sipping the honey-sweet dew of her saliva while she made mewling noises deep in her throat.

He rolled away from her to free himself of his trousers, and she drank in the sight of his strong, muscular body, marked here and there with the scars of old wounds. But beautiful though it was, her eyes kept returning to the dense dark plume spreading over his lower belly and the powerful prong rising from it: the source of pleasure by which her hunger could be appeased. Her fingers itched to touch it, but she was helplessly dependent on his will.

Now Sinclair flourished a strip of black velvet. His cock leapt and grew even bigger as he said, 'I'm going to blindfold you. Are you ready for this?'

She gulped, nodded, hoped that if she was obedient he would insert his generous spike into her yearning cunt. 'I've never done it before.'

'That's good. One should experiment with every aspect of sex play.'

His hands were gentle on her face and the velvet shut out everything as he tied the mask round her eyes. Now her other senses sharpened as sight was denied her. She became a creature of hearing, taste, smell and, above all, touch.

For a moment she lay there disoriented, lost in black silence. Then she heard him moving about, felt the mattress sag as he rejoined her. She waited in breathless anticipation, knew a thrilling stab of fear. Supposing he was unbalanced? Just supposing he was a perverted maniac? He might leave her there to starve. He might even kill her!

She could smell the sharp odour of his sweat above

the spicy deodorant and caught a whiff of his cock-juice. Then his fingers touched her right nipple, the pleasure heightened as her senses funnelled into one huge bundle of sexual hunger.

He withdrew, and it was as if she was alone. Her skin was cooling. She was aware of a draught. The smell of incense penetrated her nostrils. Had he left her? Fear rose to a cutting edge. She heard a rustling sound, then felt a touch. Not his fingers – something soft was being smoothed over her belly. She struggled to remember where she had felt it before. It wasn't leather. It had a rough nap. Suede! That was it. She'd once owned a suede skirt, supple, sensual, sinfully impractical and expensive.

The feeling was rapturous, heightening as the suede cruised down, rasping over the insides of her thighs, skating across the satin triangle covering her mound, tangling with the fur fringing her nether lips. Oh, to have it titillating her exposed clit! Karen moaned and twisted, seeking that ultimate contact. The suede was removed.

Fingers tweaked her nipples, rubbing each one with a vigour that made her gasp. The fingers were replaced by lips, sucking, nibbling, tormenting when she needed them on her wildly agitated love-bud. Her torturer refused to touch it. Spread-eagled, wrists and ankles trapped, she could do nothing to relieve her frustration. Anger and irritation with this game that had gone on a smidgen too long were now mingled with something deeper, darker, more intense.

'You want me to untie you?' Sinclair asked, a thread of mockery running through that bland voice. Karen picked up on the implication: *if you do, you'll have lost. Come on, warrior. Take everything I can hand out.*

'No!' she muttered through gritted teeth.

'Good girl.' His voice warmed with admiration.

But her whole body convulsed in an instinctive reaction when the cold bite of steel touched her pubis. She felt the knife's icy kiss slither between her skin and the tie at her right hip bone. A jerk, a chill as the thong fell away. The blade inched lovingly across to the other fragile strap. A slight scratch, a nick not deep enough to draw blood, a tension as the material surrendered. Then slowly, tenderly, the knife tip trailed up her body, heated by her skin, making contact with each nipple in turn. Would it caress or cut?

Hovering between terror and desire, she felt an ache in her bladder, pressure building up unbearably.

'I need to pee,' she said.

'Then do it,' Sinclair murmured.

'I can't – not here. The bed?—'

'Is protected. Go on, darling, piss for me.'

*My God*, she thought, eyelids fluttering against the blackness of the blindfold. *How many other women have lain here like this? What sort of a man is he?* Yet the excitement was acute, the fear sending adrenalin roaring through her veins, the need to pass water increasingly urgent. Now she began to have a glimmer of the true meaning of relinquishing her will.

Karen clenched her muscles. There was no way she was going to obey Sinclair's last command. He was touching her again, a soft textured touch this time – the touch of velvet. Starting with her feet, he allowed the fabric to whisper round each toe, over her instep, glide past her knee, caress her inner thigh. He moved it slowly, tauntingly, the strokes delicate, lascivious, as he gently parted her warm, moist lips, moving the plush pile over her swollen crack, allowing it to flirt with her clitoris, which stood proud and erect, starving for attention.

Her breath shortened, her skin flushed. Climax was so near, her clit ached for a firmer touch, ready to explode into pleasure. With a sudden change of pace Sinclair replaced the velvet with a hard object – inhuman, rubbery, infinitely strange yet deliriously pleasant. He teased her by running the tip of the dildo around her vulva, then slid the whole thing deep inside her. Karen could feel her body expanding to take it, slippery wet, the end butting her cervix. Her bladder throbbed demandingly, its need accentuated by the size and force of the alien object. She wanted desperately to let go but was too inhibited.

Slowly, Sinclair withdrew the penis substitute almost completely, then equally slowly pushed it right back in again, twisting it slightly on the return stroke. He eased it out to let it fondle her perineum and slip between her buttocks, nudging against her rectum. More pressure, and the artificial glans was penetrating her anus, inch by slow inch. Karen moaned. With his free hand, Sinclair deftly stimulated her nipples, moving back and forth between them, the vibrator returned to her silken haven, bumping her G-spot.

'More,' she wailed, thrashing against her bonds, longing to feel him ploughing through her female parts. 'Give me more! I want your cock!'

'Tut, tut, such impatience,' he chided, and she felt him shift down, his hair brushing her thighs, his breath warming her labia.

She wriggled, lifted her pubis in supplication, and he removed the remnants of her thong, grasping the gusset in his fingers, pulling it aside and exposing her full, pouting lips. He pressed hard on the engorged button swelling shamelessly from its hood. Karen waited with bated breath as he lapped at her juices and placed his mouth against her thickened lower lips, nuzzling in, finding the head of her clitoris and starting to suck and tongue it. The surge of orgasm soared through her, a shuddering, earth-shattering climax.

She screamed, and felt her bladder relax – a few powerful jets and then a longer trickle as her bladder emptied, the relief coupled with the thrill of orgasm making her forget that her urine was running into Sinclair's mouth and over his face.

'Gorgeous,' he muttered harshly. 'The ultimate turn on.'

The control he had shown so far vanished. With rough impatience he covered her body with his, and she felt his penis plunging like tempered steel between her soaking pussy lips. The scarf was snatched from her eyes, and she saw him above her, weight supported on knees and elbows. Looked down to see that mighty cock as it pistoned her, working in and out, faster and faster, till it finally exploded. He slumped on her, face buried in her hair, lipping over her neck and ear lobe.

'Now Mallory can't say he was the first of us to have you,' he whispered, and moved over to the other side of the bed, taking her with him and settling her down so she lay with her head pillowed on his shoulder.

'Does that mean so much?' She was sleepy, sated and utterly relaxed. Having someone else control your will was not so bad, not if it was a man like Sinclair.

'Hmmm, maybe. I get a kick out of putting one over on him.'

'Like when you screwed his wife?'

She felt him stiffen. 'Who told you that?'

'Never mind. It's true, isn't it? You are a bastard, aren't you?'

'The Honourable Lady Burnet was game for anything. I've never met such a horny bitch. She'd have anyone, given half the chance. Mallory took it badly, played the outraged husband to perfection. I enjoyed riling him.'

'What makes you think you've done so now? He's given no indication of the slightest interest in me.' She nestled against him, one of his large brown hands cupping her breast while she toyed with his chest hair and the small dark nimbus of his nipples. *He's totally unscrupulous and amoral, but I could grow to like this*, she thought hazily.

She could feel laughter rumbling in his chest. 'Don't be deceived by his standoffishness. He's interested all right. I know him, Karen, probably better than anyone alive. My brother wants you, and what Mallory wants he usually gets. I try to spoil it for him, that's all.'

The eastern sky was tawny red banded with grey, then came an expanse of lemon-yellow light, and above it pure clarity with here and there a small cloud tipped with gold floating like an island in a fairy sea. Mist hung at the base of the heavily wooded hills, curving in and out of the gullies, presaging another fine day, and bird calls fluted from the tree tops as Karen walked out into the garden.

The storm had passed: the fecund earth was washed clean and the crystal air felt like chilled wine. Karen stood for a moment, breathing deeply, absorbing the sounds and scents, taking the dawn into herself. The grass beneath the trees sparkled with diamond dew, wetting her bare feet. She curled her toes downwards, rejoicing in this contact with the chthonian realms beneath that green carpet. The grasses were coarse and she could almost feel the tremor of their fibres.

She closed her eyes, cleared her mind, raised her arms and began the slow, meditative moves of *T'ai Chi* by which she could draw out the essence of earth power, making it a part of herself. Dressed in her pure white *gi*, her body swayed like a graceful sapling, the ritualistic hand and leg movements bringing her ever closer to tranquillity. Her spirit soared to the tops of the trees towering above her, sensing their urge towards growth. Carried higher, she drifted far from Blackmoor Towers to ethereal planes where physical sensations no longer existed.

Gradually she came back to herself, aware of the stirrings in the great root systems sucking up gallons of water, breathing out vapour through their leaves to ensure the survival of the planet. She was conscious once more of the beauty surrounding her, the verdant lawns and flowers seeming to possess an extra brilliance, the brooding ivy-hung walls of the manor standing foursquare like age-old rocks. Ecstasy saturated every corner of her being, the joy of being young and alive and ready to take up any challenges life offered.

Slowly she retraced her steps, heading through the

silent corridors towards the gymnasium. There Sinclair had said she would find a *makiwara* board fixed to the floor, a padded pole which she could use in the absence of a sparring partner. It was necessary to train if she was to enter the contests to be held in London next year. So far she hadn't found a local *dojo*. Sinclair thought the nearest was in Exeter and had offered to help her start one by hiring a hall in the village one or two nights a week and taking advertising space in the *Porthcombe Times*.

Karen ruminated on the complexity of Sinclair's personality, sometimes bordering on cruelty, at others the acme of gentle understanding. Last night had been a first in one respect: never before had she met a man who celebrated the tender act of urination. Bodily juices and secretions enriched lovemaking, but it had been a complete surprise to find that the sight of her coming and peeing had proved a massive turn-on for him.

All in all, her time with him had been well spent. Not only had she discovered hidden depths to herself, but she had found another martial arts enthusiast into the bargain. And, perhaps more important than either of these, she had learned a little more about Mallory. *Not that I'm interested*, she told herself firmly as she approached the door of the gym. *Interest suggests caring, and the last person on this globe I care about is my irritating, arrogant boss.*

The house was quiet as the grave, but now sounds from behind the door shattered the silence – the hard, bright ring of steel meeting steel. She frowned, paused, then stepped inside.

Two men were fighting, instantly recognisable, though wearing white padded fencing jackets, their faces hidden by protective masks. Tall men, equally matched in height, vigour and skill, they were wielding rapiers. Their feet pounded the cork matting as if strictly choreographed – lunge, parry, riposte: backward and forwards. They were so intent that they ignored Karen, were probably not even aware of her presence.

Sinclair seemed indolently relaxed in style yet gave Mallory no opportunity to pierce his guard, unhurriedly retreating before his slashing attacks, parrying easily, almost lazily. The air whistled and rang with the clash of expertly handled steel. It hummed with fierce antagonism that communicated itself to Karen. Her reaction to the fighting men was visceral. She felt it in her blood, guts and vagina, was overwhelmed with molten desire, her descent from a higher plane rapid and absolute.

A gasp escaped her lips, and Sinclair glanced across, momentarily off guard. Mallory's blade slipped like a serpent under his guard. For an instant the rapiers locked, the duellists close as lovers. Then with a flick of his wrist, Mallory hooked his quillon under his brother's, and the sword was jerked from Sinclair's hand to sail across the room in a flashing arc, hitting the floor with a clunk.

'Fuck!' Sinclair exploded.

Mallory bowed ironically. 'You always did lose concentration when pussy appeared,' he chided acidly, pulling off his gauntlets then removing his mask. Sweat drenched his face and ran in rivulets from his matted black hair.

'It was bloody bad luck. I slipped,' Sinclair lied, tugging at his helmet and tossing it aside. He looked furious enough to hurl himself on Mallory and garrotte him.

With haughty unconcern, Mallory stripped off his padded jacket, torso bare as he towelled over his chest and armpits. Karen's vaginal muscles clenched, her sex dampened and her nipples rose as the coarse linen of her *gi* chafed them. He possessed such a perfect physique, iron-muscled arms, wide shoulders tapering to a narrow waist, and below it the tell-tale line of his cock pressed against the close fit of his jeans.

Sinclair watched her with a wry, cynical smile. He, too, was part naked and had Mallory not been there her lust would have been directed towards him.

'I'm going to take a shower,' Sinclair announced. 'Are you coming, Karen? I could do with a handmaiden in more ways than one.'

In a few well-chosen words he had indicated to Mallory that he was on intimate terms with her. Karen was angry yet satisfied. Mallory might have beaten him in sword play but Sinclair had shafted her last night: screwed and pleasured her while Mallory fucked his bevy of mistresses. Somehow this adjusted the balance in her book.

'Sorry to spoil your fun, but I need Miss Heyward in the library,' Mallory said with a wolfish smile. 'You'll have to shower alone, Sinclair, and take yourself in hand, if that's what's on your mind.'

He turned to Karen, the towel draped round his neck. She could smell the musky odour of his sweat, see his wet hair clinging to his brow, and her hand almost lifted to the zipper of his Levi's, almost caressed the heavy bulge between his thighs. Almost, but not quite.

'I'll change first,' she replied, distrusting this trembling, knee-weakening emotion that shook her.

He cast a supercilious glance at her *gi*. 'Ah, the very nearly black belt,' he said sarcastically. 'Have you been training this morning, Miss Heyward?'

'No, sir. I did *T'ai Chi*. I came here to practise, but it doesn't matter.'

'Too right it doesn't,' he rapped out smartly. 'I've important things to discuss with you. Are you fit?'

'Yes, sir.'

The library was dim, a warm, dawn-pink dimness. The perfume of roses mingled with the spice of leather – Persian, Russian, Moroccan calf – and with the pungency of old parchment and old print on ancient pages. The air was filled with the breath of ages, the room enfolding them in dusty, spangled intimate silence.

Karen wondered why Tony had not been summoned but was glad that she and Mallory were alone, and impatient with herself for that gladness. It was the first time. Would it be the last? What was it he wanted of her?

He was so tall. Her head did not quite reach the pit of his throat, yet she stubbornly held her ground. 'There was no need to be so rude. I would have been more comfortable in ordinary clothes.'

'You can skip off and change in a minute,' he replied, a new expression creeping into the amber eyes that were regarding her thoughtfully, hypnotic eyes under black brows that soared like wings. A hint of regret, a glimmer of interest, the beginning of respect?

'Why the urgency? What's wrong? And where's Tony?' She held herself erect, hands loosely at her sides, her head thrown back, awaiting his next move.

'Wrong, Miss Heyward? Should anything be wrong? As for Tony, I imagine he's still in bed with a congenial companion or nursing a hangover. Did you enjoy the party?'

She was fascinated by the cadences of his voice, a deep, rich baritone, soft, steeped in honey now, whereas before it had been crisp, authoritative, even scathing. Pulling herself together, she said, 'It was unusual, to say the least. But why this early morning meeting?'

'I want to check on the Bedwell cartoons. Irwin Dwyer is arriving in under a week.'

'The American? Tony told me about him. I'm sorry you're selling the drawings. It's a shame when they've been in the family for so long.'

'"Needs must when the devil drives",' he quoted coolly, staring at her with those forceful eyes, his look seeming to penetrate her very soul. 'Anyway, what's it to you? You're merely working for me, and can't possibly understand what it's like to be the owner of Blackwood. It's not just a house. It carries massive responsibilities and needs a mint to keep it going. I have my son's future to consider and don't want to hand it over to the National Trust. Irwin Dwyer did offer an alternative. Everything would remain as it has always been, and he would advise me how to increase the estate's income.'

'I'm so glad,' she countered, swallowing hard, aware that she had been staring at him. 'This is more than a job to me. I love the house and want to see it preserved.'

'You do?' He raised a sceptical eyebrow. 'Most people are out for what they can get these days. The old feudal loyalty is a thing of the past.' His voice hardened, his eyes too. It was as if he had forgotten Karen as he continued in a voice charged with bitterness. 'My wife was a prime example of this, a greedy, mercenary woman. She didn't care about Blackwood.'

He was restless, unsure, taking a few irate strides, then whirling round and coming back to her, driving his fist into his palm. 'I can't trust anyone. Even my own brother has betrayed me.'

She felt his unhappiness like a bleeding wound in her

own heart, and touched his shoulder impulsively. Fire leapt through her fingers to her womb at the contact with his bare skin. She realised that her panties were soaking wet beneath the *gi*, his very presence rousing her to melting, lubricious excitement.

'You can trust me,' she whispered.

'Can I?' Their eyes held, and she could feel herself drowning in those golden depths, wanting it, needing it, willing to lose herself in him for ever.

He moved towards the door leading to the inner sanctum and she followed, mesmerised, her mind lighting up, her body shaking as if racked by fever. All sound in the little room was muffled, sunshine pouring in at the diamond-paned windows. Mallory did not open the cabinet as she had expected. Instead he went over to the fireplace and pressed a Tudor rose decorating the mantel. There was a click and a panel opened, revealing an aperture. He lifted out a canvas.

'I wanted to show you this,' he said, propping it up against the far wall and whipping away the covering.

Karen moved closer, feeling herself growing hotter. The power flowing from this man augmented by the power of the painting caused a maelstrom of arousal within her that dissolved her will.

'Is it Dick Bedwell's work?' she managed to croak.

Mallory shook his head, adoring the picture with his eyes. 'No, it's a Giovanni, but based on one of the cartoons. He paints like Goya.'

'The girls on the swings.' She recognised it, though it shone as never before, luscious, vibrant with colour. It was almost possible to hear the girls giggling as they displayed their pink, wet and wonderful lower lips to their beaux.

Flower-wreathed, breathing out a corrupted innocence, the wanton girls were tempting, the skill of the artist portraying every nuance. Their young breasts, their nubile flesh, the subtle hues, the detailed sketchwork combined to produce a work of art both pleasing in an aesthetic sense and torrid in the extreme. Involuntarily Karen's hand dipped down to the apex of her thighs. Through the linen she could feel the warmth of her pubic hair. She felt strangely hazy, breasts tingling, her clitoris beginning to stir.

'Giovanni was a master. He's captured the spirit of the scene to perfection. Look at the colouring and detail,' Mallory said, giving her a slanting glance.

'Why hide it away? Wouldn't it be better to show it?' Karen was inching towards him, unable to prevent her feet from moving in his direction.

'It pleases me to keep it for myself or share it with a very close friend. No one has seen it except me since Caroline left.'

'Your wife?'

'My wife.'

*A close friend? He can't mean me, can he?* The idea made Karen's head reel. 'Then why me?' she faltered.

He shrugged. 'Call it an impulse. You'll not tell anyone where it is, will you? Particularly Sinclair. Even Tony doesn't know about it.'

'And Irwin Dwyer? Is he to be informed?'

'I never want to sell this one.'

*Our secret*, she thought, burning, aching, close to tears, close to joy. He was near her, his arm brushing her shoulder as they looked at the painting. The proof of his arousal was visible, as clear to her as if he was naked, that long protuberance swelling under the thin covering of denim. Karen stood beside him with a soaking gusset and the triple ache of nipples and clitoris demanding relief, and he made no attempt to touch her.

Minutes passed and then he walked to the door, saying over his shoulder, 'Make sure the cartoons are in order and the contents of the library catalogued as far as possible in the time left before Dwyer arrives. I'm relying on you, Miss Heyward.'

Karen sank against the table when he had gone, unable to believe that he could leave her, just like that. For her part, she was shaken and exhausted, disordered and confused. The hot waves of sensation that had swept her were still there. She sank into a chair, opened her legs wide and inserted a hand into her *gi*, letting her fingers walk down over her belly, brush through the crisp hair and dip into her cleft.

Her clitoris was thrumming. Karen wetted a finger in her love-hole and smoothed it over the hot little head, gently easing back the cowl. Her left hand found her breasts, skimming from one aching nipple to the other, teasing, pinching, their need echoed in her nub. She was not in the mood for delay, and frigged herself vigorously, bringing on a sharp, frenzied climax.

In the priest-hole, Mallory watched her masturbating, his eyes serious, mouth too. He held his erect phallus in one hand, rubbing it, pulling back the foreskin, anointing it with the pearly drops oozing from the slit.

Like Karen, he could not restrain himself and poured out a hot stream of abundant seed within seconds. Even as he watched her playing with herself and reaching climax, he was wondering how it would have been if he had yielded to the impulse to make love to her, which was the main reason he had asked her to go to the library.

But it was better this way. If he didn't tempt fate then he couldn't be hurt again. Better to watch her, better to pretend that it was her hand on his cock instead of his own – better anything than the raw pain he had suffered when Caroline left him.

# Chapter Eight

'Well, what d'you think of her?'

Sinclair started at the sound of Armina's voice and looked up, appreciating her beauty as she walked across the conservatory – a blonde, curly-headed sylph wearing a sleeveless, backless, button-through cotton dress, deceptively simple, but from a top Italian fashion house.

He knew all about her extravagant tastes, having paid for the ball gown she had worn to the dinner party. A bribe, of course, but then Armina was always open to bribes, out for herself and pledging loyalty to none. He accepted this and liked her no less for it. Besides which, she was one of the sexiest ladies around, with a penchant for the bizarre that matched his own. His spine tingled and the blood thickened his phallus as his eyes caressed her tiny, upward tilting breasts and the shadow where her skirt pressed between her thighs.

'Would you like a cup of coffee?' he asked, speculating on what might have brought her there.

From the depths of a deeply cushioned wicker armchair, she smiled to herself, noting the swelling in his beige linen slacks and then lifting those innocent seeming blue eyes to his.

'I'd love some, darling. I've only just got up. What a night! I had a most amusing time. How about you? Did you manage to seduce our lovely academic?'

'I did.' He found it impossible not to sound smug.

'Tell me about it,' she demanded eagerly with that flush and sparkle he recognised as sex oriented.

He concentrated on the cups and coffee-pot set out on the round rattan table. The conservatory was humid, the afternoon sun striking through the glass roof, every rare and exotic plant giving forth steamy tropical aromas. He and Armina were old friends, or rather associates, each wary of the other, withholding information they suspected could be used against them at a later date. Yet at times collaboration was essential for their mutual advantage.

He placed a cup, the sugar bowl and cream jug before her.

'Black, no sugar,' she said.

After pouring, he flicked his lighter, little flames, jets of amber, reflected in his inky pupils as he held it to the end of her cigarette. Armina inhaled luxuriously and crossed one slim leg over the other, a delicately arched foot swinging in a fragile gold leather sandal, toenails lacquered to match. Sinclair caught the smell of *Joy* emanating from between her breasts and the wonderful seaweed perfume of her secret parts.

He wanted to take her there and then on the Spanish ceramic tiles, to release his burgeoning cock and guide it into that lithe, lascivious body. His mouth filled with spittle, tormented by the killing need to taste her, to dabble his fingers in her fluids, to suck and flick and rouse her rosebud teats – to pinch and hurt her as she liked to be hurt.

Her eyes darkened from blue to violet, slightly out of focus as she stared at him from beneath black-tipped lashes. She uncoiled her legs, opened them, slipped a hand down to cradle her nest, her every movement suggestive, even lewd. This was her charm, this dichotomy between the upper-class girl from finishing school and the rapacious vampire, ready to drain her victims dry, physically, mentally and materially.

'Let's make love, Armina,' he murmured, his chair creaking as he edged it closer.

'You haven't told me what happened between you and Karen,' she pouted, stroking her breasts, pulling at the nipples through the cotton, teasing him by remaining in her seat.

'Everything happened,' he grunted, sitting back, legs apart, making her fully aware of the slant of his penis lifting the lightweight fabric of his trousers. 'I tied her up, frigged her, sucked her, made her come. She loved it. Couldn't get enough.'

'I told you she was a natural, didn't I?' Armina said unsteadily.

Talking about it ignited her fire and made her wet. Still fondling her breasts, she rested her foot on the table bracing the other leg against the floor so that her thighs were spread wide. Her skirt fell back. She wore no panties, her depilated mons shiny pink, the lips opening like a sea anemone in search of prey.

Sinclair dropped to his hunkers between her knees, his eyes level with that honey-sweet furrow. He didn't touch, simply admired, a connoisseur of female genitalia. Hers were perhaps the most perfect he had seen. Firm, full, glossy, surmounted by a prominent clitoris. He drank in the sight of her pearly organ, then stroked its head with a dry fingertip. Armina squealed and pushed her pubis upwards.

Sinclair denied her, rising to lean an arm on either side of her chair. He smiled down into her face. 'Of course, there's more she can learn. I thought a visit to Mistress Raquel might be in order.'

'When?' Armina's fingers were busy, taking over where he had left off. Her hips pumped slowly, the rhythm deep and steady.

'When you've finished wanking,' he replied, remaining where he was, lighting up a cigarette and watching her.

The Lamborghini purred like a sleek panther as it ate up the miles. Karen nestled her bottom into the voluptuous leather of the passenger seat beside Sinclair, who mastered this feral beast. Armina and Jo were crammed into the back, for this was a sports model, not some run around people carrier designed for transporting families to supermarkets. The speed was ferocious, the monster roaring belligerently when given its head, Sinclair handling it with the aplomb of a contestant in the Monte Carlo Rally.

It was a sultry evening, the sky flaming crimson. Framed against the distant luminous background, the branches and foliage looked black. Above hung a single large star like the earring of a giantess gazing dreamily across the cosmos.

The car shot through a couple of sleepy hamlets and careered along a succession of side roads, eventually braking at a pair of imposing gates flanked by a lodge house. A man in shirtsleeves came out. His head was shaved, his neck bull-like, and he had a broken nose and cauliflower ears.

Sinclair leaned from the car window and stated his business. The man nodded, grunted, returned to the lodge and within seconds the gates opened.

'He's one of Raquel's minders,' Armina said, leaning over the back of the seat, her breath tickling Karen's ear, followed by her tongue tracing the rim gently, then darting inside, mimicking a more intimate penetration.

The fine down rose on Karen's skin, her blood warming, breasts swelling, longing for the touch of lips, teeth, hands. Although she had reached orgasm alone in the library, her interview with Mallory had left her burning and unsatisfied.

What was this place? she wondered as Sinclair drove

up a long beech avenue. And who was Raquel? He hadn't told her, merely called at Laurel Cottage and asked if she'd care to visit a friend. Karen had been working all day, rushing to get everything in order for Irwin Dwyer, and had thankfully accepted the respite.

The trees parted, framing a fine example of Palladian architecture, a simple but elegant building with a central block connected by white colonnades to wings on either side. Nothing could have been more gracious than this splendid mansion surrounded by lawns and gardens.

As the car rolled towards it, another vehicle appeared from round the side of the house. It resembled a Roman chariot, carved and gilded and supported on iron-bound wooden wheels.

The rays of the sinking sun glittered on the charioteer, on metal rings and straps, on scarlet leather and naked flesh. She held the reins in one black-gloved hand, whip in the other fist landing with a resounding crack on the steed tethered between the shafts.

'Oh – ooh – thank you – thank you,' he moaned through the bit in his teeth.

'What else?' his tormentor demanded, adding emphasis by hauling on the reins and lashing his bare shoulders. 'What else, you miserable slave?'

'*Mistress!* Thank you, mistress!'

The chariot jolted to a standstill below the ornamented entrance reached by two flights of stone steps.

'Hello, Raquel,' Sinclair shouted, stopping the car
alongside.

The big woman remained in a spread-legged stance,
giving him a haughty stare. Coarse black hair flowed
across her wide shoulders. Her body was encased in a
red leather basque, her opulent breasts spilling over the
cups, white, fleshy, with brown pebbly nipples. Her bare
buttocks swelled out from under the tight leather.
Crimson suspenders cross her naked belly, connecting
with the tops of black fishnet stockings. Her pubis was
fully exposed, a wiry thatch with salmon-pink labia.

Thigh-length black PVC boots with six-inch heels
added to her formidable stature.

Goddess. Witch. Artemis. Astarte. Kali. Earth mother.
Whore priestess. Bringer of destruction, ecstasy and
release. This was Mistress Raquel.

'Good evening, Sinclair,' she said, her theatrical accent
ringing across the grass. Her steed shifted between the
shafts and the darting tip of the whip seared his buttocks. 'Don't dare move till I give permission!' she
thundered.

He cringed and shook, no wimp but a big, deep-chested man, his muscles slack, belly hanging over his tumescent penis. He was naked, apart from leather accoutrements, a spiked dog collar with chains indenting his skin as they strained down to the rings piercing his nipples, a studded belt attached to the harness binding him to the chariot. It was a replica of that worn by carriage horses, with highly polished brass buckles, a tribute to the lorimer's art.

At the back a leather thong was craftily fashioned to pass from his waist into the deep umber crease of his behind, down between his legs to loop round balls the size of goose eggs, pushing them forward, his upright dick held high. The strap was tight, but his mistress could make it tighter, creating the pain for which her slave hungered and paid handsomely to endure.

Raquel leapt down, striding round to stand in front of him, legs apart, arms akimbo. He quivered, gazing at her adoringly. She propped one foot on the first tread of the stone steps, the dark wilderness of her female parts exposed.

'Suck my cunt!' she commanded.

The slave groaned, bending with difficulty, his bonds excruciating, but an expression of ecstatic delight lit his heavily jowled face as his big, fat tongue came out to lap at her. Raquel showed no emotion, though her slit glistened with juice. She arched her hips, rubbing the moisture over his lips and cheeks, then suddenly changed position, grabbing hold of his erection and massaging his balls.

'I'll bet you'd like to let go of this spunk, wouldn't you, slave?' she sneered. 'But you can't. Masturbation is forbidden till I say you can do it. Take the chariot back to the stable and clean it thoroughly. I order you to lick the mud off the wheels with your tongue. D'you hear me? Put some effort into it. You're pathetic, lazy and disgusting.'

'Yes, mistress. Thank you, mistress. You're so good to me,' he whined.

'Too good, I agree,' she snarled, and caught him a hard slap on his dimpled arse that made drops of pre-come juice dribble from his cock. 'Go away! Get out of my sight, you useless, ugly object.'

'Humiliation. Lesson number one in being a dominatrix,' Armina murmured to Karen. 'Would you like to try? Does it appeal? I'll admit it floats my boat. Men are such bastards, it's fun to torment them, even though one knows they're enjoying it.'

Sinclair introduced Karen to Raquel. Armina and Jo were already acquainted with her. Had they taken part in these SM games? Karen wondered. Her clit twitched and a skein of something dark and vengeful tightened in the heartland of her being.

'Welcome to my home,' Raquel said, beaming at her. 'Come inside. We'll have a drink and then I'll give you a conducted tour of the torture chambers.' She laughed loudly. 'Don't look so horrified! They love it and pay vast sums of money for the privilege of being ill-treated. The slave pulling my chariot is a high-court judge and can't get enough of trotting barefoot along the cinder path my other slaves have constructed. The more his feet bleed, the happier he is, and the bigger my fee!' She gestured towards the magnificent façade. 'This place was given to me by a satisfied customer. He wanted somewhere safe where he could put on his mother's dresses and have me whip him till he came. Oh, yes, we cater for all sorts here.'

They followed her to where there were several more chariots with willing steeds commanded by war-like Amazons.

One of the stables had been converted into a double fronted garage housing a collection of gleaming cars.

Karen's head snapped up as she saw a tattooed man with windblown blond hair sitting side-saddle on a blue and chrome Harley. He glanced towards her, his expression one of total unconcern. He looked more gorgeous and sexy than ever.

Raquel clocked her interest, a smile curving her red lips. 'That's Spike. He services my cars, and me, too, when I'm in the mood for cock, which isn't often. My job's equivalent to working in a chocolate factory.'

'Karen already knows him, don't you, darling?' purred Armina, her arm linked with the willowy Jo's, both women presenting their bodies as near naked as public appearance allowed, in miniskirts and cropped tops.

Spike just sat there without speaking, his booted legs crossed in front of him, his neat tush parked on the seat of his mean machine. He wore faded, ragged, obscenely short cutoffs. Only a skimpy vest covered his upper body, and his muscles bulged, matching the impressive lump in his crutch. His pectorals were crowned by erect nipples on an almost hairless chest turned golden brown by the sun.

Then Raquel said, 'Let's go inside. I've a client waiting, and he likes an audience.'

She started off in the direction of the terrace.

Gardeners were working on the herbaceous borders and there was the distant purr of a lawn-mower. Raquel strode among them, cracking her whip.

'Faster!' she cried, prodding one wearing a sequinned evening gown and stiletto heels. 'Haven't you finished weeding that patch yet? I've never met such a worthless bunch. No treats for you tonight!'

'I'm sorry, mistress,' he bleated. 'I keep breaking my nails.'

Raquel let out a harsh, barking laugh and landed a well-aimed kick on his rear. 'Tough! I'll see you break more than that if you don't get on with it.'

The others stood watching with hangdog expressions, longing for her to reprimand them. She cast a scathing glance over her slaves and swished the whip, making them yelp at the touch of its fiery kiss. With a final disdainful glance, she abandoned them, leading her guests into the house.

Sinclair slipped a hand under Karen's elbow, managing at the same time to caress the side of her breast. 'I expect you're finding this weird,' he said quietly. 'Look at it this way. Raquel and women like her provide a harmless outlet for the cravings of certain men. In real life they're probably solid, stable, respectable chaps who love their wives, their children and the world they've carved out for themselves. They're usually men who wield power in their daily lives and who like to relax by being controlled and manipulated by someone else.'

The reception room was huge, with a large fireplace at each end and a row of tall, graceful windows facing the garden. It was superbly elegant yet comfortable, with chesterfields and wing chairs grouped in cosy conversation areas on the parquet floor. Oversized Limoges bowls filled with aromatic potpourri stood on Louis XIV buhl tables. Flowers were arranged in ornate jardinières to give the effect of a tumbling, natural profusion. Eggshell-blue paintwork picked out in white decorated the walls between pilasters of fluted marble. The high ceiling was a riot of exquisite plaster ornamentation.

'It looks sedate enough to invite the vicar for tea,' Karen commented.

Sinclair grinned. 'I believe she has had one or two vicars, as patrons though, not shepherds of their flock.'

Raquel swaggered across the room, crying, 'Sit down! Sit down! Don't stand on ceremony!'

She spoke in the bossy manner with which she addressed her slaves. After tugging imperiously at the embroidered worsted bell-pull near one of the fireplaces, she dropped on to a cushioned day bed, accepted the cigarette Sinclair offered, inserted it into a long jade holder and held it to her red slash of a mouth.

A servant answered her call, wearing the pert outfit of a French maid: a short black skirt over taffeta petticoats, a brief bodice, black stockings and court shoes, a frilly apron. The maid was skinny but fairly convincing till one noticed the military moustache on the upper lip and the clipped iron-grey hair beneath the white cap with flying streamers.

'Madame?' he asked, his voice gruff though years of bawling across barrack squares.

'Bring drinks, Fifi, and look sharp about it! And some canapés, I hope you've been hard at work making them, for if you haven't I shall be extremely displeased, and you know what that means, my girl!'

Karen sat quietly observing this Mad Hatter's cocktail party, where nothing was as it seemed. Fifi returned, staggering under the burden of heavily loaded trays. People wandered in, some dressed as schoolboys, some in furry dog suits, others in women's clothes. One man was wrapped in clingfilm, limbs, body, every part of him, with the exception of his face and the penis rearing out of a gash in the plastic.

A stern-faced nanny in a severe grey uniform led in a giant infant wearing a pink frilled frock over a nappy and plastic pants, a matinée jacket, a bib, ankle socks, white bootees and a woolly bonnet.

Raquel chucked the child under one of its several chins. 'And how is Baby Debbie today?' she cooed.

'She's been a very naughty girl,' answered Nanny, standing stiffly to attention. 'She spat her dinner everywhere and nearly fell out of the highchair. I had to pull down her nappy and smack her little botty. And then she wet herself all over the nursery floor.'

'Did she indeed? Well, Baby Debbie, we can't have this, can we? I'll have to get out my cane, won't I?' Raquel scolded.

Baby Debbie started to blubber loudly, the dummy drooping from between jutting, masculine lips. After a thorough shake and a hard slap, Nanny marched her charge away.

'*Chacun à son goût*,' murmured Sinclair. 'Becoming a baby's not my bag but it turns a lot of men on.'

Karen found herself in a sumptuous, candle-lit apartment, the curtains pulled across the windows. A man was bending over the bed, arse in the air, a large white towel spread beneath him. He was forty-something, well-preserved and handsome, and wore a taffeta frock tucked up to his waist, his buttocks and thighs naked, hairy balls dangling between them, the incongruous sight of socks and desert boots sticking out below.

'D'you want to assist?' Raquel asked Karen.

'Why not?' she answered with a shrug, willing by now to try anything once, the scene excitingly reminiscent of one of the Bedwell cartoons.

'Change into these. Over there, behind that screen.'

Raquel gave her a bundle of clothes, and Karen found Armina and Jo already stripping and donning the costumes supplied. They were giggling, roused at the prospect of the next act.

Armina wore a skin-tight body suit in black plastic. Jo was dressed in a gymslip over a white blouse with bare thighs, navy-blue knickers, grey knee socks and her hair in two pigtails.

Karen shook out her own costume. It consisted of a short white tutu with a boned bodice and slender straps – no panties – and flat ballet pumps crisscrossed with ribbon round the ankles. A birch lay to hand.

Raquel, all powerful, approached the man, asking, 'And have you been a good boy today?'

'Yes, Mistress, I have,' he whispered, and looked across at Spike, adding, 'I want to see his prick.'

'I don't know if you can. I'll have to ask him. Spike, can this gentleman look at your plonker?'

Undaunted, Spike unsnapped his shorts and his semi-hard cock bounded out, the ring glinting in the foreskin. Sinclair smiled salaciously at Armina, and Karen, who had been positioned at the man's head, birch at the ready, became impatient with this perverted game, wanting Spike to herself somewhere private.

'Let me touch it,' begged the man, fingertips pressed together as if in prayer.

'You can't. Now be a good boy or Mistress will beat you,' Raquel commanded, flexing a whip-like cane in her hands.

'Oh, no! Don't do that,' he whispered in reply.

'Why not? You're a dreadful sinner, very, very wicked, and Mistress shall punish you,' Raquel continued, signalling to Jo who leaned forward and jiggled the man's half-erect prick. He grabbed her bare knee and slid a hand under her gymslip, moaning as he fondled her sex through her knickers.

With a rushing swish the rod contacted his bare rump. He howled, jerked. The rod rose, gathered momentum and fell again. This time Karen was motioned to feel his cock. It was stiffer, getting bigger still as he reached sideways, diving under her gauze skirt and fingering her cleft.

He laid his head against the bedpost and grasped it with both hands as the birch rose and fell, his buttocks reddening, bright weals appearing on the pasty white skin. His whispering sobs and infantile protests carried no weight with his strict mistress.

'Let me play with his willie,' breathed Armina, unzipping the catsuit, her breasts, belly and smooth mound showing through the opening.

She took his weapon in her hand and rubbed it vigorously while the cane thwacked his writhing backside. Armina gave his prick a few more firm strokes, handed it over to Jo who did the same and then passed it on to Karen. She made a fist, slid the foreskin up and down over its bulbous tip. He sobbed his pleasure and spurted out a shower of semen, covering her fingers with creamy jism and spattering the towel beneath him. He cried out in the tumult of release and fell across the bed, quiet and appeased.

Spike gave Karen no time to change back into her own clothes, rushing her down the backstairs to the garage.

Hazy, drugged by the wine they had drunk, probably laced with an aphrodisiac, every person who had taken part in the flagellation had been roused to uncontrollable lust. Sinclair had fallen into bed with Armina, while Raquel and Jo had pleasured one another.

Once they reached the garage, Spike crushed Karen to him, grinding his penis into her belly, his mouth against hers, plundering the lush cave with his tongue, drinking her spittle, crushing her lips with his. He was harsh, brutal, worked into a frenzy of desire by the atmosphere created by Raquel. He pressed Karen back and back till she could go no further, meeting the barrier of the hard, shiny surface of a midnight-blue Mercedes.

Hands beneath her buttocks he lifted her, spread her over the bonnet, spread her legs wide open, pressed up against her, shorts undone, hips thrust out, that thick hard rod pumping into her slick, wet opening. The surface of the car was slippery, his cock ramming against the muscles of her womb. She wasn't comfortable, but he was heedless of this, driving into her savagely, and a part of her revelled in this harsh way of taking.

Her breasts swelled from the low bodice, and his mouth seized a nipple, sucking, pulling at it, till she was ready to explode with frustration. Her clit wanted the same treatment. Wildly she brought up her legs and wound them round his waist, thrusting her pubis against him, grinding the stem of her hungry bud on the base of his penis, attempting to capture that elusive pressure. His deepening strokes missed it, even though she enjoyed the friction of his pubic hair against hers, the rap of his hardening testicles bumping that sensitive area between vulva and rectum.

'I want more,' she gasped, pulling out from under him. 'I can't come like this.'

'Sorry, babe,' he whispered, suddenly humble, and drew back, cradling her mound in his hand. 'I didn't realise ...'

He found her core, pinching the aching clitoris, and she sighed and sighed, knowing he wasn't going to disappoint her. It took so little to tip her over the edge, but it had to be done in the right way. Clumsy, selfish lovers were no use to her, no matter how handsome and macho they might be.

Cooling his own passions, Spike worked his fingers round the stalk of her love-bud, wetting it, stroking it, parting the lips and sliding across one side then the other before returning to the centre point. His other hand plucked at her nipples, toying, rubbing, matching his movements to those rousing her clit. Up he went to the miniature hood, easing it back, making her jewel stand out, bending to admire it, lick it, coax it to climax.

The dark-blue lacquer beneath her warmed. She was no longer conscious of discomfort, focused on the pulse beating at her epicentre, arms coming up to clasp him, body moving into his. She started to convulse, felt the spasms shaking her, swept up in the mindless, glorious eruption of orgasm. Swiftly he poised over her entrance, and she reached down a hand and guided his huge member into her, her muscles gripping it as he groaned and shot into her with furious driving force.

'Spike, Spike,' she whispered, sinking down, the after-shocks of her climax still roaring through her. 'Take me back to the cottage. Stay with me tonight.'

'Anything for you, love,' he murmured into her neck.

Normally, she liked to sleep alone, but not this time. They rode back on the Harley, stumbled up the stairs, played music on the CD, drank coffee, talked and made love again. It was comforting to have him there, sharing her bed, having him fold himself against her, spoon fash-ion, his penis swelling again, moving against her backside, slipping between her legs to rest against her nether lips, the ring piercing its head nudging her clitoris.

His attention made her feel so alive, so female, so happy with herself. It dispelled the loneliness she dreaded. That time between sleep and daydreaming, the soul's midnight, when she might lie thinking about a pair of piercing amber eyes and sensual lips, a haughty look, power, a sense of mystery, a promise of magic. And a name that slipped like liquid honey over her tongue, one she could not forget no matter how many men she fucked.

'Oh, God, my back aches,' Karen complained, arching her spine and stretching, the operator's chair swivelling towards Tony.

'You've been at that computer for hours,' he said, pushing the horn-rimmed spectacles up to his forehead. 'Bloody Dwyer and this damn rush!'

'It's OK. It's got us motivated. We might have dawdled for ever if he hadn't been expected. Too fussy, too particular, that's our trouble. Now we've just had to get a move on.'

'Hard at it for almost a week! And the weather's glorious, and every other bugger is having fun,' he groused, glaring out of the library window at the sun-drenched garden.

Karen chuckled and picked up her bag. 'Let's have a change. Lunch at my place. OK?'

'You're on.'

They stopped off in the village and picked up fish and chips, the hot little shop reeking of frying fat, mushy peas and fast-food treats.

'How decadently unhealthy. Oozing cholesterol,' Karen said as she unwrapped the steaming parcels on the kitchen table, offering plates and cutlery.

'I'll put that on my fret list,' Tony grinned and waved them away. 'No thanks, I'd rather eat it with my fingers. Pity it doesn't come in newspaper any longer, it loses a certain *je ne sais quoi* without the flavour of printer's ink. Pass the salt and vinegar – oh, and the tomato ketchup.'

'You're a slob,' she remarked, scalding her mouth on a sizzling chip.

'I am. Haven't you white sliced? Put the kettle on. Nothing goes better with fish-shop chips than buttered bread and hot strong tea. A meal fit for a king.'

'How common!' she taunted.

'As muck,' he agreed.

They idled at the table, mugs in their hands, then, by mutual consent, wandered up to her bedroom. Heat breathed in at the dormer window, spiced with the scent of warm grass and roses. The stillness of noon held the countryside in thrall.

'Let's go skinny-dipping before we get back to the treadmill,' Tony suggested as they undressed. 'When we've done this, of course. I haven't had a fuck since the night of the party.'

'You're slipping,' she mocked, smiling as she stood naked by the bed.

He reached up to hold her breasts in his hands. 'And you're not? How many men have you bonked since the last time I shafted you?'

'None of your business.'

The cool sheet warmed quickly, heated by their bodies. Karen lay on her side, facing away from him but with her back pressed against his stomach and chest. Reaching round he fondled her nipples. She ground her naked buttocks against his erection, wriggling as it pushed between her nether cheeks. He lifted her thigh and spread it over his, half turning her as his cock slipped into her wet love channel from the rear. She was partly on top of him and his tongue dipped into her ear, slurping, licking, sending little shocks right through her.

Now he was embedded deeply inside her, one hand

plucking at her upthrusting nipples, the other gliding over her belly to her mound. She stretched her thigh to open her silky avenue wider. Tony's finger worked her clitoris as he pumped his prick into her, faster and faster till she climaxed, her inner muscles pulsating round his cock as she felt him reach his own *petite mort*.

Driving back to the house, Tony looked at her sideways and said, 'There's something different about you, darling. It's puzzling me. Could it be to do with Lord Burnet?'

The car was open topped, and she lifted her chin, letting the wind cool her face and tug at her hair. 'Why should it be?' she answered casually.

He grinned, shrugged and watched the white road unwinding ahead. 'No reason. Just a hunch.'

'Hunches aren't always right,' she snapped, and remained silent till they swung round to the back of the house, parked the car and headed for the pool, a shining blue oval surrounded by stone tubs massed with brilliantly coloured flowers.

They had it to themselves and stripped naked before plunging in. Karen swam several lengths, arms cleaving effortlessly through the sun-warmed water, and then lay back, resting against the rim and closing her eyes, her body floating as she drifted and dreamed.

'I've been looking for you.' A crisp voice roused her and she bobbed down, hiding her body. Mallory was standing on the tiled edge of the pool just above her.

'It's our lunch-time,' answered Tony levelly, seated on the steps, his hair and beard spiked and wet.

'I've just had a phone call. Irwin Dwyer's in London, staying at the Dorchester. He's arriving here tomorrow.'

It was impossible to fathom Mallory's expression behind his dark glasses, but he sounded impatient, even harassed. He wore a white T-shirt and white Armani jeans, so tight that it was obvious he wore nothing beneath them. Karen could see no line denoting boxer-shorts or even a jockstrap, but was achingly aware of the shape of his cock. The sunlight glittered on his blue-black hair and touched sparks from the gold Seiko banding his wrist.

'Everything's under control,' Tony said calmly, the water cascading from his limbs as he climbed from the pool.

'Are the print-outs ready?'

'More than a dozen copies. He'll have everything he wants to know.' Tony stood on the side unconcernedly, shaking himself before reaching for his trousers.

Karen wanted to get out too but was embarrassed to

be naked in front of Mallory. She told herself sternly not to be such an idiot. After all, he had seen her nude before. Had it been anyone else, she'd not have given it a second thought.

He was obviously waiting for her to make a move. *He's only worried about his library and the American*, she thought angrily. *Any other man might get a hard-on watching me. Not him! For some reason he's denying the chemistry sparking between us.* She had no idea why or how it had happened, but a huge wave of sadness overpowered her.

She tossed up her head, her tangled mane dark with water, swam to the steps and hauled herself out, ignoring Mallory. She struggled into her briefs, the material sticking awkwardly to her damp skin, and shrugged her arms into her cotton shirtwaister, never looking once in his direction.

Behind her, she heard him say to Tony, 'Will you meet him at Exeter Station tomorrow? I gather he's bringing his aide along.'

'No problem,' Tony replied calmly. 'Don't worry, sir. It's sorted.'

'I hope so,' Mallory answered gloomily. 'There's a lot at stake.'

Karen kept her face hidden behind the fall of her wet hair, fighting the temptation to look in his direction. Every nerve alive, she knew the instant he had gone inside the house. Suddenly it seemed as if a cloud had passed across the sun, a chill running through her.

'Back to work, girl.' Tony touched her arm, put a finger under her chin and lifted her face to his. 'Let's show him what a team we are, eh?'

# Chapter Nine

'I owe you an apology, Miss Heyward.'

Karen, about to close and lock the library door, could hardly believe her own ears. 'I beg your pardon?' she said, looking up at him, stunned.

'I've been unfair. Can we start again?'

This was incredible. Mallory, the lordly and arrogant, was actually expressing regret for something he had done, and to a woman, too!

The corridor was filled with the somnolence of a summer afternoon, a time when the servants had absented themselves from that part of the house, idling in their quarters or quietly undertaking some task that was not too taxing.

Sinclair had gone to London that morning, roaring off in the Lamborghini, taking Celine and Jo with him. He had spoken airily of business in town. The singer was working with her *répétiteur* in preparation for the starring role in *Carmen* due to open in Vienna in October. Jo had the opportunity to glide the catwalk for a leading fashion designer. Armina was absent, presumably humping Tayte or getting her kicks at Raquel's establishment. Patty was busy in the greenhouse, interested not only in the horticulture but in the well-endowed young gardeners.

Karen, the work completed as far as she and Tony were able to take it before Dwyer's arrival, had made certain that all was in order for the important visitor and had decided to head for home. The last person she had expected to see was Mallory.

'You don't have to apologise to me, sir,' she replied tartly. 'I'm just doing a job. That's all.'

'It's not all,' he insisted, leaning a shoulder against the panelling, the angle of his body preventing her from passing him without being downright rude. 'You told me you loved the house, and I think that is true.'

He was heart-stoppingly sexy – lean, masculine, casually chic, his sleek hips, long thighs and divine arse displayed in an unbroken line from waist to knee, riding breeches fitting without a wrinkle. The ridge of his penis drew Karen's eyes like a magnet.

'It is,' She was trembling, wanting, the hot lava of desire soaking the gusset of her panties.

'And I've treated you badly.' He held out a hand, his frank smile making him look even more devastatingly handsome. 'Let's shake on it and be friends. What d'you say?'

What *could* she say? What could any red-blooded woman say in the circumstances? An electric charge shot through her as his warm, dry hand closed over hers. She felt the hardness of his palm, accustomed to riding and hawking, the strength of his fingers practised in coaxing beautiful music from piano strings, the touch she had seen encountering Armina's body, and Celine's. Her need was appalling, her nipples contracting, womb yearning, clitoris avid.

Karen returned his smile, felt the hesitant release of her hand, felt hope striking cautious roots. Till now his mind had been opaque, his body in denial. She had an intense desire to open up both shuttered, enigmatic areas.

'I'm fascinated by the history of the house,' she managed to say through the lump in her throat. 'There's absolutely no need for you to worry about the library. Tony and I are dedicated to it. He can't wait to show it to Mr Dwyer.'

'Ah, yes – our millionaire. He's gone to fetch him. I suggested he drive the Rolls. Americans are usually most impressed by that symbol of English gentility. Irwin asked me how he could get his hands on a title.' Humour flashed in his eyes, an unsuspected quality.

Karen suddenly realised Mallory might be fun, with maybe a keener sense of humour than the satirical wit favoured by his brother. It was possible they could laugh together once her stabbing, dragging, obsessional passion had been slaked.

'They're sometimes sold, aren't they?' she responded conversationally, attempting nonchalance to hide the raging lust urging her to dive a hand between the unbuttoned front of his blue cotton shirt, caress the sepia chest hair and tweak the dark nipples.

'I believe so. Unfortunately some of our oldest families are forced to sell up, can no longer afford to be choosy. Acres of English soil are being sold off to foreigners.' His voice was cutting again, all humour leaving his face, replaced by that sombre expression lurking there at all times.

Karen wanted to draw his head down to her breasts, to hold him like a child and kiss away the pain. *Don't be a hypocrite*, she lectured herself. *It's common or garden lust you feel, nothing more. You want him close to your tits so he can suck them, draw the nipples between his even white teeth, driving you mad with longing. And then – ah, then – down to your clit. You'd open to him like a flower opening to the sun and, once ripened, would absorb him into the depths of your rampant, lecherous cunt.*

Her eyes misted as she cartwheeled back in time to when she had first seen his erect phallus, recalling the length and girth disappearing into Armina's mouth:

'Are you all right?' His concerned voice recalled her.

'Oh, yes. I was just thinking – the cartoons, you know. Mr Dwyer is bound to be over the moon about them,' she spluttered, the heat receding from her belly and cleft, leaving a dull ache.

'They are splendid, aren't they?' He sounded amused, a trifle puzzled, his amber eyes boring into hers.

'I must go,' she said, longing to escape, to rush back to the seclusion of Laurel Cottage and there gloat over this meeting while relieving herself with the vibrator Celine had insisted she accept as a present.

'Must you?' There was a hint of regret in his voice. 'I'd rather hoped you might have time to ride with me. I'm taking Leila out. Have you ever seen a hawk strike?'

She wasn't to be dismissed! Her heart fluttered like that of an infatuated girl or a tripping groupie backstage at a rock concert, but she despised her weakness. He was, after all, only a man, not a god to be worshipped.

'I'd like to watch you put her through her paces.' She consulted her wristwatch in a businesslike fashion. 'I am rather busy, but I can spare an hour or so. I'm hardly dressed for it,' she added with a gesture towards her linen shorts, thin blouse and espadrilles.

'It will do. We won't go far. You look lovely,' he said, heaving his shoulders from the wall.

*If I were a Victorian maiden I'd probably swoon at his feet right now*, she thought.

A golden glow covered the earth, the sun high in a cloud-less heaven, skylarks soaring into the azure depths, their song vibrating on the thermals. Ringdoves gave vent to their doleful, amorous calls from the dark bank of woods the riders left behind as they rose to the open ground beyond – the wide sweep of moor that bordered the sea.

Heat on her cheeks, wind in her hair, tumult in her sex, Karen rode beside Mallory like a comrade from far-off times. It felt right, as if she had entered an existence long remembered, secretly missed and desired, beyond recollection or comprehension.

*There are some moments so magical that nothing thereafter ever quite measures up to them*, she mused. *This afternoon is one of them*. The conviction grew as they paused near a great outcrop of granite which a mysterious people had raised into a barrow thousands of years before.

'It's reputed to be the haunt of hobgoblins,' Mallory said, looking at her gravely. 'Are you afraid, Miss Heyward?'

*Not of spirits*, she wanted to retort, *only of you, or rather my erratic emotions concerning you. I don't fancy becoming your doormat, my Lord Marquis of Ainsworth.*

Then she forgot everything, completely captivated by Leila's performance. The falcon was a diva of the skies – powerful, heavy and perfectly mannered, but temperamental nevertheless.

'Don't stare at her,' Mallory warned as he removed the hawk's hood. 'She'll get upset if you look directly into her eyes.'

*I'm jealous*, Karen decided, watching the tender way in which he handled the bird, whispering endearments as he prepared to cast her off from his wrist. *And Leila's jealous of me. She loves him and doesn't want any other female around. Possessive bitch of a thing! I'll bet she'd peck me if she could, go for the throat – no, the eyes! And, hell! I don't blame her.*

'Watch this,' Mallory commanded and tossed up his arm. Leila, who had started to bate restlessly, shot upwards at speed. 'See her go! The most exciting part is the stoop from perhaps one thousand feet. She drives down on her quarry at a hundred miles an hour and strikes with her foot closed like a fist, killing it stone dead. Let's follow her.'

The dash across the moor in pursuit was mind-blowing, hounds and horses going full tilt. Once Leila struck she had to be coaxed away from the kill, and Mallory did this on foot, whirling a long rope with feathers tied to it round and round above his head while whistling her special call.

Leila obeyed, descending on the lure, which Mallory dropped to the ground. Then he made after her, taking her on to his glove, rewarding her with a titbit. The strike was repeated, and Karen and the dogs were given the job of locating the dead rabbit, hare or grouse and bringing it back to him, Karen's only lure being the promise of that wide, sensual mouth, his fiery eyes and the firm bough of his penis temptingly displayed by his form-hugging breeches.

They jogged home through the twilight, and Karen wished Blackwood Towers would remain for ever in the distance, a mirage seen but never attained. When they clopped into the yard, Tayte came forward to assist but, to her amazement, Mallory handed the hooded falcon to him, swung down and appeared by her side before she had time to slide a foot out of the stirrup.

She felt his hands at her waist, the strength of him as he lifted her effortlessly to the ground, remaining there holding her lightly, looking down into her face. 'Thank you, Karen,' he murmured. 'I've enjoyed this afternoon. Will you come to dinner? I'll be entertaining the American and his assistant. I could use your support.'

'Will Tony be there?' She could hardly speak. He had used her first name, but even now she did not quite dare to return the intimacy. Her thighs ached from riding, the inner sides sweaty from contact with leather, slippery with love-juice through contact with him.

'Oh, yes. You'll come?'

'I will.'

Armina had said he liked fellatio after hunting. Would he want it now? She could feel the grip of the flimsy triangle cupping her mons, feel how wet it was, how taut against her clit.

'Shall I take the horses, sir?' a guttural voice enquired.

'Yes, and tell the kitchen staff to make sure the game is hung.'

Karen was plummeted from Disneyland to the reality of the darkening stables and Tayte grinning knowingly at her, a reminder of sexual congress in the loft, of the big pink serpent he kept in his jeans and his willingness to share it.

Wantonly, she lusted to see it again, to compare it with Sinclair's. Maybe tonight after dinner, if Mallory didn't come up with a more alluring proposition. The thought that he might, plus the heat of his hand imprinted on her waist, made her even more conscious of her breasts and nipples unfettered by a brassière under the light, almost transparent covering of her Indian cheesecloth shirt.

'We're back,' Tony's voice carolled cheerfully down the mobile phone. 'Mission accomplished.'

'What's he like?' Karen, naked, her hair tied up in a

towel, balanced the headset between her ear and raised shoulder and lit a cigarette.

'The tycoon? Seems an OK sort of guy. Down-to-earth – easy to get on with. Crazy about England.'

'And the aide?' She sat on the side of the bath tub and blew smoke rings.

'Earnest, eager to learn, very much an all-American girl. Not bad looking but repressed. Wears specs. Terrible dress sense. She's got the hots for her boss. Typical secretary type.'

'Oh, I somehow thought it would be a man.'

Tony's disembodied chuckle rippled through the ether between his cottage and hers. 'Sorry to disappoint you, love. Isn't there enough cock at Blackwood Towers?'

'Don't be crude.' She smiled and tapped her cigarette into a shell-shaped ashtray.

'Me? Crude? You sure you're talking about the right bloke? Anyway, Mallory tells me he's invited us to dinner. Is that right? He also said you two had been riding this afternoon. What's been going on during my absence? I can't trust you, can I? As soon as my back's turned you're off dicking it. I thought you hated his guts.'

'I wanted to see Leila at work. There was absolutely

no sex involved,' Karen lied coolly. She didn't intend to have Tony prying and teasing and generally making her feel foolish.

'Ah, I understand. You rode with His Lordship in the interests of falconry,' he said sceptically.

'You know I like to find out about things.'

'Of course, ducky – I quite understand. Now then, about tonight. Dinner first, followed by a grand viewing of the library and Dirty Dick's porn.'

Nervousness clawed at her vitals as she realised just how heavy a responsibility she and Tony had taken on. It *must* go well. She had worked without let, giving herself no spare time. While managing to maintain the daily ritual of *T'ai Chi*, plans for the *dojo* had been temporarily shelved.

'Who else will be there?'

'Armina and Patty. Irwin likes quim, so get on your best bib and tucker and forget your drawers.'

Karen could feel her hackles rising. 'Fuck off, Tony!' she shouted down the phone. 'I'm not turning tricks, if that's what Lord Burnet expects.'

'Chill out. No one's asking you to. You'll like Irwin, anyway. All we've got to do is make him feel welcome. If there's any shagging to be done I'm sure Armina will oblige. Shall I pick you up, or d'you want to play Miss Independent?'

'I'll drive the Golf, then I can leave when I've had enough.'

She laid the mobile by the bath, within reach should it ring while she was immersed. Everything was to hand and she was looking forward to preparing herself. She had brought up a bottle of white wine, slightly over-chilled. It felt good on her tongue, the cold snapping her into a greater awareness. She relaxed in the luxury of the warm, jasmine-scented water, eyes closed as she listened to the music swelling from her portable CD player.

Celine's interest in *Salome* had reawakened her own love of that high-camp opera, and she had bought the latest recording. The thrilling soprano voice plucked every ounce of feeling from Strauss's music as the unhinged princess, victim of a dysfunctional family, sang. Dark, brooding, desperate, her plaintive elegy for the prophet who had been slain so she might kiss his lips made the hair stand up at the back of Karen's neck.

She lay in the bath languorously fondling her nipples and seeing Mallory's sherry-gold eyes with her inner vision. The music welled to a crescendo as Salome took Jochanaan's severed head in her hands and placed her lips over the dead ones. It flowed over Karen's body, culminating between her legs. Jochanaan. Mallory. Her fingers found her wet pubic hair, parting it, seeking the tiny, hard, essential kernel.

She shared Salome's anguish. Tears pricked behind her closed eyelids, ran from the corners to fall across her cheeks. She could taste them, salty on her tongue. The princess knew that killing Jochanaan had given her no peace. Kissing him wasn't enough. She wanted his body and this was now impossible. She had destroyed the thing she loved.

Karen circled her clitoris, played with it, stimulated it and, as the final, dissonant chords reverberated through the air, she surrendered herself to the violence of an explosive orgasm.

Salome died, crushed by the shields of Herod's soldiers. The compact disc finished. Karen came out of her sensual trance. She left the tub, towelled her hair, went through the routine of preparing for an important evening, the same as on other occasions, yet with a major difference: in her heart she knew why she was taking extra care, and it wasn't on the American's account.

Her bedroom became a sacred place, consecrated to

the worship of her womanhood. Pouring a puddle of lotion in her palm she worked it into her skin till her flesh felt as soft and tender as a rose petal. Every toe was massaged, the nails manicured, painted the colour of sand. Armpits were shaved of every trace of hair, her pubis left in its natural state, covered in short, feathery, reddish curls, several shades lighter than the ringlets corkscrewing across her bare shoulders.

Last summer her parents had visited Turkey and brought her back a present. There had never seemed an appropriate moment to wear it, until now. The jellaba was long, dyed in the vibrant hues of the desert at sunrise. Made of hand-spun wild silk, it was bordered with gold embroidery and seed pearls. The wide, loose sleeves were ornamented, and the deep slash between her breasts fastened with loops over buttons covered in gilt thread.

She twisted a rope of variegated semi-precious stones about her neck, and hooked a pair of dangling beaded earrings into her lobes. Beautifully crafted jewelled sandals had come with the outfit, a copy of those found in a pharaoh's tomb, flat soled, supported by a thong between the big toe and its neighbour, the kind of footwear in which she was most at ease.

Beneath this exotic creation Karen wore absolutely nothing, the silk caressing her skin like a lover's lips. Such attire called for equally colourful make-up and she didn't hesitate, eyes accentuated by kohl, slanting at the outer corners, cheekbones dusted with gold blusher, mouth shaded a deep, warm apricot. She sprayed on *Shalimar*, a sensual perfume, the very name conjuring up images of the mystic East.

Cigarettes and lighter went into a drawstring pouch, with her keys and some loose change. Her pulse was beating rapidly, her root chakra throbbing with molten fire. Tonight she'd share Mallory's ancestral couch. She was ready. For anything? Almost anything.

'It's great to meet you, Karen. Lord Burnet has told me so much about you,' said Irwin Dwyer, clasping her fingers in a firm handshake with that innate politeness of the educated, well-heeled American male.

'How d'you do, Mr Dwyer. I'm sure he's been exaggerating,' Karen answered, pleased and confused, even a little shy.

Before her she saw a genial, smiling man, but guessed at hardness beneath the marshmallow exterior. He was handsome, wearing a hand-tailored tuxedo.

Clever plastic surgery made him look closer to fifty than sixty, his jaw tight, eyes unlined. He was a bulky bull of a man, flab kept at bay by rigorous work-outs, thinning dark blond hair streaked by the sun. His eyes were a twinkling blue, his face broad, his skin deeply tanned. He had a narrow mouth that could have looked mean but for the lips. These were full, sensual, the lips of a successful tycoon who enjoyed every aspect of sex, was able to buy it, to win it, to woo women into loving him.

'Hey, call me Irwin. Exaggerating? I think he sure played it down. He certainly didn't tell me you were cute as well as clever.' There was no doubt that he charmed on a grand scale.

Power emanated from him, a potent aphrodisiac. It would set women's hearts racing and make them cream their knickers. It had that effect on Karen, her nipples puckering as she wondered how it would be to have him kiss them and if sleeping with a great man performed a kind of magic: was one able to absorb his success along with his spunk?

They had gathered in the salon, so full of antiquities it resembled a museum, but with a lived-in look. Tony was already there, and Patty, wearing an oyster satin dress with off-the-shoulder puffed sleeves and a boned bodice that accentuated her breasts, an ingénue with a single white camellia in her dark curls in contrast to the gamine, racy Armina.

She had arrived late, her slinky silver lamé gown clinging to every curve, naked under the glittering fabric, displaying the hint of a nipple, the tautness of her buttocks, the shaded valley between them opening and closing intriguingly as she walked. Tiny, waiflike, she was sin incarnate. Surrounded by gorgeous woman, Irwin appeared to be in seventh heaven, but he paid Karen the most attention, making her feel special.

Mallory's dark head bent towards Martha Reiner, Irwin's secretary, a thin woman wearing a shade of heliotrope that did nothing for her sallow complexion. Her brown hair had been scraped into an upswept style, and she peered at him through the lenses of her expensively framed glasses while trying to catch what Irwin was saying to the other women. It was obvious she was cock struck and hero-worshipped her employer, her notebook and ballpoint poised, attempting to cushion him from life's vicissitudes when he was more than capable of coping alone.

'D'you think he screws her when there's nothing else

on offer?' Tony whispered to Karen, debonair with his rakish beard, dark-blue velvet bow tie and cummerbund.

'Probably,' she replied, sipping a Margarita, savouring the salt rimming the glass.

'Poor dear,' he continued, swirling his whisky, the shaved ice tinkling. 'Maybe I should step in. Give her a rogering.'

'Maybe you should.' Karen was hardly listening, watching Mallory without appearing to do so.

Dinner was superbly cooked, the hors d'oeuvre delectable fruits of the sea, followed by a traditional saddle of beef, crispy roast potatoes, plump Yorkshire puddings and verdant home-grown vegetables swimming in butter. Then the exotic surprise of peach and meringue pudding, covered with cream and served with hot brandy sauce. Coffee was brought out to the terrace.

Mallory leaned against the stone balustrade, wearing his dinner jacket with as much ease as his riding clothes. He held one of Irwin's cigars between his fingers, its tip glowing, sometimes near his lips, sometimes a red beacon emphasising a point as he gestured.

'I thought a series of mazes to intrigue the punters when we go public,' he said, his eyes cutting to Karen.

'There used to be a maze. Have you seen it on the old plans of the grounds?'

'It was situated beyond the lawn near the lake.' She was feeling full of food and wine, slightly light-headed. It seemed incredible that he was actually asking her opinion, his voice caressing her ears, vibrating down her spine, a melting sensation pooling in her groin.

'But a maze will take a long time to grow, won't it?' Irwin put in sensibly.

He was seated on a Regency bergère chair, opulent with gilt fantasies – chimera heads, animal legs, stars and Egyptian winged sun motifs. Armina and Patty were close at hand, determined not to lose sight of this important visitor, acting on Mallory's behalf but also on their own: Irwin would be generous.

'Not if we construct one of roses, or buy semi-mature box hedging. I'm even considering a Zen garden, with pebbled paths, bamboo screens and unexpected views of water and bonsai trees.'

'I've a Japanese friend who could advise you,' Karen said, transported back to Kan's flat at the mention of dwarf trees and thinking of the lovers she'd enjoyed – and the as yet untested one.

'I think different mazes are a great idea,' Irwin

enthused, beaming at Armina who coiled nearer, arranging her legs in such a way that her skirt slipped open affording a brief glimpse of her hairless mons. 'We'll get a landscape gardener working on designs. Make a note of that, Martha.'

'Yes, Mr Dwyer.' Her face was flushed, and she fumbled with her notebook, obviously affected by the wine and the majesty of her surroundings.

Karen sympathised, guessing that this romantic setting must be playing havoc with her libido. The terrace was softly illumined, the garden clear and dramatic in the radiance of the full moon sailing serenely across the sky attended by her retinue of stars.

'Have you ever been to the States, Karen?' Irwin asked, and something in his tone made her think of a world hyped with promise and excitement.

'No, but my parents are there at the moment.'

'You must visit. Come to LA as my guest.' He gave an expansive gesture, a great cuddly cat at play, claws sheathed momentarily. 'You must all come.'

'I'd love to.' Armina leaned over to rest her hand on his knee, sliding it higher, flirting with the substantial bulge of the mature tackle cradled between his legs.

'So would I,' breathed Patty, angled so that he could

look down at the curve of both breasts and the tips of rosy areolae.

'That's settled. Come back with me at the end of the month. You too, Karen. I fly Concorde and have my private jet meet me the other end.'

Martha's face was blotched, a flush spreading up from her neck. Tears sparkled behind her lenses. Tony, lounging on a cane-backed settee of Art Deco vintage, looked on with his Pan-like smile. Karen noticed Mallory had vanished.

Piano music sounded from the distance. She drifted towards the door, lured by the cascading arpeggios. She found him in the salon, thundering out dark, stormy cadences as if to relieve some torment deep in his soul, face carved in hard lines of concentration. She walked across the space separating them like someone under a hypnotic spell, gravid with desire.

Beneath the raw-silk jellaba she could feel drops of perspiration trickling down her spine. Her labia were unfolding, moistening, her clitoris aching like a nipple waiting to be sucked. He ignored her and she inched closer, till her arms rested on the polished black lid of the Steinway.

*It's not true that a pianist's hands should be slender*

*and delicate.* The thought fired her mind. *His are strong, positive, each sequence of notes attacked mercilessly yet with rapier-like precision. He plays as he fences, knowing when to attack. Like everything else he attempts, he'll want to be the best there is.*

The softness of the silk was an irritation now, her nipples erect, almost painfully sensitive. She opened the front of her robe, spreading it wide till her breasts were bare, then circling the dark rings, pinching them into peaks. There was something profoundly erotic in arousing herself while he sat there interpreting a Beethoven sonata as if nothing else existed.

Mallory raised his eyes but kept playing, the most delicious, searing heat radiating through her as he watched her pinching her nipples harder, rolling them between her fingers. As he fed on her hands, so she continued to gaze at his. She could see the sinews, the dark down on the backs, the way they bunched to attack a chord or spread wide to coax a melody. 'I want them to touch me,' she gasped, no longer simply wet between the legs, now flooding in a hot tide.

As the final, climactic notes resounded, he sat back, hands on his knees, still looking at her. Something seemed to come from his eyes into hers, just as light fills a cloud at sunset. She dropped her hands, let him see her swollen, aching breasts, the tips red with arousal. He reached up and touched one. A shiver of delight raced through her.

'Music is the greatest art form,' he said, and she pushed against his hand. 'Emotions can only be expressed through music.'

She reeled under the impact of his touch, nerve endings quivering as he rose and stood behind her, hands sliding under her armpits to reach her breasts again. She strained back against him, felt his breath whispering over her skin, felt one hand trailing down over her belly. Through the silk she felt his pressure on her clitoris, could feel the juices soaking it, dampening his fingers. His hardened phallus moved, restricted by his trousers and her robe, but even so she felt its hot strength as she parted her thighs, lifting her backside to rub over it.

Now his seeking fingers became impatient, undoing the jellaba, seeking the texture beneath. Karen sighed, shuddering at the ecstasy of his touch, turning her head to meet his searching lips.

'Ah, there you are, Mallory,' said Armina, gliding into the room. 'I wondered what had happened to you. Irwin wants to see the cartoons.'

He froze, stood back, released Karen. Her body was suddenly chilled, bereft of his warmth, the sensations that had been surging through her slackening with cruel abruptness.

'Hope we haven't interrupted anything,' Irwin grinned, appearing in the doorway, his entourage in tow. 'Thought we'd get down to business first, then concentrate on having a ball.'

Mallory became the perfect host, conducting Irwin through the house to the library. Tony unlocked the door and stood back for them to precede him.

'Wow! Will you look at that?' Irwin gasped. 'Gee, I'd like it in my ranch house!'

Several thousand books stood behind the fronts of tall bookcases in this baroque room designed especially for study. Karen and Tony exchanged a congratulatory glance. They had produced order out of chaos. Irwin almost tiptoed, his voice hushed as if he was in church.

'It's all so *old*,' whispered Martha, taking her cue from him.

'Fantastic!' He was craning his neck, staring up at the richness of the ceiling, then pummelling Mallory on the shoulder. 'You're sitting on a gold mine. No need to open it to the public. We'll advertise it in trade magazines. Shoot a video. Turn part of the place into an exclusive guesthouse. Seminars, business conferences, literary conventions. What a venue!'

He swung round to his goggle-eyed secretary. 'Make a note of this, Martha.'

'Yes, Mr Dwyer.'

Irwin was launched, cash registers ringing in his ears. He looked directly at Karen. The pussy cat had gone back to sleep, a tiger taking its place. 'D'you have a fax machine?'

'We're on the Net.'

He rubbed his hands gleefully. 'Great. You get on to it first thing tomorrow, Martha.'

'You've not yet seen the *pièce de résistance*,' Mallory interjected quietly. 'Follow me.'

He had a key for the sanctum and, grinning like a child about to be presented with a new toy, Irwin was at his heels. Karen's hands clenched into fists. This was the moment of truth.

The little room was bathed in soft light, glowing, intimate. Mallory crossed to the cabinet, then stopped. 'What's this?' he said sharply. 'It's open.'

'It can't be,' Karen exclaimed. 'Everything was secure when I left this morning.'

But he was right. She could see the catch had been forced. Mallory dragged the drawer open. It was empty. The Bedwell cartoons had gone. He turned on her, the rage in his eyes paralysing.

'Where are they? What have you done with them? My God, if I find out you've stolen them I'll see you go down for years!'

# Chapter Ten

Blackwood Towers swarmed with uniformed police and a dash of plain-clothes officers disguised in jeans, Reeboks and anoraks.

'But you can tell a copper a mile off, can't you?' Armina said, so aroused it was all she could do to keep her hands off her crotch.

'Daddy was in the army,' Patty confided, sitting close to her in the salon, where suspects had been herded. 'I just adore men in uniform. I hope I get interrogated by one.'

'Kinky,' Armina responded, eyes bright as they wandered over every constable, male or female. 'I thought you were keen on Neanderthal studs dripping testosterone. I'll settle for the inspector. He can grill me any time.'

Mallory had reported the robbery to Porthcombe sub-station and Exeter had been alerted. Panda cars had come screaming up the drive and disgorged a stalwart band led by Detective Inspector Callard. He wasn't in uniform, just an ordinary suit, but his authoritative aura had almost brought Patty to climax. Everyone was ordered to remain in the house for questioning while the boys from forensic dusted powder all over the library and took fingerprints.

Mallory, in the blackest mood on record, accused Karen, the newest recruit to staff and the least known. Even Tony was suspect in his eyes, for she was his protégée.

'I think they may be in partnership,' he said, alone with Callard and a constable in the study, which had been commandeered as an interview room. 'They know the value of the drawings.'

'But the window was tampered with, sir, and the alarm system disconnected,' Callard reminded him patiently, used to dealing with all sorts and having insurance fraud in mind.

Mallory bit his lip, face pale under the tan. 'I know, but don't you think that could be a blind?'

'I'll question everyone,' Callard said, drumming on the desk top with his fingers. 'Can you provide me with a list of people who've visited recently and photographs of the missing articles?'

Mallory had prints and was able to show Callard one of the Giovanni painting, though reluctantly as no one knew of its existence, with the exception of Karen. He now regretted bitterly his impulse. His life and plans had been disrupted, and he blamed her for it. Irwin might still be interested in the development scheme, but without an injection of American dollars Mallory would be hard put to manage.

'Works of art are ordered by rich collectors,' Callard continued, watching Mallory's reaction. 'Thieves are given a shopping list of requirements and where to find them. This won't be an open-market job. It's unlikely that whoever took the drawings will be touting them round. Still, we must explore every avenue.'

'But that's ridiculous!' Mallory exploded, hardly able to remain in his chair. 'That means if a dishonest collector's got them they can never go on show – they'd be kept hidden away in a vault.'

'Have you had them on show, sir?' Callard fixed him with a stern eye.

'No, but I was about to. Mr Dwyer and I planned to exhibit them.'

Mallory fetched a folder, and Callard examined the prints, then said, 'We'll make some copies.'

'Don't worry, honey,' Irwin said soothingly.

He and Karen were sitting in the conservatory where they had been permitted to have breakfast though they were still under surveillance. It was a scrappy meal as the servants were in a ferment – toast and marmalade, a pot of strong coffee, another of Earl Grey tea.

'Of course I'm worried,' she cried, hand shaking as she refilled her cup. 'He's accusing me!'

'That's crazy. I'll talk to him.'

'You don't believe I stole them?'

'No way, babe. I judge character pretty good, and you're no thief, but my gut reaction says it was an inside job.'

She frowned. 'One of the staff?'

Could it have been Tayte? she wondered. He was always short of money. Or maybe Spike? It seemed unlikely, though he did have expensive taste in fast bikes. Maybe they were in league. Armina? Possibly. Patty? Not really; she was too straightforward. The horrible thought struck her that Tony might have been tempted. It was too preposterous to contemplate yet lingered on the periphery of her mind.

Karen drooped in her chair, and Irwin patted her shoulder kindly, his touch far from avuncular. 'You like your boss? Did you have something going with him?'

She shook her head, tousled russet curls glinting. 'Our relationship never really got off the starting blocks.'

'And you're sad about that?'

'Not really. It's best to keep work and pleasure separate.'

'I'd like to have you work for me. Does this mean what I think it means? No fooling around?' His voice was as seductive as silk and he leaned forward, raised her hand and just grazed his lips over the back of it.

Karen came out in goose-pimples. She was surprised how attractive she found him, even in the harsh morning light when his clothing was crumpled and he needed a shave. Something warm flowed from his fingers, tingling through her nerves into her core. Mallory had wounded her deeply, being so quick to name her as the culprit. She wanted to retreat like a sick animal, to hide away till she had healed. Irwin could help that healing process.

She rose. So did he. She slipped her arms round his neck and placed her lips on his, leaning her body into his. She took command, tasting coffee on his tongue, winding her own into the cavern of his mouth, feeling his broad back under her hands, the long solid stalk of his phallus pressing against her belly.

He licked her lips, tasted and savoured them, then said in a husky undertone, 'Where can we go?'

'My cottage. If the police will let us.'

'Leave it to me.'

She waited for his return. He was not gone long. 'What did Callard say?' she asked, as he strode across and picked up her wrap, placing it across her shoulders.

'It's OK. But we mustn't leave the estate.'

Karen drove to Laurel Cottage through the early-morning freshness, dazed by lack of sleep, trying not to remember the mood in which she had left it last evening. Hopeful? Anticipatory? She battened down the hatches on her emotions. No commitment, no entanglement. Carnal pleasure would do nicely from now on, just as it had in the past.

While she took orange juice from the fridge and carried it upstairs, Irwin showered, coming to her bed squeaky clean. The full, thick, arching length of his cock was completely exposed, all the swellings and veins standing out, and the hard, red naked head. Luxuriant folds of hairy skin joined the base of his shaft to the heavy balls pulsating and moving in their energy and excitement. Karen slithered out of the jellaba and lay back, taking comfort from the admiration in his eyes.

'Oh, baby, you're beautiful,' he whispered, a catch in his voice. 'I've wanted you since the moment you walked in the door last night.'

He stood looking down at her, massive, powerful, overwhelming her with a superabundance of sexual fire. His hand came to rest on her breasts as he stretched out beside her, firm experienced fingers playing with the teats. She gasped, twisted in his embrace, rubbed her face against his coarse chest hair smelling of her shower gel, his skill, gentleness and controlled passion obliterating the memory of any other man. He knew what he was doing, his caresses following a pathway down her torso, around her navel and hovering over her bush.

Karen's hands wandered his fine body. He was past middle age but firm muscled, such heaviness as there was adding to her sense of well-being and security. Here was the father she had wanted but never had, to adore her, admire her, fulfil her.

Irwin's fingers parted her cleft, dipped down into the fluid running from her vulva. He spread some of it lightly over her engorged lips, teased and petted the erect crown of her clitoris. She moaned her pleasure as he rubbed it, and could hear by his ragged breathing that he desired her as much as she wanted him. Then he dived down to her furrow, drinking in her juices. She felt the sensual warmth of his tongue. Pleasure shattered her. White-hot waves roared and rippled, bearing her to a swamping orgasm.

Still convulsing she shifted her thighs up and apart, offering him entrance. She wrapped her arms and legs around him, leaving love bites on his neck. He drove into her, a sword thrust reaching her womb. Karen looked down, watching that great weapon pulling out, lingering, then sliding back, the tense sac of his scrotum tapping against her anus.

'Oh, honey,' he groaned, and his movements quickened.

Now he was almost hurting her with his size. All she could do was take it, hanging on to him as he coasted towards climax, the final shuddering dilation of his cocktip telling her that he had arrived.

Martha cried when she came. Tony was glad. A satisfied woman was the best of allies, an unsatisfied one the worst of enemies. He thought the famous quotation should have been changed to, 'Hell hath no fury like a woman cheated of her orgasm.' Men would do well to remember that when they humped and grunted their way to climax with scant regard for their frustrated partner.

'I shouldn't have done that,' she murmured smugly. 'You'll think I'm an easy lay.'

'Not at all,' he said gallantly. 'It was just one of those things. Too strong for both of us.' *What a load of bullshit!* he thought.

She disposed of the condom, washed his dick and wiped it on a pink hand towel. It was pleasant, rather like being attended by a maiden aunt or one's mother.

'How old are you, Martha?' he asked, tucking the sheet around him and fumbling for his cigarettes and lighter.

'That's not the sort of question to ask a lady,' she simpered, flapping her hand at the smoke and adding, 'I do wish you wouldn't do that, honey. It's so bad for you. Anyhow, you're not exactly a spring chicken.'

Whoops! A teensy bit sharp there. Could she turn into a nag? Yet he found even this sweet: he was genuinely fond of her and glad to bring a little sunshine into her life.

He had barrelled up to her room on the pretext of delivering a message from Irwin and found her in tears. She had seen her beloved boss go off with Karen.

He knew Karen and he were in a spot, the finger of suspicion well and truly pointing at them. They needed friends in high places. Karen was sensibly screwing Irwin. Tony could do nothing less. He had never seen a woman so much in need of a thorough shafting as Martha.

'I've been unfaithful to Mr Dwyer,' she continued, snuggling down beside him. She had put on her dressing gown, but he slid his free hand in the front and found one of her ample, nicely shaped breasts. The nipple immediately hardened.

'Does he hump you?' Tony asked, rubbing his thumb over the appreciative teat.

'Not exactly,' she confessed, looking younger, prettier with her hair falling in thick brown waves over her shoulders. 'He likes me to give him a blow job when he's tense. Says it relaxes him.'

'And he doesn't return the favour?'

She blushed. 'No, he's never – I mean no one has ever ...'

'Sucked you off? Dear me, we'll have to do something

about that, won't we?' And Tony disappeared under the bedclothes.

He found her lush thicket, spread the wings of her cleft and fastened on her well-developed clitoris with all the aptitude at his command. She came almost at once, crying again.

*How lucky I am to enjoy my work*, Tony thought, smiling to himself as he subjected her to a series of mini-climaxes that reduced her to putty in his hands. *She'll do her utmost to see that I'm not picked on. Mallory'll have a hard time dismissing me, and Irwin will defend Karen. We're home and dry, or rather home and wet.*

The press gathered at the gates like a conclave of vultures. TV cameras were in evidence. Mallory gave an interview. Facsimiles of the rollicking Bedwell cartoons flashed across screens throughout the nation well before the watershed. No doubt letters of complaint would appear in the *Radio Times*.

The police made discreet enquiries in Porthcombe and the surrounding district. Nothing came to light. Patty, by now rampant with desire for anything in uniform, got into her car and drove to the station, her sights set on

Sergeant Harvey, briefly glimpsed when he came to Blackwood with the inspector.

She parked outside the police station, now closed for the night, and knocked on the door of the adjoining house. Harvey answered, in his shirtsleeves and in the middle of his supper.

'What you doing here, miss?' he asked, frowning. 'Aren't you supposed to stay put? No one's allowed out till Inspector Callard says.'

'I know,' Patty confessed, artless in a brief skirt and figure-hugging jumper, nipples pointing directly at him. 'But I had to see you.'

His interest was roused, both by the nipples and the hope of information. 'Is it in connection with the burglary?' It would do his career a power of good if he could put one over on the big boys from Exeter.

'Can we go to the station? I'd rather talk there.'

He put on his regulation jacket with the three stripes, fastened the polished buttons and lifted his peaked cap from the hall stand. The whole of Patty's pelvic floor was aflame, the fire leaping upwards to her breasts. She regretted not wearing panties to soak up the essence bedewing the inside tops of her legs.

The station was empty. He led her through the

reception area to his office. It was plain, functional, ideal for the scenario she planned.

'Please sit down, miss,' he said, indicating a chair facing the desk.

'I'd rather stand.'

Harvey's rugged face became stern. 'Look here, miss. What's all this about? You've interrupted my supper, and if I find you're wasting my time ...'

'What will you do, sergeant?' she breathed, leaning languorously against the wall. 'Will you punish me?'

'Punish you, miss? I don't know what you mean.'

Harvey was out of his depth, a bachelor whose only experience had been with a barmaid at the Ainsworth Arms. He recognised Patty, knew all about the goings on at Blackwood Towers. She was one of His Lordship's girlfriends, a scarlet woman according to the desiccated hags who ran the Women's Institute.

Patty arched her back and lifted her ribs, tits pointing to Jesus. Harvey started as her breasts brushed the front of his coat. He retreated, tightening the grip on his cap, held under one elbow.

'I have been naughty, haven't I? Coming here under false pretences,' she whispered, cushiony red lips pouting.

'Why did you come?' He realised as soon as he said it that the word had another connotation. A flush reddened his weather-browned cheeks.

'I wanted to see the inside of a police station.' Marlene Dietrich as *Mata Hari* could not have been more seductive. 'Is it true that you carry handcuffs and a truncheon?'

He fumbled at his belt and produced a leather pouch from which he took a pair of manacles. 'Here you are, and here's my truncheon.' That too was in a special pocket, about the same size as the solid rod she could see lying thick and inflated under his dark-blue trousers.

'I've always wondered what it would be like to be handcuffed,' she murmured, the tip of her pink tongue wetting her lips. 'Could I try?'

Sweat broke out on Harvey's brow beneath the short haircut. His control snapped. 'Arms behind your back!' he ordered in that terse, clipped tone he used when apprehending malcontents.

She obeyed, turning around. 'But, Sergeant, I shan't be able to reach my love button. Supposing I want to frig myself? Will you do it for me?'

'Stop that dirty talk!'

She heard the snap of steel meeting steel, felt cold

metal banding her wrists. 'Are you cross with me?' she asked, so wet she could smell her juices wafting from beneath her mini-skirt.

'I bloody well am! Dragging me away from my supper.' He was breathing heavily, the upward arc of his cock distorting the shape of his pants.

'Go on! Tell me off!' she begged, edging closer.

'And Sergeant, please put your hat on. It makes you look so sexy!'

Harvey did as she asked, then pressed up against her, her locked hands contacting the emulsion-painted wall. He ravished her lips, forceful tongue plunging and plundering, aping the motion of coition.

Patty kept her eyes open, wanting to see the black and white band of his hat, reduced to jelly at the feel of coarse serge as his collar brushed her throat and the discomfort of buttons marking her flesh.

'You're a tart!' he shouted. 'A filthy little whore. I should give you a good seeing-to.'

He jerked at the buttons of his jacket. Disappointment mingled with Patty's rampaging desire. 'Don't take it off!' she cried.

'I'm not. Just want to get at my old man easier. That's what you want, isn't it?'

His flies gaped open. His lively member sprang out, the purple glans rising from the wrinkled foreskin. Patty gasped as he rucked up her skirt, cock hopping at the sight of her bare belly and fluffy pubes. He gripped her brutally, lifting her with a palm under each bum cheek. She opened her legs and felt the blunt tip of his tool nudging her opening. He pushed upwards, spearing her, filling and stretching her till it was buried deep inside.

Keeping her positioned, her back supported by the wall, one of his hands worked under her sweater, raising it above her breasts where it lay like a crimson band.

'God, you've got nice titties!' he muttered, pinching the tips till she screamed. 'I'm going to suck 'em raw, bitch!'

He slid out of her, and her feet touched the floor. He freed her hands and propelled her across to the desk, stiff phallus sticking out from his flies. Patty sprawled across the surface, scattering papers and files, gazing up at a framed photograph of the queen on the wall above her head. Her Majesty was shaking hands with officers-in-chief (all uniformed) on an official visit to her guardians of law and order.

Harvey pounced on Patty's naked breasts, gnawing her nipples. Jolted between pleasure and pain, her hand found his phallus. She ran her nail across its weeping eye, relishing the feel of the smooth shaft between her fingers.

'Make a fist,' he commanded. 'Rub it hard. That's right. Oh – yes – yes!'

Now her own odours were joined by his – the gamey smell of cock-fluid, sweat, Old Spice aftershave, fabric in need of dry-cleaning. It was a potent brew and she was crazy for orgasm, jerking her hips in an effort to contact something, anything, on which to masturbate her clit. She grabbed at the shape hanging from his loosened belt, tugged at it impatiently, pulled out the wooden truncheon.

A libidinous smile on her wide mouth, she stroked its smooth end up her slippery cleft. Harvey watched her, his prick growing larger, dribbling its need. She guided the makeshift dildo into her love-hole, just the end to begin with, then pressing in further. Its brown, polished length almost disappeared.

The sensation in her vagina was making her clit envious. It stirred, demanding a share of the action. Slowly she slid her new plaything out of her cunt, across her streaming avenue and touched the head against the very tip of her love button. It electrified the glowing bud, sharp waves of delight shooting through her as she came in a blinding rush.

Harvey thrust his prick between the swollen lips of her sex. He rammed against her ferociously and she heard herself cry out, the tight muscles of her sheath clenching over his width as he pounded his way to completion.

Later, over a cup of hot, sweet tea in the police house, he said, 'What was it you were going to tell me, miss?'

She smiled at him, catlike and content. 'It doesn't matter. I got what I came for,' and she was thinking, *This will be something to tell the girls when I get home.*

'What the hell's going on, Mallory?' Sinclair asked as he entered the Red Drawing-Room two days later. 'Police ringing me up at dead of night.'

'It couldn't have been.' Mallory fixed him with a jaundiced eye. 'They contacted you hours after the event.'

'Oh, Christ, picky as ever!' Sinclair helped himself to a brandy from the tantalus on the chiffonier. 'So? Have they got whoever stole the damn things?'

'Not yet. I'm sure it was Karen or Tony, or both of them,' Mallory gloomed from the depths of a crimson-upholstered armchair.

'Really? Could it be you made an error of judgement

when you employed her? I remember thinking she was a little too clever, a tad too keen,' Sinclair mused, nursing the goblet between his palms.

'And how was your alibi?' Mallory barked. 'Perfect, I suppose?'

'Well, I did have to embarrass a married lady by asking her to confess I'd spent the afternoon in question at her pied-à-terre in Knightsbridge.'

'And had you?'

'Too right I had. What a screw! Frustrated, poor cow. Wife of a Tory MP.'

Mallory stared at him through slitted eyes. 'Celine and Jo?'

'Both working their rocks off. Lots of witnesses. Which leaves us precisely nowhere. Looks like you've lost your drawings, brother.'

Inspector Callard had withdrawn but police presence was still felt. The press had simmered down, having wrung every last ounce out of Mallory's habit of living like an Eastern potentate with his harem of beauties. They hadn't dropped the story entirely, but had rushed off to cover a more salacious news item concerning a member of the royal family.

Karen, incarcerated in Laurel Cottage by choice, was

avoiding contact with anyone except Tony and Irwin, trying to calm her jangled nerves through meditation and failing miserably. It was horrible to feel like a criminal when she had done nothing. She hadn't been charged but was obviously the prime suspect. The case was bound to be dropped through lack of evidence but mud stuck and she doubted she'd be able to find a similar post elsewhere.

It was a shock when Sinclair turned up on her doorstep, insouciant in Calvin Klein sunglasses and a camel double-breasted suit, beige cotton shirt, herringbone tie and plaited leather belt all by Giorgio Armani. He looked relaxed and fit and carefree. Too full of himself, in fact.

Karen wondered, not for the first time, what he knew about the theft. He had been absent, it was true, but could easily have had an accomplice. She clearly recalled checking on the cartoons before she went hawking with Mallory. Every one had been in place.

'Sorry to hear you're in trouble,' he began, stepping inside without being invited. 'Is there anything I can do?'

'Thank you, but no.' Karen was aware of looking scruffy, in a sweatshirt and peg-top trousers.

He, on the other hand, was bandbox fresh, his bold

glance sliding over her impudently. 'You look great, Karen. Is the prisoner on parole? Can I take you out to dinner?'

She grinned wryly; he had the power to charm and amuse her, even now, when she distrusted him. She had little to go on, but it would be in character for him to sit back and let someone else take the rap. She told herself it was immaterial to her whether Mallory recovered his precious cartoons or not. All she was concerned about was clearing her name.

Sinclair wined and dined her in an exclusive restaurant between Porthcombe and Exeter, but she drank little, offering to drive back through the moonlight. It was no longer a full moon but lying on its side like a drunken woman with a mottled face.

'I can't wait to get away from here and never come back,' she said grittily.

'That's a pity.' Sinclair's voice was slurred, his body sunk low in the passenger seat. He gazed at her owlishly, wagged a finger and added, 'Did you take the drawings?'

'No!'

'Course you didn't. Mallory's a fool to pin it on you. You know you didn't steal them, and I know you didn't steal them.'

'How do you know?' Karen slowed going through the woods, on the lookout for deer but also to listen carefully to his words and their subtext.

Sinclair tapped the side of his nose with drunken solemnity. 'Ah, that would be telling. Come back to my place and we'll talk some more.'

His bedroom in the disused wing was every bit as bizarre as she remembered, but this time there was a difference: she was in absolute command of herself.

'D'you want a drink?' he asked, shrugging his arms out of his coat and slinging it over a throne-like chair upholstered in leather.

'No, I've other pleasures in mind,' she murmured, sidling up to him and slipping her arms around his body. Despite herself, her pulse was racing, his very presence making her nipples harden and juices flow. He was a rogue, but then weren't the bad boys always the most exciting?

His response was immediate, and she unzipped his trousers and lifted out his massive prick until it was vertical against his taut belly. He groaned, sobering by the minute, hands delving under the long floral muslin skirt till he touched bare flesh and the hem of her panties trapped between her buttocks. She flinched at the surprise of his finger edging past the damp, flimsy fabric and finding her tight nether hole. Desire was lashing through her, making it difficult to carry out her intentions.

'We make a fine pair, Karen,' he whispered, mouth close to hers. 'You don't really love Mallory, do you?'

'What gave you that idea?' She raised one leg and hooked it round his hips, pressed the other against his thigh, gyrating her pelvis to bring the much needed friction to her clitoris.

'Because the bastard always gets everything I want.' His hands grabbed at her breasts through the sheer cotton, manipulating the nipples till she was ready to yell with frustration.

'And you want to punish him?' Her brain was still functioning clearly, even though under assault from her senses. 'You like to dominate people, don't you? Remember how you did it to me?'

'Ummm ... yes. D'you want some more?' He was backing her towards the four-poster, almost carrying her.

'How about if I do it to you?' The visit to Mistress Raquel had taught her a salutary lesson: even the most powerful of men liked to reverse roles. 'Mutual sub-dom – you first, then me.'

He collapsed across the bed, grinning up at her, amused by her keenness to explore sexual deviations. 'OK. I get off on being tied up. You'll have to do everything – even undress me.'

'It will be a pleasure.'

Soon he was spread-eagled on the black silk sheet, multi-hued Hermès scarves tethering his wrists and ankles to the posts. Karen surveyed him, possessed of a primitive satisfaction at seeing him naked and helpless like a victim about to be sacrificed to the Great Earth Mother.

His skin was sheened with sweat, phallus jutting aggressively from the tangled mass of pubic hair, balls cushioned on the sheet between his splayed legs. Karen smiled to herself as she shed her dress and knickers, seeing Sinclair's weapon thicken at the sight of her naked breasts, slim thighs and wet pussy.

It was time to begin the ordeal. She wheeled over two floor-standing pier glasses and angled them so he could see her from several viewpoints and also himself wriggling uselessly like a landed fish. Excitement bit deep, her loins red hot, lovebud straining from its enfolding cowl. She felt powerful, omnipotent, woman incarnate, with the male roped out before her in all his weakness and vulnerability.

He was her creature to pleasure or abuse as fancy dictated. Standing, legs spread, Karen stroked her breasts, playing with the stiff nipples, then walked her hand down to her mound, almost idly fingering herself, wetting a digit in her juices and leaning over to trail it across his lips.

Sinclair, nostrils flaring as he inhaled the spicy odour, shot out his tongue to lick it. Smiling she withdrew her hand, tormenting this horny man who was unable to do anything about it. She straddled him, lowering herself on his chest while his cock strained to reach her pink and parted avenue. She inched up to make this impossible.

'Karen, for God's sake!' he rasped. 'Get on it! Ride me!'

'Impatient,' she chided, sliding higher, a trail of silvery fluid glittering on his chest hair. She reached her goal, stopping with knees spread wide over his face.

His head lifted, tongue darted out to caress her labia and clit. She sighed, sank down, let him fill his mouth with her fragrant essences, feeling the heaviness in her loins, the surging waves predicting orgasm. This was not to be permitted – not yet – and the pleasure of denying herself, and him, was exquisite. She moved, lithe as a cobra, coiling down to examine his genitals. It was fun to lift and weigh the bulky testicles, tense in their downy pouch, to run light fingers up his shaft, hearing him moan, seeing the pearly fluid poised on the tip of his glans. She rubbed his erection, but not enough to relieve him.

Her control was slipping, almost yielding to the burning desire to feel him inside her. Should she indulge? How close could she bring herself without tipping over the edge? Well aware that intercourse had never given her orgasm, she permitted that ardent cock head to brush against her pudenda. Sinclair was a wily protagonist in the torrid sexual duel. With a sudden lift of his hips he thrust upwards and in, but Karen was on guard, rising to her knees to deny him full access.

'Damn you!' he muttered, furious.

There were adult toys on the bedside cabinet, curious objects to heighten sensation – oriental duo balls, penis rings, a vibro vagina, a choice of dildoes. She selected a huge black one. It felt and looked like the real thing. A flick of the switch and it hummed busily. Moving away from Sinclair, but well within sight, she rubbed it over her clitoris, neck arched, eyes closed, moaning at the intense pleasure it evoked.

Don't give in, she told herself. Moving position, she

sat in a chair close by, her legs open so that he could see the vibrator protruding from her pussy. She ignored it, lit a cigarette and picked up a magazine, flicking the pages. One foot lifted, straying across the bed, toes rubbing absently at his bulge.

He moved against that impertinent caress, and she wondered if this might be enough to bring him to climax, waiting to see a fountain of spunk shoot upwards before creaming his belly and chest. This would have been entertaining, and she might have lapped his tool to make it stand again. Keeping the vibrator aimed at her clit, she could have impaled herself on his cock, lunging furiously till the heat shattered within, exploding into orgasm.

*Don't even think about it*, she warned herself. *This isn't your mission.* She slowly eased her foot away.

'All right. What is it you want?' he panted, penis hard as a rock, so near and yet so far from ejaculation.

'Want? *Moi?*' She did a Miss Piggy impersonation, tossing her head.

'Stop winding me up. Are you going to fuck me?'

She removed the vibrator, leaned over him, put the buzzing rubber against his lips, let him lick her fluid from it. 'Are you going to tell the truth?' she countered.

'Concerning what?' The smell and taste of her was sweet agony.

'Concerning the cartoons.' She ran the pseudo penis over his blunt male nipples. Then she switched it off and laid it down.

'Jesus, you demand blood, don't you?'

'No, only the facts. I don't like being called a thief.'

Her free hand encountered that erogenous area between his balls and his arsehole, tickling and caressing before moving away. 'The Inquisition should have employed you,' he groaned, sweating. 'For God's sake, Karen, fuck me!'

There was a phone near the bed. She picked it up and held it above him. 'I'm going to ring your brother. I want you to speak to him. Tell him the truth. Will you do that?'

'Blasted female,' he raged. 'It was a joke, that's all. I wanted to rattle him.'

'And make a small fortune into the bargain.'

He grinned suddenly, totally unashamed, and Karen's lips twitched. Bastard he might be, but an irresistible one. 'Will you shag me blind if I do?'

'Perhaps.' She connected with Mallory. His voice crackled down the line. 'I've Sinclair here, sir,' she said. 'He was something to tell you.'

'Put him on,' the deep voice breathed in her ear, and she visualised, hated, wanted him, despised herself for that wanting.

She held the receiver so Sinclair could speak into it. 'Mallory? Look here – it was a hoax. Yes, I took the damn things. Where are they? Quite safe, old boy – hidden in the west wing. I say, there's no need to speak to me like that! All right, I'll come and see you – and bring them with me. Calm down. You'll burst a blood vessel.'

The phone went dead. Karen took it away. Sinclair looked at her with hot eyes. She placed herself on his face so that he could dip into her spicy nest. He found her clit, his tongue slick smooth, working over it while she added her own frantic movements, spasm after spasm rolling and rolling in the pit of her belly, till climax roared through her like a hurricane and she collapsed on his chest.

An instant later she was riding his prick, rising and falling, lunging and pumping, rewarding him for his confession with a wild trip to the highest peaks of sensation.

# Chapter Eleven

Karen took the path winding down to the beach, the uneven surface jabbing through the soles of her sandals. She had come to say goodbye to a spot she had grown to love during the hectic days following Sinclair's confession.

Though now vindicated, she was still angry and hurt, seeking solace in the cave-pitted cliffs and miles of beach washed by an ever-changing sea. Let Mallory sort out his own problems.

A statement had been issued to the press: Lord Sinclair Burnet had perpetrated a hoax, not expecting it to be taken seriously. He expressed regret for any upset caused. Mallory dropped charges and made an official apology to the police, but only the timely intervention of an influential uncle at Scotland Yard had prevented Sinclair from landing in serious trouble. He had taken himself off to South America till the dust settled.

Tony was prepared to forgive and forget. Karen wasn't. That morning a hand-delivered letter had arrived at Laurel Cottage formally reinstating her.

Suppressing her first impulse to trash it, she had told the messenger to wait, sat down and dashed off her resignation.

There was one option open to her. Irwin wanted her as his secretary now Martha had elected to stay on at Blackwood Towers and organise the exhibition of Bedwell cartoons and the manor's emergence as a conference centre. Tony would still be head librarian, and it was obvious they were now an item.

Irwin had offered not only a job: he wanted her to become his mistress, possibly something more in the fullness of time. But he already paid alimony to five wives and supported numerous offspring. There must be a major flaw in his character with that amount of failed forays into matrimony. Karen had no ambition to find out.

It was a backward step, but there seemed to be no

alternative to living with her parents while she looked for work. Her indignation blazed. She wanted to slap Mallory, scratch him, thump and kick him into admitting he had treated her unjustly. No chance of that. He was avoiding her as if she had the plague.

Her toes sank into dry sand as she reached the huge rocky amphitheatre. Noisy gulls wheeled overhead or picked over the dead fish, stranded crabs and other flotsam drifting in the shallows. A deep rock pool glinted at the base of a tumbled mound of boulders. Karen quickly untied her bikini bra, wriggled out of her shorts and removed the matching G-string. The tangy breeze played over her, stippling her nipples, her body losing tension under the sun's warm caress.

Her spirits rose as she waded in. It was icy; the tide only just receding. Cool fingers crept up her thighs and dipped into the secret places concealed by her curling pubic hair. The water was transparent, light touching the molluscs clinging to the rocks. She ran a hand under the surface, seeing how the droplets sparkled on her tanned skin, her worries dissolving.

'I want to talk to you, Karen.' Mallory's sudden, unexpected voice sent fiery arrows darting through her.

'Leave me alone,' she stammered, crossing her arms

over her breasts and thinking, *Christ! How clichéd! I'm behaving like a maiden in a melodrama. In a moment I'll be saying, Unhand me, villain!*

'No.' He loomed above her, barefoot, bare chested, legs astride in stonewashed jeans. Gone was the austere expression. His amber eyes were as mild as the ocean, deep pits of pain and rage. 'You can't resign. I won't let you.'

'Get real!' she stormed. He couldn't have chosen a worse tack if he'd tried. Hadn't he learnt anything? 'No one tells me what to do.'

His eyes snapped. 'You're the most bloody-minded female I've ever met!' he snarled. 'Get out of that damn pool. We've got to talk about this.'

She held out her hand. He clasped it and she deliberately pulled him off balance. He landed beside her, a tidal wave swamping them.

'Bitch! You did that on purpose!' he bellowed, drenched and furious.

'Now will you leave me alone?' She scrambled to her feet, and lust blossomed in her as his eyes fastened on the globes of her breasts.

*Get out of this, my girl*, she scolded herself, heading for the towel that lay on a rock with her clothes. *You don't want anything to do with him. You're your own woman again and it's great!*

Mallory leapt out. He reached the towel first, planted a sandy foot on it. The soaking denim emphasised his penis, so clearly that she could see the bump of his foreskin. That huge weapon menaced and frightened her, yet filled her with a scalding flood of desire.

'You're going to listen to me, Karen.' He seized her by the upper arms, shook her till her breasts bounced, then dragged her closer, his mouth on her throat, kissing, sucking, leaving the imprints of his teeth.

She groaned in unwilling response as his lips fastened on a naked nipple, dragging on it till she was nearly mindless with need. 'Don't, Mallory – please.' She barely knew what she was saying, her hard-won resolve disappearing.

Making one last desperate bid for freedom, she resorted to a karate chop and pelted towards the sea. He was after her, she knew, hearing his panting breath carried by the wind. Her mind was in turmoil – she abhorred the idea of surrender but felt she would die if she didn't.

The water was ice cold, clutching at her thighs, freezing her vitals to aching numbness. She waded further in till the sea was waist high, the swirling current threatening to sweep her feet from under her.

'Let go, Karen,' Mallory shouted above the noise of crashing waves. 'Don't fight it any more. You want me in the same way that I want you.'

'What are you saying? I don't understand,' she yelled back.

His hair was dripping, spume milling round his crotch. He clutched at her, caught her, pulled her towards him, crying, 'I was afraid of how I felt about you. I tried to ignore you, but it was no use. Then, when I'd weakened, the drawings disappeared. I thought I'd been made a fool of again, and that you'd betrayed me – like Caroline.'

'Oh, no, it wasn't like that,' she gasped, shivering with cold and passion.

'I know that now.'

He kissed her, his lips tasting of brine, and she warmed in his arms, heated by his hard muscles and the stiff promise of his cock. She struggled with his buttons, released the mighty, uncoiling python, supporting it in her hands, while he opened her honeypot to the lecherous wave tongues lapping and licking at her.

Locked together, they stumbled to the shore, a tepid

bath warmed by hot sand and sun. Tiny wavelets bubbled over their bodies as they lay there oblivious to everything. Karen lifted her breasts to his hands, the nipples steel-hard with cold and arousal. This was what she had dreamed of, yearned for, yet all the while a part of her – the reasoning, sensible part – told her it was only a dream.

His mouth was on her labia, sucking in seawater and her juices. Riven by exquisite pleasure, she felt his tongue probe and explore that most sensitive portion of her body. Her groping fingers fondled his wet black hair as she urged him to go on, the blood drumming in her ears, the incandescence growing, the sea rippling round her thighs and penetrating her vagina. The sky started to spin, forming a brilliant kaleidoscope, as she twisted her head from side to side in her extremity.

The most acute pleasure carried her to the peak, then tumbled her down to reality, and she felt him rise to his knees between her relaxed thighs and drive his penis into her. She thrust against it with every vestige of strength, her muscles expanding to take him – big, bigger, a final surge distending it even more as he surrendered to his own passion. She felt him convulse, heard him give a husky cry of satisfaction as he poured out his tribute.

She had him! He was hers. With her fingertips she

explored his face, the soft, silky brows, the aquiline nose, the sensual lips. She could tell that he was smiling as she moulded her body round his lean hardness in the balmy wash of the sea.

Then, just as she was preparing to sink herself into him, to subjugate her will, her ambitions, her very soul, words spoken to her long ago by her wise mentor, Tony, drifted into her mind: 'Be very careful what you ask for – the gods might be listening and give it to you.'

Karen lay sunning herself on a lounger near the swimming pool. It was early September but still hot; her tan was deep and golden after the continual exposure of summer. Armina was with her, lithe, supple, nude – no longer the tenant of the Dower House, having banished herself to Raquel's mansion. She sometimes visited the girl who had succeeded her, but without the slightest trace of rancour. Sinclair, with an odd spark of chivalry, had not implicated Armina, but Mallory had guessed that she had been his partner and had told her she was no longer welcome.

'*C'est la vie!*' she remarked, rising up on one elbow and reaching for a Martini in the shade of the umbrella. 'It was time to move on.'

'I don't imagine you mind fending for yourself.' Karen sat up and applied another layer of coconut oil to her body, adding to its bronze lustre.

'I'm hardly doing that, darling.' Armina gave her a shrewd stare through her dark shades as she sipped her drink. 'Money's never been a problem, and Raquel runs a funhouse. It'll amuse me for a while, and that, after all, is what life's about – being amused. You should try it sometime.'

Karen smiled across at her. 'I have. You've introduced me to a number of amusing things.'

Armina moved her lounger a little closer and pointed to the sun oil. 'Would you like me to do your back?' she offered, rising gracefully to her naked feet.

Karen rolled on her stomach and gave herself over to Armina's skilled ministrations, a sigh escaping her lips as she felt those soft hands working over her shoulder muscles, down her spine, around her buttocks, slipping between, delicate fingertips massaging the sweet-scented lotion into her cleft. Her thighs and calves received attention till she felt she was melting into the padded cushions beneath her, languorous, pleasure-loving, under the guidance of her hedonistic friend.

It was quiet, peaceful, idyllic. Sappho's island of

Lesbos must have had the same atmosphere, she thought dreamily. Women sunning themselves, pleasuring one another – gentle, understanding beings whose sensuality was so much more advanced than men's.

'Does he satisfy you?' Armina murmured, and her hand returned to Karen's twin entrances. She opened her legs a little to make its passage easier.

'Mallory? Oh, yes. He's good, but you should know that, Armina.'

'He has a big cock, I'll grant you. A little too big, maybe. And he is terribly handsome. I hope you haven't fallen in love with him.'

Her finger had found Karen's love-bud and was massaging the oiled head softly, bringing her closer and closer to climax. The tiny nub of erectile tissue transmitted waves of sensation to every part of Karen's body, gathering, concentrating, pulling all her energies into itself.

'I think I may have loved him, or been on the verge of it,' she gasped, moving her hips in appreciation of the experienced finger. 'But I've never felt quite the same about him since he accused me—'

'Or since you actually had him? Sometimes the fantasy is better than the reality,' Armina murmured, pausing, fingertip hovering over Karen's throbbing clit, prolonging the build-up to orgasm. 'He seems smitten with you. You're the only mistress now – Celine's launched on her career, Jo's face is on the cover of every fashion magazine.'

'And Patty's fucking most of Devon's constabulary,' Karen added, wriggling to indicate her eagerness for Armina to continue masturbating her. 'Mallory wants me to marry him. He has sentimental ideas of having his son live with us.'

'So that you can play Mummy?' Armina crouched by the sunbed, knees apart, her bare, rosy pubis nicely aligned with Karen's eyes, the subtle perfume of her damp avenue blending with that of coconut oil.

'Exactly,' Karen was finding it hard to concentrate on anything except the waves of desire coursing through her groin.

'Have you said yes?' Faster, that finger now, working busily up and down on the swollen nub.

'Oh – oh! Ah – yes! Do it! Go on! Bring me off!' Karen cried piteously, suddenly swept to the top of a beautiful, exquisitely orchestrated climax. Limp and saturated with pleasure she collapsed, heated by passion, heated by the sun. What more could she ask?

She smiled into Armina's eyes and spread herself out on her back, her friend returning to her couch, smoothing her wet finger over her own moist clit. 'You haven't answered me,' she said. 'Are you going to marry him? I think the title of marchioness would suit you.'

'I haven't made up my mind.' Karen stretched her arms above her head, resting them on the plump pillow. 'And the more I prevaricate, the keener he gets.'

'Good,' Armina said, with a grin. 'Keep him insecure. I know him, and he'd soon lose interest if he was sure of you. Play him at his own game.'

The phone trilled and Karen reached for the handset, pulling a face at Armina as Mallory's voice caressed her ear.

'Hello, darling. Thought I'd give you a ring.'

'That's sweet of you. How's the London meeting going?'

'Fine, fine. We're off to have lunch at Irwin's hotel. The plans for Blackwood are in the bag.' He sounded jubilant.

'I'm pleased. So you'll be able to start alterations? Hold the first conference very soon?'

'So Irwin says. I'll be back tomorrow. What are you doing right now?'

Karen smiled and watched Armina playing with herself. Supposing she were to tell him the truth, say that orgasmic spasms were still rippling in her sex? She decided against it. 'Me? I've been working in the library. You still employ me, you know.'

'Don't do too much. There's no point in getting overtired. I want you fresh for my return.'

'Worry not, my love. I'm lazing in the sun.'

'And tonight?' He sounded vaguely uneasy and Karen liked that.

'Oh, don't really know. I've been invited to a gay party and may go along. They can be fun, as long as one isn't looking for a fuck.'

'What d'you mean? Are you looking for a fuck?'

'I didn't say that,' Karen answered sweetly and winked across at Armina who held up one hand, thumb and forefinger pressed together in a gesture of success. 'Anyway, I thought you weren't sexually jealous.'

'I'm not,' he replied, a shade too quickly.

'Then it's no problem. I may stay in, of course, or go for a drink with Tony.'

'And Martha, I hope. They're a couple, aren't they?'

'I believe so.'

'That's good. Darling, when can we plan our wedding?'

'I'm not sure. We'll be so busy for the next few months.'

'That shouldn't stop us.' He was getting agitated, and London was a long way off. It wasn't her intention to discourage him too much.

She murmured sweet, soothing nothings in his ear and when he had hung up, turned to Armina, saying, 'He's promised to ring me again, and he will, maybe several times. I'll leave on the answerphone whether I'm in or not, just to keep him on tenterhooks.'

'That's my girl,' Armina said approvingly. 'It's the best way. And what exactly have you planned for tonight?'

Karen flopped back on the cushions, almost purring with contentment. Only that day a card had arrived from Jeremy bearing a Greek stamp and a 'wish you were here' message that sounded sincere, though she wouldn't hold her breath. Also a letter had come from Kan, reminding her to keep in training for the May event. Sinclair had rung her, suggesting she might like to visit Rio. Irwin had not given up, and then there was Mallory himself, her gorgeous, sexy, mean and moody aristocrat with the biggest cock she'd ever sucked.

'I thought we might spend it together,' she answered, reaching across the space between the loungers and linking her fingers with those of her female paramour.

'There's always Tayte, should we fancy playing with a dick,' Armina suggested.

Eyes closed, the two women lay on the terrace, the sun burning down on their naked bodies, lazy, dreaming, content. Then from the distance came a sound – the throbbing, blood-stirring, throaty roar of a powerful machine.

'It's the Harley,' Karen murmured sleepily. 'What say we invite Spike along, too?'

'That's a brilliant idea!' Armina agreed. 'Oh, and remind me to show you the secret passages sometime. They could prove useful, especially if you do become the lady of the manor and want to play away from home. A girl has to look after herself, you know.'

'And you'll be my ally?'

'Bet your sweet life I will. I helped Sinclair, didn't I?'

Karen listened and agreed, though knew she could never entirely trust Armina. But she'd look out for herself, all right, marry Mallory and work at the relationship one hundred per cent. But should it not prove to be an alliance made in heaven, then there were other roads open to her, and she wouldn't hesitate to take them.